MURDER ON A FROSTY NIGHT

BOOKS BY VERITY BRIGHT

THE LADY ELEANOR SWIFT MYSTERY SERIES

1. *A Very English Murder*
2. *Death at the Dance*
3. *A Witness to Murder*
4. *Murder in the Snow*
5. *Mystery by the Sea*
6. *Murder at the Fair*
7. *A Lesson in Murder*
8. *Death on a Winter's Day*
9. *A Royal Murder*
10. *The French for Murder*
11. *Death Down the Aisle*
12. *Murder in an Irish Castle*
13. *Death on Deck*
14. *Murder in Manhattan*
15. *Murder by Invitation*
16. *Murder on the Cornish Cliffs*
17. *A Death in Venice*
18. *Murder in Mayfair*
19. *Murder on the Nile*
20. *A Midwinter Murder*
21. *A Recipe for Murder*

22. *Death at a Paris Hotel*
23. *Murder at the Royal Palace*

MURDER ON A FROSTY NIGHT

VERITY BRIGHT

bookouture

Published by Bookouture in 2025

An imprint of Storyfire Ltd.
Carmelite House
50 Victoria Embankment
London EC4Y 0DZ

www.bookouture.com

The authorised representative in the EEA is Hachette Ireland
8 Castlecourt Centre
Dublin 15 D15 XTP3
Ireland
(email: info@hbgi.ie)

Copyright © Verity Bright, 2025

Verity Bright have asserted their right to be identified
as the author of this work.

All rights reserved. No part of this publication may be reproduced, stored in any retrieval system, or transmitted, in any form or by any means, electronic, mechanical, photocopying, recording or otherwise, without the prior written permission of the publishers.

ISBN: 978-1-80550-019-3
eBook ISBN: 978-1-80550-018-6

This book is a work of fiction. Names, characters, businesses, organizations, places and events other than those clearly in the public domain, are either the product of the author's imagination or are used fictitiously. Any resemblance to actual persons, living or dead, events or locales is entirely coincidental.

To all the wonderful readers of the Lady Swift series.

The truth is rarely pure and never simple.

— OSCAR WILDE

1

'Oh my!'

Lady Eleanor Swift stared at her ribbon-entangled bulldog and tomcat. They were chasing each other around and around on the wrapping paper she was trying to rescue. The villagers were due at Henley Hall, her inherited country estate, in a little over two hours, and she still hadn't even managed to wrap their presents.

Despite this, her mouth broke into a smile. 'Isn't Christmas just so magical!'

She glanced out of leaded windows at the ornate wrought-iron stakes lining the snow-blanketed drive. Each one was decorated with giant holly-and-ivy wreaths decorated with red ribbons and gold baubles, now dusted in glistening snowflakes. Her best friends, Lord and Lady Langham, had upgraded their Christmas decorations in their monumental mansion, Langham Manor, and Eleanor had happily accepted the cast-out decorations. She hated waste and her own – much more modest – country house, Henley Hall, was now decked out with almost unimaginable festive finery.

Returning to the job in hand, she hitched up her silk and

cashmere skirt and threw one knee onto her desk to trap the flailing red tissue paper. As her pets tried to steal the partially wrapped gift for the umpteenth time, she tickled their noses.

'Gladstone, and you, Tomkins, you'd better watch out! Otherwise, I'll wrap you both up and foist you off onto one of our unsuspecting villagers as their festive gift!'

Before she could carry out her threat, a familiar tap heralded her morning-suited butler. He took a single step into the room and froze, surveying the chaos with a pointed sniff.

'It's not as bad as you think,' she said airily.

He raised an eyebrow, but his eyes twinkled with festive fun. 'What isn't, my lady? The shudder-inducing mess? The lack of progress regarding the gift wrapping? Or my mistress, the lady of the manor, disgracefully spreadeagled across her desk in a hurricane of crumpled tissue paper? The very lady who, incidentally, is booked to play elegant hostess to the entire village of Little Buckford shortly.'

She glanced at the mantelpiece clock. 'We've hours before... Oh!' Blanching at how the afternoon had run away from her, she shrugged. 'Really, if there's that little time to finish the preparations for the villagers' traditional Christmas Eve festivities, I can't fathom why you're wasting precious minutes scolding me. Especially over making such a teensy mess. Even though telling me off is your most favourite thing. After squabbling, of course. And don't try to deny it.'

Despite his pursed lips, his eyes sparkled. 'And anyway...' She waved her scissors at him harder than she intended. They slipped from her grasp and narrowly avoided spearing him. But only because he deftly caught them with one hand. She winced apologetically.

'Neither squabbling nor issuing respectful admonishments were the reason for my venturing into the' – his lips twitched – 'wreckage of your office, my lady.'

She groaned. 'It hardly matters. We converted it so I could

use it for our new detective agency. But as you well know, clients have hardly been flocking to the door.' She sighed. 'It hasn't managed anything like the successful first few months we'd hoped for since launching.'

Clifford came further into the room, stepping over the wrapping paper and gambolling pets. 'Merely an unfortunate period of slack water, as it were, my lady. As I have oft repeated, slow and steady is—'

'Infuriating. And troubling. As *I* have often repeated, Clifford. We've only had a handful of minor cases after our inaugural success. And none of them have really expanded our reputation or been very lucrative. Uncle Byron left me Henley Hall and I'm determined to preserve his memory. After all, that's why we named the agency "The Byron Detective Agency", isn't it? But so far, I seem to have only detracted, not added, to his legacy. And Hugh even resigned as chief inspector so the three of us could start it together! Where is he, by the way?'

'In the "dungeon", as you have aptly designated his office, my lady.'

She sighed. 'Let me guess. My wonderful husband is trying to make a dent on his part-time consultancy work for Scotland Yard?'

'I really couldn't say, my lady. However, on his desk I noticed this newspaper.'

He handed it to her. Three headlines had been circled.

POLICE STILL HUNTING PARK LANE JEWEL THIEVES

POLICE CONFIRM MAN KILLED IN BUTTERTON IN
STAFFORDSHIRE WAS INVENTOR WORKING FOR
GOVERNMENT

CRIME FIGURES ROSE IN THE HOME COUNTIES FOR
THIRD MONTH IN A ROW

She shook her head. 'Even though he's all but left the force, he's obviously still finding it difficult to stop being a policeman twenty-four seven!' She felt a sudden wash of dismay. 'Perhaps starting a detective agency wasn't our greatest idea?'

In reply, Clifford stepped around the desk and whispered to Gladstone and Tomkins, 'Paws over your ears, please. Lest you hear her ladyship's uncharacteristic defeatism.' He glanced sideways at her. 'Especially during this festive period and at, possibly, ahem, the most misplaced of timings.'

With a magician's flourish, he produced a small silver tray. On it was an envelope.

She stared at it, her eyes widening. 'A telegram?'

He nodded. 'I was just checking the last ribbons had been tied to the seasonal wreath on the front door, my lady, when it arrived.'

The welcome wreath was a long-standing Henley Hall tradition. Everyone in the household, including all the staff, contributed something to it.

She peered closer. 'Addressed to "The Byron Detective Agency"! Clifford, could it be a case?'

He nodded. 'Possibly. One is assuredly due if the new year is to see a turnaround for our fledgling venture.'

She swept the telegram from the tray and herded through the sea of tissue paper, dodging the dog-and-cat-shaped mounds now surging joyfully back and forth under it again. 'Come on. Let's open this with Hugh.'

Too eager to care about propriety, she grabbed the newspaper and her skirts and ran down the corridor which was decorated with gold paper lanterns and rows of flickering candles lining either side. In the marbled hallway she just had to pause for a moment and admire the Christmas tree planted in a huge earthenware pot. It soared up to the ceiling, decorated with red, gold and green baubles and velvet bows. At the end of each branch hung miniature rocking horses, nutcracker dolls and Lilliputian silver lanterns, all rescued from her friends' Christmas decoration upgrade. The only bare part of the tree was the lower branches. Her naughty bulldog had a habit of stealing any low-hanging baubles and burying them!

As she hurried down the next corridor, Clifford lengthened his stride and arrived two steps behind her at the door marked with an engraved brass plate 'The Dungeon'.

'My lady!' he hissed in a horrified tone. 'It is Christmas Eve!'

She frowned. 'So? Hugh's not going to be dancing naked around his office. And even if he was, he and I were married some months ago, remember? Oh!' She paused, her hand on the handle. 'You mean he might be wrapping a present for me?'

He nodded as he knocked loudly.

'Come in, Clifford,' her husband's deep voice rumbled out.

'Her ladyship is with me, sir.'

'Blast it! I mean, wonderful. Just... umm, hang on.'

'And she might have good news!' she called through the keyhole.

There was the sound of filing cabinet drawers slamming shut, then the door opened, revealing her divinely tall and athletically built husband, Hugh Seldon. Or Sir Hugh, as he had been knighted a few months back. Not that he would use his new title. He was far too humble. He smiled, raking his hand through his chestnut curls. 'Hello, Eleanor. Umm, good news, eh? Are the preparations for the villagers' celebrations all finished? Because if so, I wasn't trying to duck out of helping.'

She slid her arm into his. 'I know, silly.'

He ran his hand around his neck. 'I was just trying to clear enough work to ensure we have a proper first Christmas here at Henley Hall now that we're married.'

'By working on extra cases, Hugh?' She brandished the newspaper. 'I don't remember you telling me anything about' – she pointed at the circled headlines – 'these.'

He winced. 'No. They're not... officially on the list of the ones I'm advising about. But' – his tone became more animated – 'I was trying to catch that jewel gang before I resigned. They've been operating in that part of London since last year. They've run rings around the authorities for too long. So I thought I'd just keep tabs on them, you know.' He shrugged and hurried on at her expression. 'And the police haven't released the man's name who was found dead, but it was Professor Charles Hunt. I met him a few years back when he was designing something very hush-hush. Anyway, Morrison's working on the case, and it would be a feather in his cap if he could solve it. Apparently, some important plans for his latest invention went missing. And the crime figures rising—'

'Hugh Seldon!' She crossed her arms. 'You are supposed to have all but retired, remember?' Her tone softened. 'Although, I love the fact that you won't let go once you've sunk your teeth into something.'

Clifford coughed. 'In which, if I may be so bold to say, my lady, you and the master are similarly matched. Although, in your case, it is more likely to be a well-done steak you sink your teeth into, perhaps? Or a—'

'Clifford!' She tried to sound stern, but Seldon's laughter set her off too. She rolled her eyes. 'Don't think you can distract me. Either of you. Anyway, Hugh, you may be too busy to pursue all these unofficial cases, because...' She waved the telegram. 'You'll never guess who this is addressed to?'

'The agency?' he said hopefully. At her nod, his face lit up. 'What does it say?'

'We've no idea. I wanted to wait to open it together.'

Before she could tear it open, a letter opener was respectfully slid into her hand.

'To avoid having to contact the telegraph office on Christmas Eve to request the message be re-sent because it was rendered illegible on opening, my lady.'

She tutted good-humouredly as she opened the envelope and whipped out the thin blue paper inside.

Seldon and Clifford both held up their crossed fingers as she unfolded it and read aloud…

2

'"Sir, madam. £300 deposited in agency bank account. Further £300 payable on accepting case. Further £300 payable on completion."' She gasped. 'Listen to this, chaps! "Initial £300 to be retained regardless case taken or not."' She lowered the telegram and stared at the others. 'It's signed "IOU Esq".'

'"Esq" for "esquire", one presumes,' Clifford said. 'And the postscript, my lady?'

'What post— Oh, over the page.' She read on. '"To accept case, arrive no later than midnight tonight."' She handed Clifford the paper. 'There's an address.' She frowned. '"Waketon Court, Yorelow, Westhamshire". I've never even heard of the county, let alone the town.'

Clifford pulled out his pince-nez and glanced at it. 'Hardly surprising, my lady. It was the smallest county in England. That is until it was dissolved in 1876, if memory serves.'

'If it does, it would seem our would-be client is living in the past!' She cursed her lack of English geography, having spent much of her life abroad until she'd inherited Henley Hall five years ago. 'How far is it?'

'A good six to seven hours by motor car, I would estimate.

Given we will have to do much of it on country roads once past Oxford. To say nothing of the fact it will be dark by quarter past four this afternoon. Plus, snow is threatening.'

Seldon raised a hand. 'One moment! Keen though I am for a change in fortune for the agency, we can't go tonight. The villagers are arriving soon and will party here until at least eleven o'clock. And as Lady of the Manor, surely you need to be here, Eleanor? That telegram explicitly stated we had to arrive before midnight. To have any chance of that, we'd have to set off almost immediately!'

Clifford nodded. 'If not sooner. All the same, sir, if I might be permitted to telephone the bank to at least check the veracity that three hundred pounds has been deposited in the agency's account?'

As he left the room, Eleanor slid her arm back into Seldon's. 'Hugh, I desperately want to be here to welcome the villagers, but equally we desperately need the agency to start showing a profit. Henley Hall is very costly to keep running. And even though the wolf is hardly at our door yet...' She shrugged.

He pulled her to his chest. 'I know, my love. But the villagers coming here on Christmas Eve is a tradition your late uncle started and held to religiously every year. It means the world to them. And to you.'

She nodded. 'It does. And it feels a huge responsibility, if I'm honest.' She stared at the telegram. 'Dash it! Why didn't the sender include their telephone number?'

'More to the point, why didn't they telephone us in the first place? And who demands someone travels to them on Christmas Eve with no notice?' His brow furrowed. 'That telegram is odd in other ways as well. The sender made it as short as possible. I presume because telegrams are charged by the word. Yet they think nothing of handing over three hundred pounds. Non-refundable at that!' He shook his head. 'It's probably a hoax.'

'Actually, sir, I think not.' Clifford strode back in, holding a map. 'At exactly midday today, the agency's bank account became three hundred pounds the richer!'

Eleanor's eyes lit up. 'So the sender is serious.' Her brow furrowed. 'If we can't telephone, can we send a telegram in time to receive a reply?'

Clifford shook his head. 'Regrettably, my lady, there is no time.'

He spread the map out on Seldon's desk, and pointed at a tiny village place name. 'Yorelow', set in the middle of... nothing. Even the few minor roads shown passed either side of it by a wide margin.

She shrugged. 'Just because our potential client lives somewhere a little... remote, we can't turn it down flat.'

'But we don't even know what the case is, Eleanor.' Seldon winced. 'It might be a divorce case. We promised we wouldn't take one of those yet!'

'Yes. Or it might be a case of missing jewels. Or a lost relative,' she said enthusiastically. 'If we just went up and found out, we could accept it if it looked good and arrange to return to Yorelow to complete the case straight after Christmas. Then, if we drove back through the night, we'd still be home in time for Christmas Day breakfast.'

Clifford glanced up from tracing a tiny brass wheel set in a wooden handle across the map to measure the distance. 'Leastways in time for luncheon. Which would leave the arrangements for Boxing Day unaffected also.'

'But the villagers, Eleanor?' Seldon said.

'Clifford, any thoughts?' she said hopefully.

'Several, my lady. The principal ones being the second and third amounts of three hundred pounds offered in that telegram.'

'Ever the terrier over the purse strings! Thankfully,' she muttered.

'And the second thought which strikes is the memory of just how many of these Christmas Eve festivities his lordship, your late uncle, was regrettably forced to miss. Due to business, or... other matters.'

'Other more dubious matters with you alongside him, you mean?' For the umpteenth time, she wished she knew what the pair of them had really been involved in when Clifford had been her late uncle's batman in the army. After her uncle had resigned his commission, Clifford had been his butler and partner in adventure. Their shared experiences had led to them becoming firm friends despite their class differences. And so it was proving with her.

Clifford adjusted his perfectly aligned cufflinks. 'Ahem. I am sure the preparations for the festivities are close enough to completion that your band of aproned elves can finish them without too much fluster. They would be beyond proud to be entrusted with running the event.'

Eleanor smiled at the mention of her loyal staff of ladies. 'And the Women's Institute are all coming. They're always up for pitching in with anything needed.' She bit her lip. Despite her words, she was still feeling torn. She was the Lady of the Manor. And the villagers had welcomed her in with open arms from day one. But with the number of noble families across England losing their estates to the ravages of increased taxation and death duty, she had to put securing Henley Hall's finances first. Or the villagers might have nowhere to celebrate Christmas Eve next year! 'Please call Mrs Butters, Clifford.'

He strode to the fireplace and pulled the bell sash. A few moments later, Eleanor's rosy-cheeked housekeeper appeared. She stepped in and curtseyed.

'Sorry to call you when you're so busy,' Eleanor said.

Mrs Butters tutted gently, her grey curls bobbing. 'Goodness, m'lady, you can never have need of apologising. In fact, I was just on my way to report on progress; the treasure hunt is all set up and the crafting table is filled with all the spare holly, ivy and fir cones Lizzie and Polly have collected so the young 'uns can turn them into festive decorations they can take home with them. And Lizzie and Polly have also set up a cosy corner where they can read the real young 'uns *A Christmas Carol* as they do each year until they fall asleep. Gives the parents a few hours to really let their hair down without worrying about the little 'uns. Speaking of which, the dancing room is ready, too. There's just the finishing touches to one of the games' rooms and the dressing of the long dining tables in the ballroom. But 'tis only the Christmas decorations as is left to be added to them.'

'Well done!' Eleanor said. 'Now, we want to ask you and the ladies a favour.'

Seldon stepped forward. 'And feel no pressure that you should say yes.'

Mrs Butters beamed back at both of them. 'If it's not overstepping to ask, is it summat for the agency as has come up?'

'It is. But the problem is, we would need to leave soon,' Eleanor said.

'Would have left already, ideally,' Clifford added, consulting his pocket watch.

Mrs Butters clapped her hands. 'Then there's no time for any more discussion. Save to say, perhaps you might take Master Gladstone with you? And we'll keep Tomkins. The pair of them have got each other as frothed up as a bowl of whipped cream! You can't see your office floor for shredded tissue paper now, my lady.'

'Gracious, of course.'

With a, 'Right you are then, m'lady,' Mrs Butters bustled out.

'Gracious, what a wonderful blessing our ladies are!'

'Absolutely, Eleanor!' Seldon shook his head ruefully. 'But I still can't believe we're actually going to drive what... three hundred odd miles?'

'Closer to four hundred and ten, in fact, sir.'

'Thank you, Clifford. Four hundred odd miles on Christmas Eve with snow threatening, to some forsaken village in the middle of nowhere with no idea what we're being asked to investigate?'

'Yes, we are, Hugh,' Eleanor said, now fully resolved. 'Because needs must. And whoever our mysterious client is, they're obviously serious. And, it seems, in need of help.'

Seldon let out a long breath. 'We agreed we would vote on whether to take each case, remember?' To her surprise, he raised his hand. 'I vote for all three of us that we go. Only let's set off without delay so we can be back as soon as possible so we still get some Christmas at home.'

'I shall begin fettling the Rolls immediately, as she needs some additional adjustments for such a long trip in this bitter weather,' Clifford said.

'We could go up in my motor car?'

Clifford cleared his throat quietly.

Seldon nodded resignedly. 'Ah, yes. My little Austin Seven might not be quite up for it. And the Rolls will give the impression the agency is flourishing.'

'And in this freezing weather, sir, it will be rather more comfortable for her ladyship. Shall we rendezvous in forty-five minutes on the entrance steps?' Clifford glanced at her out of the corner of his eye. 'And not a Lady Swift's forty-five?'

'By which you mean three hours, you terror!' As they headed for the door, she clapped her hands. 'So, The Byron Detective Agency is still in business!'

'Though what business we're getting involved in, who knows,' Seldon muttered.

She slapped his arm. 'Let's hope one as festive as the season!'

But in her heart, she wasn't so sure.

3

The only sound was the rumble of the Rolls's tyres on the uneven road surface and the swish of the wipers as they swept the falling snow from the windscreen.

Eleanor stared out into the blackest of winter nights. The last street light they had passed had been on the outskirts of Oxford over five hours ago. Since then, only sporadic huddles of stone cottages and barns had shown any form of light, although the moon occasionally broke through the blanket of brooding cloud. Despite this, she couldn't help feeling a festive thrill.

It's still Christmas Eve, Ellie, and I'm with my two most favourite men in the world.

She leaned forward in the back seat. 'Clifford, surely you can motor the Rolls at more than the speed of a decrepit donkey? After all, it's only snowing lightly.'

He raised an eyebrow. 'Indubitably, my lady. If you wish to spend the remainder of Christmas in a ditch. And miss our rendezvous?'

'It must be time I relieved you at the wheel, Clifford,' Seldon called from the back seat, too. 'You've driven the whole way so far.'

'Most kind, sir. But with no implied slight upon your driving skills, the Rolls can be another, ahem, inconstant lady in such conditions.'

Eleanor ignored the mischievous jibe. She had found out first-hand just how right he was one previous Christmas when Clifford had broken his arm and she'd taken over driving duties. 'Come now, children. We haven't got time to squabble. Our midnight deadline is looming!'

Seldon discreetly pulled her closer into his side under the thick cashmere blanket her butler had thoughtfully packed, along with two flasks of coffee and a basket of festive treats which was now severely depleted. Mrs Trotman, Eleanor's no-nonsense cook, could always be relied upon to conjure up a splendid picnic at a moment's notice.

'One silver lining,' he murmured. 'As Clifford is clearly as stubborn as you are, I get to snuggle up with you for at least some of Christmas Eve while he continues to drive.' He cocked his head. 'Although, honestly, I'd hoped to enjoy listening to you two trumping each with the sort of ridiculous games I've always imagined you played on long journeys.'

She laughed. 'He does have a seemingly endless arsenal of competitive diversions.'

'However, her ladyship is not a fan of repeatedly coming second, sir,' Clifford added.

She tutted. 'It's true. But that's not the reason I'm not playing. It's pitch-dark out there and for once I was letting you concentrate on driving.'

In the passenger seat up front, Gladstone poked his head out from under the map Clifford was consulting and yawned.

She leaned forward between the seats and cupped his wrinkled jowls as Clifford negotiated the leviathan Rolls around another tortuous bend. He then took the right-hand fork at the top of a steep rise before stopping in a precarious passing place on the edge of a deep gully. Below, the side vanished into blackness. He clicked on his pocket torch and studied the map intently.

'Problem?' Seldon said.

'Not exactly, sir. Only according to the map, the village we seek should already have appeared.'

'Your mental compass doesn't usually fail us,' she said genuinely. 'Trust your intuition, Clifford.'

They motored on until a signpost materialised in the headlights' halo.

'Tell me it says "Yorelow"?' she murmured hopefully.

'It might have, my lady, if there was anything written on it!'

With little choice, he took the turning and set off down a rough track, the snow falling heavily now. The exposed roots of the thick trees on either side left the car lurching and pitching as if they were driving down a dried-up river bed. After a while the road forked in two again. With no indication which way led to the village, they opted for the left one.

Finally, they reached more level ground. But only a moment later, the track ended at the edge of small lake, ringed by trees.

Eleanor hid a smile and tutted. 'Shall I take over map reading duties now, Clifford?'

'Be my guest, my lady,' he said. 'But it is not navigator error. The map, roads, and signposts simply do not agree.'

She looked around. 'Well, it's almost midnight already! So we'd better retrace our steps and try that other fork in the road.'

In the gloom, Seldon was the only one who spotted the turning.

'Bravo, sir!' Clifford said as they bumped along the marginally improved surface.

'Fingers crossed it leads to Yorelow. Or at least to somewhere inhabited where we can ask for directions,' Seldon muttered.

A moment later, as the track swung around a sharp curve, Clifford stamped on the brakes.

Through the windscreen, Eleanor saw the figure of a woman dart across the path of the car, only an inch from the Rolls's bonnet. She was wearing a long black gown, her head covered. As they lurched to a stop, the woman locked eyes with Eleanor.

Then she was gone.

Eleanor jumped out and looked around, then peered under the car. She sighed in relief. 'Not there! Which means she must have been unscathed.'

'Naturally,' Clifford said, joining her, his breath freezing in front of him as he spoke. 'The Rolls's brakes are second to none.' He then called through cupped hands, 'I say, madam! Are you alright?'

Eleanor strained her eyes into the gloom. 'Even if she hadn't been unscathed, it wasn't your fault. She shot out in front of you. And she was dressed head to toe in black! But you definitely missed her, thank goodness. What on earth was she doing out here, at this time of night. And in this wonderfully seasonal, but witheringly chilly weather?'

She wrapped her arms around her sides as a shiver overtook her. But not only from the bitter cold. She had the impression someone was watching them. She hastily slid her mittens on, Jack Frost already nipping at her fingertips.

Seldon joined her, rubbing his neck. 'I was looking out the back window when we braked. What did I miss?'

'A strangely dressed woman in a shawl, Hugh. Who we thankfully also missed with the Rolls.'

Clifford's brow furrowed as he bent forward to stare at the radiator grille.

'What is it?'

He straightened up and held out his hand. On the palm was a thin tube, two or three inches in length. Clearly it was part of a longer item as one end was jagged, as if broken off.

She stared at it in the glare of the headlights. 'It looks like... clay?'

Seldon nodded. 'How it got lodged in the radiator grille, who knows?' He glanced at his watch. 'If this woman's gone, we'd better do the same. That deadline is getting desperately close.'

They climbed back into the relative warmth of the car and set off again. But at an even slower speed. Perhaps the women in this area had a bizarre penchant for throwing themselves in the path of passing vehicles, she mused. Even as she had the thought, she shook her head. Just how many vehicles would ever likely pass along here? She peered ahead into the gloom, mystified again why anyone would be out in such a remote spot in such wintery weather. Why hadn't the woman at least paused to regain her breath, seeing as she'd missed serious injury by only a whisker? Or stayed to speak to them? And surely that hadn't been a wreath of greenery poking from her hood? But what she really couldn't get out of her head was that stare.

How many minutes later it was, she couldn't say, but a light up ahead glinted through the swirling snowflakes. All three of them let out a sigh of relief.

Clifford pulled up outside an ancient, black-timbered building where the light seemed to come from.

'Looks like some sort of pub or tavern,' she said, leaning out of her window to read the sign above the gnarled oak door, Jack Frost nipping at her nose this time. '"The Angel's Summons". Unusual name, but very apt for Christmas.'

'It's well after licensing hours for it to still be open, though,' Seldon said.

Eleanor smiled. 'You're not a policeman any more, remember? Besides, when away from home, Clifford and I have always stood by the age-old maxim, "When in Rome, do as the Romans do." On this occasion, I for one am glad the landlord has less than perfect regard for the law.'

'*Landlady!*' a sharp voice called from the doorway.

A woman dressed in a blue cable-knit cardigan and brown twill trousers stalked out onto the tavern's front step. Her vivacious, fair hair seemed at odds with her stiff demeanour. Yet even with the suspicious, narrow-eyed look dogging her face, there was an attractiveness about her, Eleanor thought. Strong features, set above a capable but still feminine frame which spoke of hard work and an iron will. She estimated her to be in her forties.

'I won't stand for no trouble,' the woman said. ''Specially from strangers poking their nose into my affairs, even if it is Christmas Eve. So, you can turn your fancy motor right around!'

Clifford stepped out of the Rolls, his footsteps crunching in the newly fallen, newly frozen snow. He doffed his bowler hat. 'Actually, madam—'

'I'm no madam! Mathilde Frisham is my name. Miss.' She ended with a hint of regret to Eleanor's ears. Or was it bitterness?

Eleanor hurried out of the car to join Clifford, with Gladstone scrambling after her. As the eager bulldog scrabbled up the woman's legs, the landlady bent down and ran her hand over his head.

'Making trouble couldn't be further from the reason we are here, Miss Frisham,' Eleanor said. 'We've got lost, you see, and would be grateful if you could point us in the direction of Waketon Court.'

The landlady's brows shot up. 'There? And of a night-time, too.' She hesitated, then shook her head. 'If that's how it is, so be it. Go along yonder. Eastways, straight after church's netherside. Call back for a tot to see you home if it is fine and dandy for the place still to be open! If you can,' she ended in a mutter.

The door swung shut behind her.

Eleanor grimaced. 'If we can?'

Clifford arched a brow.

'She must have meant if we have time. It's pretty late already,' Seldon said. 'I think my, er, remark about it being after licensing hours might have upset her a little.'

Trusting her butler's interpretation of 'along yonder' as being in the direction they had been heading in, they set off again. Soon they arrived at a triangle of snow-flecked grass, with several unmarked turnings. They finally found the church, but only by trying the first two options, both of which ended at dead ends.

The church itself was a dark stone building, set amidst a small graveyard, which was surrounded by a wall that was so low it seemed to have little purpose. Mind you, she mused, why did that surprise her? Nothing was as one expected here. No village green. Not even a hint of a high street. And where were all the houses?

'There!' Eleanor cried, pointing. 'Opposite the church!' The Rolls's headlights picked out a dilapidated sign, half the top letters missing: W-K--O- C--RT. FIFTY YARDS BACK.

Seldon rolled his eyes. 'Then why not put the sign fifty yards back?'

'Who cares!' she said ecstatically. 'We've found it!'

'And it is, ahem, only just gone midnight,' Clifford added as he carefully turned the car around and drove towards a set of impressively tall, but battered gates.

'This must be the place,' she said gleefully. 'I'll open them. No fussing, Clifford. I'm stiff from sitting anyway.'

She leapt out before he, or Seldon, could argue, immediately being coated in the softly falling snow.

'What the—' She jumped back. A flicker of a match was followed by the dim glow of a lantern. It threw an eerie yellow light on a set of wizened features.

'Umm... sorry to have bumped into you. Is this Waketon Court?'

'Per'aps, it is. Per'aps, it isn't,' the man said warily.

As Seldon joined her, the man shuffled off, his lantern fading into the gloom until it was suddenly extinguished.

Seldon looked at her quizzically. 'Who was that?'

She shook her rapidly whitening head, a halo of dislodged snowflakes shimmering around her before fading into the night. 'No idea. He could have been coming from the house or the other side of the road.' She waved for Clifford to drive closer. Only then could she see the sign half-hidden by the thick vines running riot down the gate pillar.

'Aha! So it is Waketon Court. We're finally here!' she cheered.

The driveway ended after less than ten car lengths. As Clifford eased them to a stop, the headlights picked up a dark-red painted façade, criss-crossed by aged and wonky black timbers. Much like the tavern.

They all stepped out onto the soft carpet of newly fallen snow and approached the front door.

'Best behaviour please, Master Gladstone,' Clifford muttered, clipping the bulldog's lead on.

'Here goes,' Eleanor whispered, pulling on the ancient bell rod.

A distant jangle filtered out to them.

After a long minute, the sound of several bolts being pulled back and locks being turned reached them. The door opened slowly to reveal a stocky man in his sixties. He was wearing a uniform similar to her butler's, but cut from a style popular decades earlier.

'Yes?' he said in a surprisingly reedy voice for one of such a robust build.

'Good evening. I am Lady Swift. This is my husband, Mr... Sir Hugh Seldon. And this is Mr Clifford. The three of us are here for an appointment with the master of the house.'

The manservant's brow furrowed. 'That will not be possible, m'lady.'

Seldon took half a step forward. 'Listen, my man. We've driven over seven hours to get here. On Christmas Eve of all times. Now, give me one good reason why your master can't see us?'

The manservant nodded stiffly. 'Certainly, sir. The master of the house is dead.'

4

Eleanor's thoughts whirled.

'Dead?'

The manservant nodded. Then, to her growing confusion, ushered them into the black-beamed entrance hall without a word. She felt as if she'd stepped back in time. So much so, an ancient Anglo-Saxon king draped in animal furs sitting in the enormous oak chair beside her wouldn't have been out of place. The gaily decorated Christmas tree next to it, however, felt frivolous given the morbid news they'd just received.

The door closed behind them, seemingly by itself.

The calm and assured policeman Eleanor had fallen for in Seldon stepped forward and addressed the manservant. 'Our condolences, Mr...?'

'Just Babcock, sir. I was Mr Pritchard's valet.'

'I see. And when exactly did your master pass away, Babcock?' Seldon said.

'Five years ago, sir.'

'What the—' Seldon's frown told her how mystified he now was, too.

She cleared her throat to regain Babcock's attention,

which had been distracted by Gladstone nuzzling his hand. Whether her bulldog was offering sympathy, or angling for treats, she wasn't sure. 'Can you shed any light on...' She scoured her coat pockets. The telegram they'd received appeared in Clifford's gloved hand. 'Ah! That's it.' She held it out to Babcock. 'This message. It was sent to us earlier today.'

The valet's eyes flicked slowly across the lines. 'In a manner of speaking, yes, m'lady. Leastways, I was told to expect you tonight.'

'Ah! That's a relief. But if it wasn't your master who sent us this telegram, who did?'

He tapped the second to last line. 'Mr... Unwin sent that telegram,' he said in a disdainful tone. 'Mr Inigo Osmund Unwin. "I.O.U." He is my late master's nephew and has been temporarily... residing here. At his own invitation.'

Eleanor caught Clifford's quiet tut of disapproval of what he clearly saw as Babcock's disrespect. She couldn't disagree, but was curious over what was behind the manservant's animosity towards their potential client.

'Thank you for clearing up our confusion over who we have actually come to meet, Babcock. Please inform Mr Unwin we have arrived.' She caught sight of an elderly grandfather clock she hadn't noticed. Despite it telling her little, having no hands on the clock face, she said confidently, 'And, er, in line with his midnight deadline.'

Babcock shook his head again. 'Apologies, but Mr Unwin is not here, m'lady.' He glanced at the handless clock. 'And it is, in fact, nearer half past. However, follow me, please.' He marched off under the low square arch on the right.

Gladstone waved his tail enthusiastically and set off in pursuit, followed by the three of them. The timber-beamed passageway ended at a studded door, a huge iron ring acting as a handle. Babcock bowed his head and entered.

'Oh my!' Eleanor couldn't help murmuring as she stepped in after him.

The room was lit by a ring of candles set in an old cartwheel hanging on thick chains. The furniture was sparse, with an oak desk and a commanding chair behind it, upholstered in leather covered in what looked like Egyptian hieroglyphics. Hanging above it was a framed portrait of a striking older man that reminded her a little of her late uncle. Off to the side of the desk, facing the windows, was a tall ebony cabinet. Through a set of French doors she could see the snow still falling.

'When do you expect Mr Unwin back?'

Babcock shrugged. 'I have no idea, m'lady. I last saw him at ten thirteen this evening when he went into the master's study.'

'How did you know the exact—' Seldon caught Clifford's look. 'Forget it. I know. You're a valet. It's your job to know.'

'Yes, sir. Mr Unwin did, however, leave this.' He pointed to a gramophone record lying on the desk's burgundy leather inlay.

Seldon stepped to her side. 'A record?' He craned his head. 'Oh! It's marked "For The Byron Detective Agency".' He frowned. 'I still don't understand.'

'Not surprising, sir,' Babcock said with a hint of sympathy. 'You see, Mr Unwin has a thing for... newfangled fads. This is his latest. I believe he acquired the contraption from the colonies.'

Clifford ran his eye over a tall, lidded cabinet along one wall. 'A fine example. From America, perchance?'

'A gramophone player?' Seldon tapped the large flared brass horn sprouting from it.

Clifford nodded, his eyes bright with animation. 'Indeed, sir. However, it is also a home-recording device. A recent, ingenious adaptation of the eminent Thomas Edison's original phonograph invention of 1877. You see, by introducing changes to a magnetic field—'

'Clifford,' Eleanor interrupted with a wince. 'We'd love you to witter our ears off with the technical details, but later perhaps?'

He bobbed his head apologetically. 'Noted, my lady.'

Babcock clucked his tongue. 'Rather than speak to anyone, Mr Unwin uses that contrivance. Even to the point of leaving instructions for the staff regarding his fancies for lunch or supper!'

Eleanor could see how that might rankle.

'Well, at least we can use it to play that record back, I suppose,' Seldon said. 'Though this is all very baffling.'

'If you need me, there's a bell rod by the fireplace, m'lady.'

She gave him a smile. 'Thank you, Babcock. You've been most helpful.'

The door closed behind him.

Clifford sniffed. 'Although the offer of a warming refreshment for you, my lady, and you, sir, after such a long journey, would not have gone amiss.'

She flapped an affectionate hand at him. 'Ever attentive of you, Clifford. But we're not here to assess Babcock's merits. Besides, we might not be meeting him at his best, given how late it is.'

Seldon nodded. 'And he doesn't seem a fan of our client. Mind you, I can't blame him. Leaving recordings of his instructions for dinner is decidedly odd. I can't imagine Mrs Trotman responding well to that.'

Clifford shuddered. 'Such a course of action would be most unwise!'

Seldon glanced at Eleanor teasingly. 'This Unwin character's not far off being a contender for your title of the epitome of the unorthodox.'

'Hilarious!' she said as he and Clifford shared an amused look. 'But let's hear what investigation we've travelled up here on speculation to agree to. Or not!'

She watched as Clifford started the gramophone. Gladstone, bored with proceedings, busied himself sniffing around the room in the hope of finding a snack.

'How would this Inigo Unwin have recorded his voice, though, Clifford?' Eleanor said.

He opened the front doors of the cabinet and pointed. 'With this ring microphone. The extended cable allows the user to record in comfort a distance from the apparatus itself while one's voice is engraved on the surface of the record. There is indeed one more blank disc still in its packaging in here.'

He set the record Babcock had given them on the turntable, the three of them sharing a look of eager anticipation.

As it started spinning, a series of muffled clunks filtered out of the brass horn. Then a protracted hiss, followed by the sound of a man clearing his throat. 'Good evening.'

The quality of the recording was poor, but by straining her ears, she could make out an educated but hoarse male voice. Eleanor pictured a man in his late twenties or early thirties, perhaps.

'I, as you have probably learned from Babcock by now, am Inigo Unwin. My apologies for asking you to come at short notice.'

Seldon rolled his eyes. 'Hmm, a bit of an understatement!'

The hiss intensified as if the snow outside had become a blizzard and found its way onto the recording. 'Especially on Christmas Eve,' the voice continued. 'But an urgent matter has arisen. You will have received the first amount of three hundred' – a loud crackle made them start – 'pounds I placed in your account earlier.'

Eleanor waved an impatient hand at the record. All of this they knew already.

'The second instalment is in the top drawer of the desk. I shall wait while you confirm this for yourselves.'

'Check please, Clifford,' she said, whispering for some reason.

He strode to the desk and opened the drawer. Pulling out an unsealed envelope, he counted the bundle of banknotes poking out.

'Two hundred and eighty... ninety... three hundred pounds exactly.'

'Excellent!' She turned back to the record. 'All checked, thank you, Mr Unwin.'

The hiss continued.

Seldon grimaced. 'If he records his dinner requirements like this, it must take Babcock an age to find out what vegetables he wants with his meat.'

'So,' Unwin's voice suddenly came through again, 'you know now I am serious in wishing to engage your services. But if you choose to accept the case, you must do so by midnight tonight.'

'A most precise stipulation,' Clifford murmured, always the one for exactitude in everything.

'We're trying to,' she muttered, ignoring Babcock's insistence the deadline had already passed. 'But you need to tell us what the wretched case is!'

Her gaze darted to the French doors. Was it just the snow whirling around or... had she seen a faint shadow through the glass? She waved for the others to carry on listening and peered harder into the night.

Nothing.

Chiding herself for being over-imaginative, she tried the handles. Finding the doors unlocked, she poked her head outside.

Again nothing, except the snow falling silently.

Yanking the doors closed, she returned to the others, who were listening intently to more hissing overlain with a clinking sound and a... gurgle?

Clifford mimed taking a swig of a drink.

'Now,' Unwin continued, 'the reason for my calling you down here...'

Eleanor rubbed her hands in anticipation. Seldon nodded thoughtfully. Clifford poised his pen over his pocketbook, hushing Gladstone's snuffling.

But the only sound was hissing. Then a clunk, as if the microphone had been put down hastily or knocked over.

'Clumsy!' Clifford tutted in horror. 'That is a delicate piece of apparatus!'

The record continued spinning, but now, behind the hissing, she could hear other noises. A chair being pushed back? Then a faint click? The gramophone needle slid onto the last groove, a loud click sounding above the hissing with each revolution.

They stared at each other.

'That can't be the end of it,' she said in disbelief. 'Turn it over, Clifford.'

He did. But as the needle reached the end of the record for the second time, it was clear there was no more from their would-be client.

'And it is now exactly thirty-seven minutes past the hour of midnight.' Clifford's pocket watch snapped shut.

Seldon shook his head slowly. 'Can someone please tell me' – he spread his hands – 'what in blazes that was all about?'

Clifford raised an eyebrow. 'I am as much in the dark as you, sir.'

Eleanor nodded. 'And me. But what I do know is that The Byron Detective Agency already has a mystery to investigate!'

5

'This place can't *still* be open at this hour on Christmas Eve, surely?' Seldon frowned. 'Actually, of course, it's gone midnight. So it's Christmas Day. Happy Christmas, Eleanor! And you, Clifford!'

'And the same to you, sir,' Clifford said.

'And you, Hugh!' she cried as he drew her into a hug.

They shared a tender kiss while Clifford averted his eyes.

As they drew back, Seldon grimaced. 'Perhaps we'd better save any more festive fun until we've worked out what we intend to do about our missing client and case details?'

Eleanor nodded. 'You're right, Hugh. We really need somewhere to regroup.'

As Clifford held her door open, she climbed out of the Rolls and up the steps to the tavern, where earlier they'd asked the landlady, Miss Mathilde Frisham, for directions.

Eleanor pressed her face to the front door. The glass was so old it was thicker at the bottom than the top and almost opaque. 'There's a light shining inside,' she said in relief, already starting to shiver in the freezing air.

Gladstone let out a hopeful woof and butted the door with his nose. The door creaked open.

Inside it was festively warm and cosy, a fire glowing in the enormous hearth. The walls were timber-framed with ancient earth-red bricks in between in a herringbone pattern. A sprinkling of mismatched tables, chairs and benches were dotted about. The low ceiling was hung with myriad ceramic pint and half-pint jugs. She sniffed. The air was tinged with the scent of hops, fragrant wood smoke and a hint of something tantalising. Her stomach rumbled. The whole place felt reassuringly forged from the annals of time itself. Whatever problems they had at the moment, this ancient tavern had clearly seen worse times and survived.

'Ah! So you did call back then.' The landlady's strident voice cut across the room. She was leaning on the counter, under a woven Christmas display of green spruce, ivy and red-berried holly running the full length of the bar.

Shaking a cloud of snowflakes from her hair, Eleanor put on her best smile. As she approached the bar, she noticed it was made from a single sawn tree trunk. 'Good evening again, Miss Frisham. I know it's terribly late. And Christmas Eve too. I just hoped, if you were still open, you might be able to furnish us with a scrap of something warming? We're ravenous.'

Mathilde looked her over, picking at her cardigan cuff. 'As it happens, this is the one day of the year we're open later than normal. The lot what come out of Midnight Mass around half past one, pop in here for summat. Wouldn't be a patch of what you're obviously used to, though.'

'You'd be surprised, Miss Frisham,' Clifford said.

Seldon nodded wryly in agreement.

Eleanor rolled her eyes good-naturedly. 'What this pair of rotters mean is that I might, on occasion, devour anything.'

Mathilde almost smiled. 'In that case, shake the fire and park yourselves.'

She disappeared through a jute curtain.

Seldon led Eleanor to a table in an alcove by the fire where Gladstone was wagging his tail at a lifelike deer. Made from woven willow, a plaited wreath of silver leaves graced its neck.

Clifford gave the glowing embers in the giant iron basket a rake of encouragement.

'That fireplace wouldn't be out of place in the great hall of a castle,' she mused. 'This old tavern must have heard some stories in its time.'

She settled onto a padded bench next to the fire, Seldon sliding in beside her.

'I'm rather more interested in the story of that gramophone record at Waketon Court!' he said. 'For starters, why did Unwin record it at all, unless he never intended to be there in the first place?'

'I never thought of that.' She shook her head. 'This case is getting more peculiar by the minute.'

He sighed in frustration. 'But that's just it. *What* case?'

Clifford cleared his throat. 'Sir. Mr Unwin paid us three hundred pounds to come up here on short notice on, of all times, Christmas Eve. I would suggest, as her ladyship did back in Mr Pritchard's study, that we already have a case. A missing person's case: our client.'

For a few moments they sat in silence, thawing their bones out until the landlady appeared with a large tray. Clifford stepped over and relieved her of it.

'No need of that,' Mathilde said defensively. 'Nothing wrong with these arms. Not after all the pints they've pulled. And the barrels humped up from the cellar. And the lack of men willing to lift a finger!'

As Clifford set the tray down on the table, she waved a hand over the three bowls. 'There's more warming in the oven.' Reaching down to cup Gladstone's wrinkled jowls, her expression softened. 'The one in the metal tin is for this 'un.'

She stalked back to the bar and disappeared through the curtain again.

Clifford set about serving Eleanor and Seldon. Strangely, what looked like a diminutive cottage loaf sat in the middle of each of the bowls, wafting out a cloud of inviting steam. To Eleanor's delight it turned out to be a lidded, thick-crusted carrier for a beefy leek and celery broth. Clifford tested Gladstone's simpler fayre with the tip of his little finger to make sure it wasn't too hot, then set it down in front of the hungry bulldog. Bobbing his head to them, he wandered away as if to study the architecture of the tavern.

'Oh no, you don't!' Eleanor hurriedly swallowed her first mouthful and pointedly put the lid back on. 'Either you eat at least a spoonful or two with us, or I shall refuse to eat mine. And then you'll be entirely responsible for me coming over all feeble and falling in a faint from lack of sustenance.'

'No, he wouldn't,' Seldon said. 'Because you have the unnerving constitution of a rhinoceros. Albeit a beautiful one,' he added quickly, dodging her swipe. He waved his spoon. 'But I'd dig in all the same if I were you, Clifford. It's superb.'

Her butler pursed his lips. 'It is not the quality of the food which prevents me, sir.'

'No, it's his terrible secret that does, Hugh.'

Clifford glanced sideways at her, his eyes giving away his curiosity.

'I've finally worked it out, Hugh,' she said conspiratorially. 'It's obvious now why Clifford never eats or sleeps. And why he glides about so silently that we never hear his footsteps. He's really a vampire!'

Seldon choked on his soup as Clifford gamefully perched on the seat opposite, but still didn't take his bowl of broth. Seldon pushed it in front of him.

'All joking aside, this is no time for worrying about the rules of butler etiquette, Clifford. You're here on agency business like the rest of us. And we all need to stay sharp-witted enough to work out what to do.'

'Very well, sir.' He lifted the lid of his breadbasket reluctantly. 'To return to the conversation you and her ladyship were having a few moments ago. Admittedly, the absence of our supposed client was as unexpected as it was confusing.'

'And Babcock apparently has no idea when Unwin will be back,' Eleanor added.

'True, my lady. But, perhaps, that is exactly why we were summoned by Mr Unwin? Perhaps he was aware something like this might happen?'

She gasped. 'You mean, he thought someone might kidnap him and he wanted us to stop them?'

Seldon swallowed his spoonful thoughtfully. 'In which case, like his midnight deadline, we were too late. However, if there is any possibility the man's in trouble, he is, by default, our client so—'

He was interrupted by the front door flying open.

It let in an icy blast of snow and wind, followed by a lanky man in his early thirties. He was dressed in a woollen cap with ear mufflers and a dark-green waxed coat. It swung open as he moved, revealing patched brown corduroy trousers belted with several loops of slim rope. And the inside pockets of his coat seemed to be stuffed with something. On seeing them staring, the man snatched it closed.

Gladstone let out a quiet growl, his hackles rising.

'Get out, Ned Yearth!' Mathilde called from behind the bar. 'You're banned, as you know well!'

The man ran his tongue down the inside of his cheek as he shook his head with a sly grin. 'Where's your charity at, Matty? It's Christmas Eve, innit?'

Her eyes narrowed. 'You're no charity case, Ned. You are nothing but trouble. And don't you dare call me Matty! Not even Mathilde. You know why you're banned. Now get out!

'You gonna try and make me, Matty, dear heart?' Ned shot back.

Seldon jumped to his feet and cleared the gap to him in three strides, Clifford beside him. 'No. Because we'll do it for the lady,' he said calmly. 'Only I'm sure you're a decent sort, and will save that being necessary.'

'There's nothing decent in him,' the landlady spat.

Ned's jaw tightened, but he was dwarfed by Clifford's commanding six feet and Seldon's even taller, athletic frame. Eleanor watched the stand-off.

Clifford gestured at the door. 'Your choice.'

Ned scowled. 'You threatening me?'

Seldon's tone turned as steely as his expression. 'Not at all. We are merely making it clear that while we are here, Miss Frisham is not going to be intimidated by you.'

For a horrible moment Eleanor thought Ned was going to take a swing at her husband. Gladstone too, evidently, as he shot across the floor, barking vociferously.

Instead, Ned seemed to think better of it. With another scowl at the landlady, he spun on his heel. 'It's not me you should be banning, *Miss* Frisham, but that cursed Inigo Unwin!' he shouted over his shoulder.

Eleanor started. It seemed not only had their client disappeared, but here was someone with a grudge against him.

'But don't fret,' Ned growled over his shoulder. 'Mark my words, that cur will get what he deserves one day!'

6

'It's the likes of that Ned what make this place more plague than profit!' Mathilde said bitterly as Seldon and Clifford sat back down.

Eleanor wondered how anyone could turn a profit in such a sparsely populated hamlet. 'Are you alright, Miss Frisham?' she asked in a sisterly tone.

The landlady shrugged. 'No choice not to be, have I? Not like some.' She walked back behind the bar. 'I'll get your pies.'

Seldon grimaced as he retook his seat beside Eleanor, discreetly squeezing her hand under the table.

She shook her head. 'I don't think she meant to be offensive, Hugh. I just think that Ned upset her more than she wants to let on.' She sighed, never more grateful for all her many blessings than now.

'Find Waketon Court, did you?' Mathilde said, returning and placing the tray down.

'With your directions, yes, thank you,' Eleanor said. 'But not our host. He wasn't at home. Perhaps you've seen him this evening? Mr Inigo Unwin?'

Mathilde glanced away. 'No. He's not one for coming in

here any more.' She shoved the tray forward with a frown. 'Fidget pie. And a jug each of fruitly.'

'Looks and smells delicious. Thank you.'

Eleanor didn't miss the landlady's knotted brows as she stalked back to the bar. Perhaps she and their absent client weren't friends? Along with Ned, and Babcock, that made three of them! Mr Unwin didn't seem to be the flavour of the month in Yorelow. His disappearance was becoming more worrying by the moment.

Seldon stared at his drink as Clifford placed the tankard in front of him. 'Fruitly? That being a pint of cider by any other name, no doubt?'

'One thing cannot be exactly another, sir. And it is likely included in the price of the meal. Thus not served illegally.'

Eleanor smiled. He was clearly trying to ease Seldon's unease at being in a tavern after hours and drinking. She noticed his fingers straying to his cufflinks. 'Now, Clifford,' she said firmly. 'Having learned a minuscule amount of your skill at reading minds, forget Hugh for the moment and tell me what is bothering *you*?'

His brow flinched. 'My lady, as your butler, it is far from my place to hold an opinion.'

She paused in admiring the layered gammon, apples, onions and potato encased in the oven-hot, golden pie crust. 'And yet, as always, you have one. Thankfully. Besides, I'm not asking you in your capacity as the best butler in the world, but as our equally treasured third partner in The Byron Detective Agency. We are, after all, on a case whether we chose to be or not.'

He nodded. 'I was hoping to save the news until after Christmas, my lady. However, maybe now is the time to mention it. You see, it has come to my attention that the Henley Hall estate is soon to undergo a tax assessment.'

Eleanor's fork clattered onto the table. 'Clifford! That will almost certainly mean a demand for goodness knows how much extra money!'

He nodded again. 'National sympathy with the Labour Party's policies continues to increase. Our Conservative Prime Minister, Mr Stanley Baldwin, has to respond to demands to "fix" the waning economy.'

She groaned. 'Of course I want to pay my way. But it does seem as if the more affluent classes have been targeted to the point of bankruptcy of late!'

'Pay *our* way, Eleanor,' Seldon said emphatically. He turned to Clifford. 'How do you know about this impending visit?'

He ran a finger around his starched white collar. 'Alas, discretion forbids, sir.'

Seldon slapped the table. 'Then it's unanimously decided. I'm voting for all of us. We stay until we find our client, as we've already decided. And then if that wasn't what he paid us the initial three hundred pounds for and then offered us two further payments of three hundred pounds, we find out what was and stay until we've earned that!'

'Agreed!' Eleanor said enthusiastically. 'In the morning we'll return to Waketon Court. And if Unwin isn't there, we'll ask Babcock for his whereabouts. If he doesn't know, we'll make a village-wide search and ask everyone we meet! Someone will know where our absent client has gone to ground!'

Clifford rose. 'Shall I enquire of Miss Frisham if her fine tavern runs to having guest rooms?'

Eleanor looked out of the window and shook her head forcefully. 'Absolutely not. Please plead that she put us up whether or not she has. Because judging by the increasing snow out there, if she doesn't, we're going to spend Christmas frozen to death in the Rolls, stuck in a ditch!'

7

'So you're wanting to stay in Yorelow this eve, I hear?' Mathilde said, returning a moment later with Clifford.

Eleanor nodded. 'It would be a shame to miss seeing it in the light. And given it's probably almost morning now, we'd be very grateful if you have space for us?'

'There's two rooms atop. But it's a rare day they're let out.'

'They will be perfect,' Eleanor said chirpily.

Mathilde frowned. 'You're a rummy sort of fancy lady, if you don't mind me saying.'

'My wife gets that quite a lot,' Seldon said wryly.

Clifford went off to retrieve the bags from the Rolls while Eleanor and Seldon followed the landlady to a narrow door tucked away in an alcove.

'The rooms are at the top of the last set of stairs. I'll sort you some bedding,' she said, leaving them to it.

The way up was barely lit, the only light being a single candle lamp at each dog leg of the ancient oak staircase. Eleanor helped Gladstone up, as he was too excited to not just throw himself at each step. She wasn't far off copying him, thinking that anywhere to lay her head would do fine, given the lateness of the hour and the increasingly treacherous weather outside.

As Seldon opened the door of the first room, however, his sigh was so deep, it fluttered her curls.

'The other one must be better,' he said, almost tripping over Gladstone, who was eager to lead the way even though he clearly had no idea where to.

At least in the second room, the bare iron bed frame was more ornate.

'Eleanor, this couldn't be further from what I wanted for you at Christmas!' he groaned, following her inside.

'Oh, I think it's a splendid adventure, Hugh,' she said genuinely. 'I've never stayed in the attic of such a historic tavern before. It's all spotless. Even the rugs dotted here and there over the beautiful old floorboards are clean. And look, the lords and ladies patterned washstand is very quaint. Plus, the little candle lamps are very romantic.'

With a still reluctant Seldon following, she stepped into the timbered alcove. 'Oh! And these amazing carved throne chairs wouldn't be out of place in an actual castle!' She turned and bobbed up on her toes to kiss him. 'You can be the knight and I can be the damsel in distress. And you can rescue me, if only from the spiders who probably live up here.' She shivered, not being a fan of waking up with a hairy-legged new friend on her pillow.

He smiled and pulled her to his chest. 'Miss Frisham was wrong. You aren't a rummy sort of fancy lady. You are an impossibly wonderful sort of one.' He buried his face in her hair and muttered, 'And I don't deserve to spend the rest of my life with you.'

The sound of a cough made them jump apart.

'It's fine to come in, Clifford,' she called out.

He appeared, balancing a double mattress in front of him.

'Even better!' she cheered. 'But have you got one too? And no fibbing!'

'Scouts honour, yes, my lady. And laundry, fresh bedding and thick quilts await. Along with two lit iron braziers to ward off any winter chills.'

'Hurrah! Come on, team,' she cried. 'This is a Christmas we'll always remember!'

All three set to making the beds, while Gladstone set to on getting in everyone's way.

To her credit, Mathilde came up and tried to insist she make up the beds. Eleanor refused, however, struck by how tired the woman looked.

She's almost haggard, Ellie, poor thing.

'The three of us will have it all done in a jiffy. I'm sorry we've kept you up so late. But your hospitality has been second to none,' Eleanor said. 'Please do retire for the night.'

Mathilde smiled. 'Kind, for sure.' But as she turned away, her face slipped into a scowl. She marched off muttering grimly, 'But there's one more thing I needs do tonight as won't wait. And it was due longaways back!'

Eleanor grimaced at Clifford, who was looking at her quizzically. 'No idea. Now, let's get this room shipshape!'

With their combined efforts, it was soon cosy and delightfully Christmassy. Clifford fetched more lamps, plus some of the spruce, ivy and red-berried holly from the bar. As well as the reindeer made from willow. He even artfully folded their towels into free-standing Christmas trees at the bottom of their bed, a tiny paper-wrapped soap balanced on top like a star. And the miniature box of chocolates that appeared from nowhere nestled on her pillow was the perfect extra treat.

'Happy now, Hugh?' she said.

Her husband nodded without hesitation. 'Absolutely!'

'Excellent! Then I suggest a short walk to let Gladstone do

whatever he needs to and help our supper go down.' She frowned. 'Oh no! But we can't. We'll be locked out.'

Clifford stepped out of the room and back in, three wellington boot bags hanging from one arm, along with her warmest hooded cloak and Seldon's full-length wool overcoat. He also held up an ancient-looking iron key.

'Acquired from Miss Frisham at a small extra cost so you might enjoy the snow on this most special of festive nights, my lady. Although technically, it is now Christmas Day morning as it is fast approaching half past one.'

She helped Gladstone into his quilted tweed coat with a snug ruff which Clifford had also produced from nowhere. Grabbing her boot bag, she led the charge down the stairs.

Outside, that singular, magical stillness and silence that only comes with thick snow having fallen was overlain with the sound of singing and organ music.

'It must be Midnight Mass at the church,' she said.

Clifford nodded. 'I would imagine it is all but over.'

'Let's go and enjoy the last of the singing anyway,' Seldon said. 'We can listen from outside.'

With Gladstone wading joyfully through the deeper patches of snow, they set off, Clifford his ever-deferential few steps behind Eleanor and Seldon.

'Please crunch and swish alongside me this once. It's Christmas, after all.' She wished he would countenance her linking arms with him, as well as Seldon.

'Respectfully crunching and swishing alongside, my lady. Inelegant though the latter is.'

She laughed, lifting her face to enjoy the feel of the snowflakes on her cheeks, despite the bitter cold. She was overcome with the childlike excitement that only came at this time of year.

'This sleepy little hamlet has treated us to the most unexpected Christmas Eve. And from what I can see of it now, it's going to treat us to a beautiful, snow-covered Christmas Day morning as well.' She waved a hand at the acres of white around them, delighting in the Dickensian thatched houses they were passing. 'It's a true winter wonderland.'

Seldon tightened his arm against hers as they reached the triangle of rough grass, taking the left fork towards the church and the sound of singing. 'I suppose you didn't see much snow as a child? Having spent at least the first nine years abroad in the tropics or thereabouts.'

She nodded. 'Maybe that's why I'm dreaming of gliding about on a frozen lake in ice skates. Like they do in those desperately sombre Russian novels Clifford devours as insatiably as Gladstone and I do sausages.'

Clifford tutted. 'As you do the antics of pirates and highwaymen in penny dreadfuls, my lady.'

Seldon chuckled and steered them down the track beside the low wall around the graveyard. Across the higgledy-piggledy gravestones, the lights of the diminutive stone church shone out of the one stained-glass window. The singers, who sounded as if they were only a handful strong, reached a crescendo.

'"Hark the Herald Angels Sing",' Clifford said. 'The recessional, or last, hymn of the service, I would conjecture.'

She sighed. 'Shame.' Her gaze fell on the gates to Waketon Court, which were still open, only one light shining out from the end window of the house. 'However, I've just thought. Our absent client, Unwin, may well not have gone missing at all! Maybe he's simply gone to Midnight Mass, though it's odd Babcock didn't know.'

'Although, my lady,' Clifford said, 'I did not get the impression Mr Unwin confided in Babcock.'

'I agree,' Seldon said keenly. 'On both points. Let's go!'

The three of them stamped through the last of the snow to the path leading to the church entrance. Here the arched windows gave out more light, as none of them were of stained glass, which made the snow shrouding the gravestones glisten.

'Look! That gravestone. Someone's slipped and fallen!' She ran forward as best she could in the snow. But on reaching the figure, she gasped.

Seldon was quickly by her side. 'Not fallen,' he said gravely. 'But dead!'

He was right. There was no mistaking the lack of life in those eyes!

8

'Oh gracious, what a tragic way to leave this world!' Eleanor breathed as Gladstone snuggled against her legs with a soft whimper.

Catching Seldon's urgent instruction to Clifford to escort her to the tavern, she shook her head. 'No. I'm alright, Hugh.'

Her gaze rove sadly over the man hanging motionless over the gravestone, a gathering cloak of snow settling on him. His head and arms hung limply down, his lifeless stare fixed on the ground.

Where he'll soon be interred, Ellie.

She became aware of Seldon's arm around her shoulders as he led her away. 'Eleanor, please,' he said gently. 'You can't do anything to help the poor fellow. And you've seen too many bodies in recent years!'

The overwhelming need to wish the dead man eternal serenity made her step back to the grave, Seldon reluctantly sliding his arm from her shoulder at Clifford's sage nod.

'Rest in peace, unmet friend. May you be forever among people who love you,' she murmured, fighting tears. Up close, she reckoned he was only thirty-something. As she watched, the body slid slowly backwards down onto the grave.

'Oh heavens! I was sure he was dead,' Seldon muttered, dropping to his knees. Wrenching off his glove, he pressed his hand to the now sprawled man's neck as she sank down beside him. After a moment, he frowned. 'Not only is he dead, he has been for a while. Maybe an hour or two?' He looked at his watch. 'One forty-five. So, that would mean he died sometime between eleven forty-five and twelve forty-five at a very rough first guess.'

She didn't need to check for herself. He had been a detective chief inspector with Scotland Yard for over fifteen years before retiring. He wouldn't have made a mistake.

'Which means he was killed just before, or just after we arrived,' she said. 'Had we been on time, we might have been able to save him!' She frowned. 'But then... then how did he suddenly move?' she whispered, her breath catching.

He stared at the body, frowning. 'If my estimation about the time he died is even halfway correct, the initial stiffening of muscles through rigor mortis would have begun. But that alone shouldn't have made him move like that.'

Clifford cleared his throat. '*Lumbricus*, sir.'

Seldon's frown deepened. 'What?'

'The eminent naturalist and geologist, Charles Darwin, devoted thirty years to a study of earthworms, or *lumbricus*, as well as writing *The Origin of Species*, on which his fame largely rests,' Clifford said. 'He divined that "worms have played a more important part in the history of the world than humans would at first suppose".'

'And what in blazes has that to do with the fact we've just seen the body of a man dead for several hours move of its own accord?'

Even Eleanor couldn't fathom where her usually infallible butler was going with his line of thinking.

Clifford held up a gloved finger. 'The last treatise Darwin published documented, among other things, how this seemingly humble creature can cause the subsidence of gravestones by their activity below ground. As in the case here. The right side is a good three inches lower than the left. You see, he concluded the average worm ejects twenty ounces of soil annually—'

'Clifford!' she said sweetly. 'Maybe now is not the time for regaling us with his full findings?'

He bobbed his head apologetically.

'Although, in truth, I'm enormously comforted by your observation,' she added.

Seldon threw him an appreciative look. 'Actually, the slowly increasing rigor mortis combined with the sloping gravestone is a perfectly plausible explanation.' He rose, gently pulling her up with him. 'Come on. We should inform someone.'

Clifford pointed up the path. 'I believe the attendees of Midnight Mass are just exiting the church.'

Seldon raked his hand through his snow-damp chestnut curls. 'Oh heck! We need to keep them from seeing the body. No one else needs their Christmas ruined by this ghoulish spectacle.'

'Allow me, sir,' Clifford said.

She noted his arched brow as he strode back up the path to the church's entrance with Gladstone trotting alongside on the lead.

Seldon turned to her with a pleading expression. 'I don't suppose I can persuade you to go with him, Eleanor?'

'I don't suppose you can, Hugh, no. Because a second set of eyes is always helpful. Besides, you need what I imagine Clifford just slipped me.'

She reached into her pocket and pulled out her butler's slim torch.

'We don't need that,' Seldon groaned. 'This man could well have died from nothing more questionable than a heart attack.'

'Brought on by what? Dancing a jig on whoever's grave this is? Think about how he was hanging over the headstone when we found him.' She shivered. 'Something's... all wrong about this. First our missing client and now... this.'

He followed her gaze along the grave to the gravestone. Slowly, he nodded. 'I see what you mean. To have finished up like that from a heart attack or similar, he would have needed to be standing on the grave itself when it struck him.'

'Exactly! It is not an accepted manner of paying your respects to the dead. Even in this far from commonplace village, I'm sure.' She shook her head, frowning. 'You know, it almost has a touch of the... *theatrical* about it.'

Seldon took the torch from her. 'At least let me be the one to examine him closer.'

But as he stepped around her, the beam picked out something that made her shudder. She hadn't noticed when the body was lying over the gravestone because his arms had been hanging either side of his head. But now, there could be no mistake.

'His hair, Hugh! Or rather the pale-crimson patch of snow clinging to it by his right temple.'

Seldon inched the torch over the area. 'Well spotted. Hmm, he received a nasty whack with something hard, for sure. And oddly shaped. Blast, I can't see well enough to—' He jumped as Clifford's gloved hand appeared over his shoulder with a fold-out pocket magnifying glass at the ready.

'The local police officer will be here shortly, sir. Fortunately, he was attending Midnight Mass himself, I was informed.'

'Then why didn't he dash back here with you, for Pete's sake?'

'Because this is Yorelow, sir. And evidently certain customs must be observed, no matter what.'

'Hurry, Hugh,' Eleanor blurted out.

'Why? We are not here to solve yet another suspicious

death,' Seldon said firmly. 'Unless...' An unspoken understanding passed between them. He continued to scrutinise the wound. 'I can't think what he was hit with though? It seemed to have had a curved end of sorts.'

'Clifford, you look too. From your angle, you might spot something different,' she said.

Whipping up his coat-tails and dropping to his haunches, her butler took the magnifying glass. 'I concur, sir. With the added observation, I believe the item had a jagged nick on its outer edge.'

She inhaled sharply. 'Obviously foul play!'

Seldon nodded. 'We might be able to find some evidence, and maybe even the murder weapon, and hand it to the local constable.'

'I'll take this side of the grave, Clifford. You take the other,' she said.

From his inside pocket, he produced a leather pouch of matches. Lighting two from the inbuilt strip of emery paper, he handed one to Eleanor along with more unspent matches to light from the first as she went.

After a minute of searching silently, Clifford muttered, 'Ah! Could this be something?'

She and Seldon were immediately beside him. He took the torch and pointed the beam at a small area of snow-cleared grass.

'Looks like fragments of what might have been pottery?'

'Whatever they are, they are almost certainly made of clay,' Clifford said.

Like the item we found earlier in the Rolls's radiator grille, Ellie?

'And given they are not buried very deep in the snow, they must have been dropped recently,' she added. 'But how did you spot them?'

'Ahem, Master Gladstone's nose, my lady.'

'Well done, boy!' She ruffled her bulldog's ears. As she glanced up again, her eyes caught the glow of light across the narrow track running between the church and Waketon Court. Blinking rapidly, she strained to see more clearly.

Isn't that the French doors of the study Babcock showed us into, Ellie?

She turned at the sound of footsteps crunching through the snow behind them. Gladstone let out a low growl. Eleanor felt a frisson of unease. It was the man who had tried intimidating the landlady in the tavern.

Seldon and Clifford stepped forward together.

'If you've come to make trouble, you'll find it was a bad decision,' Seldon said calmly.

Ned shrugged, running his tongue down the inside of his cheek. Tilting his head, he looked past Seldon at the body.

'Did you enjoy the reverend's Midnight Mass service?' Clifford said smoothly.

Ned smirked. 'Might have. Might be enjoying this more. Christmas comes but once a year as they say!' He winked at Eleanor and ambled away.

Seldon watched him go intently. 'Did either of you see him come out of the church?'

She and Clifford both shook their heads.

Then he's a definite suspect, Ellie, for our...

She left the creeping suspicion unfinished. 'Forget him for the moment. We've been so caught up, none of us have looked at the gravestone itself.'

With Seldon peering over her shoulder, she took the torch and swung the beam slowly over the front of it.

'No blood,' he murmured matter-of-factly. 'So, he was probably hit on the head and then placed there.' He glanced up the path to the church. 'Where anyone coming out of Midnight Mass would see him.'

She frowned. 'So the killer wanted him to be found?' She

finished scanning the inscription on the gravestone and shook her head. 'Goodness, nothing seems to be as one would expect in this village.'

'Hamlet, my lady. If you will forgive the correction,' Clifford said.

Seldon held up a halting hand. 'This is definitely no time for quoting Shakespeare.'

'I meant "hamlet" as in "small village", sir.'

'Now, listen up, you lot!' a high-pitched voice called. 'Ain't it time all honest folk were abed and rogues were about their business?' A man with a weathered face and large jug ears crunched through the frozen snow, a mail bag of sorts over his shoulder. He tipped his chequered cap. 'Evening to you, of course.'

There was a muddiness to his tone, which made his words run together. Unlike his sharp blue eyes, which were staring back at her, lit by the glow of the flickering lantern he was holding up. He was dressed in green woollen trousers and a dark swing-fold cape.

She smiled at him. 'Good evening. And you are?'

'Quilter, madam. Constable Farnaby Quilter. Hang fire a mo, please.' He dived into the bag hanging from his shoulder. With a yank, he produced a policeman's helmet and swapped it for the cap on his head. Then he tapped his nose with a knuckle-swollen finger. 'Our new reverend said as some fella had reported a doings in the churchyard 'ere. On what is now Christmas morn' of all times!'

'We found this man slumped over that gravestone, Constable. Dead,' Seldon said.

Behind him, the villagers who'd been attending Midnight Mass were flocking towards them.

'Dead, you say, sir?' Quilter clucked his tongue. 'That's ruined someone's Christmas! His for sure, poor codger.' He swivelled his head and held Eleanor's gaze. 'And you were 'ere to meet the deceased. Why, madam?'

'We weren't here to meet him. We were...' She hesitated. The villagers in woolly hats and coats were within earshot, most of them gawping at the body. Instinct told her the truth about why they were in Yorelow was not something to air in public. 'We were, er, just passing through, you see?'

Quilter gave her a stern look, which suggested he was unconvinced. 'Folks!' he called, making her jump. 'Get gedden to your beds, every one of you!' He lifted his police helmet and added more genially, 'And a merry Yule all round.'

With muttered returns of the same, the group reluctantly dispersed.

Seldon glanced at Eleanor and nodded. Clearly, this constable held some authority in the village. And he had shown discretion in not pressing them for more details on what three strangers were doing in the local graveyard on Christmas morning.

'Now' – Quilter adjusted his helmet – 'I'll take a look at the deceased.' He yanked on his trouser tops and knelt stiffly. With a sharp hiss, his lantern chose that moment to go out. Seldon handed him Clifford's torch, receiving a grateful nod in reply.

The beam clicked on.

'Well, well! That's the way the wind's blown then, is it?' He sat back on his heels. 'And right 'ere, too.'

'Do you know who he is, then?' Eleanor asked.

'No mistaking him, madam.'

Her mouth went dry. Her creeping suspicion had become a certainty.

'That is... *was* one Mr Inigo Unwin Jones.'

Our missing client, Ellie!

9

Amongst the white-topped gravestones, The Byron Detective Agency stared sombrely at their very deceased client.

'That rather explains why he wasn't home to meet us,' Seldon muttered grimly to Eleanor.

'And puts the agency in the middle, not of a missing person, but of a murder investigation!' she muttered back, stamping her feet as the creeping cold crept further inside her boots, numbing her toes.

Seldon nodded ruefully.

In the steady snowfall, Constable Quilter was doing his best with a scoop of paper torn from his notebook to collect the last of the clay fragments they had shown him.

'Any early thoughts as to what happened to poor Mr Unwin, Constable?' she said.

He pocketed the last of the fragments and looked around. 'If you'll take it from me, madam,' he lowered his voice to a whisper, 'we five needs be talking where the graves don't have eyes 'n ears.'

She felt a prickle down her spine at his insinuation that someone might be spying on them.

'Five?' Seldon looked over both shoulders. 'There are only four of us here.'

Quilter smiled at Gladstone, who was leaning up his trousers while getting his chin tickled. 'Mr Wrinkles here makes us a sound five in my book, sir.'

'Alas, not a very discerning book, then,' Clifford murmured mischievously to Eleanor.

Quilter jerked his head towards the track leading back to the village. 'Follow me, folks, if you will.'

Eleanor's heart clenched at the thought of leaving the dead man sprawled on a grave. Alone, in a shroud of snow on, of all days, Christmas morning.

Reading her mind, as usual, Clifford slid out of his coat. 'Perhaps until the deceased can be transported to a more suitable resting place, Constable, the gentleman might be permitted a little respite from the worst of the weather?'

Quilter nodded without hesitation, but flapped Clifford aside and laid his own cape over Unwin's body. Her heart warmed to the policeman who had already impressed her with his dutiful attitude, and now was showing his compassionate side, too.

Straightening up, he led the way through the swirling white flakes, grunting without anger as Gladstone gambolled ahead, tripping the constable up in his heavy boots.

Eleanor assumed they were heading for the police station, most likely just Quilter's front room in a hamlet like this. She was surprised, therefore, when they arrived at the Angel's Summons tavern. Pausing only long enough to offer an appreciative whistle at her stately Rolls-Royce parked outside, he started up the steps.

'You want us to talk in there, Constable?' Seldon fought a frown. 'At what must be almost two in the morning?'

'Five past, actually, sir,' Clifford said, closing his pocket watch.

Looking unfazed, Quilter nodded. 'This 'ere tavern is the safest place to talk. And I'm thinking neither of you gents will brook the lady sitting on my bed, seeing as my police room is my sleeping, eating and everything else space besides, too. But it's your choice.'

Seldon nodded. 'Your respectful attitude towards my wife is appreciated, Constable.'

'Wife?' Quilter winked and slapped him on the back. 'I'll buy it, sir. Being Christmas 'n all.'

At Seldon's reddening face, Clifford hurriedly handed him the key he had got from Mathilde.

'Looks like your inimitable charms worked as usual!' she whispered to him.

He shook his head. 'What worked was opening my wallet again, my lady!'

Inside, the fire still glowed comfortingly in the hearth. At the bar sat a slim brunette-haired woman in a crocheted pink cardigan, tied at the neck by a wide ribbon. She struck Eleanor as being close in age to her. Turning around, the woman called out, 'Bit early for decking the halls, isn't it, Quilts, old boots?'

Quilter tutted. 'Pah! I'm not here for an early pint 'o festive tidings, Blythe. Mind, we can't have these folks thinking Yorelow's hospitables is lacking, can we?' He licked his lips as he rubbed at his raw red knuckles, warming them from the freezing temperature outside.

The woman smiled at Eleanor, which made her already pretty face light up. 'Quite right. Park up, people. I'll see you right in a sec.'

Unexpectedly, she scowled at Gladstone, who was trying to say hello to her.

Not everyone is a dog lover, Ellie.

She tapped her leg for her bulldog to come away from the bar stool. 'Forgive me, I thought you were a customer.'

'Chance'd be nice! No, I'm the landlady.'

'Joint landlady,' a sharp voice called out. Mathilde stalked out from behind the curtain. 'This is my sister, Blythe. Who shouldn't be in the bar looking like that!' She waved a disapproving hand at her sister's clothes.

Eleanor could see a resemblance between them physically, but not in demeanour!

Perhaps her face had given away her thoughts as Blythe said, 'Oh, lighten up, Mathilde! It's Christmas morning. And play nice. We have customers.' She slid off the stool, revealing that her feet were encased in cosy felt slippers, embellished with little crocheted hearts ringing the toes. 'We'll fix you some warming cups. Get comfy, folks.'

'Thank you, ladies.' Eleanor took pains to smile at both of them.

'What happened to all the villagers from Midnight Mass, Quilts?' Blythe said breezily.

Quilter adjusted his helmet strap. 'There was a doings in the churchyard, so I sent 'em home. Sorry.'

Mathilde shot her sister a look. 'Well, that's the takings gone! What sort of a doings?'

'Ah, well.' He looked suddenly uncomfortable. 'Someone passed away there this eve. It was... that Mr Unwin.'

Blythe's eyes widened. 'Inigo?' she breathed, a quiver in her tone.

'Like there's ever been two in Yorelow!' Eleanor's sharp hearing caught Mathilde mutter. The woman raised her voice. 'We'll set the mull to warm.'

They both disappeared, whispering fiercely together.

Quilter led Eleanor, Clifford and Seldon to the most tucked away table, even though they were the only ones there. Before she had finished settling on the one bench, Gladstone claimed the space beside her. Seldon took the next chair with a resigned pat of the bulldog's head.

Quilter flapped a hand at Clifford. 'I've questions for you

all, so you needs park up too, sir.' He regarded the three of them suspiciously. 'Now, you can't have been passing through Yorelow as you tried to have me swallow in the churchyard. Nothing "passes through" Yorelow, seeing as it's the very definition of a dead end, so it is. Why else would it be called the Devil's Porringer?'

'A "porringer" is a fascinating geological feature akin to a punchbowl,' Clifford said. 'Water erosion of the upper sand strata occurs until it reaches the impervious layer of clay beneath. Resulting in a place such as Yorelow being at the bottom of a steep-sided circular depression.'

No wonder this place feels like the village time forgot, Ellie.

Quilter grimaced. 'Only one way in and out, too. Which is a devil when the road gets blocked by snow. Or washed away. Now, 'scuse me changing the conversation, but suppose you tell me the truth as to what you three is actually doing 'ere?'

She glanced at the other two, receiving nods of agreement. 'I am Lady Eleanor Swift. And this *is* my husband—'

'Hugh Seldon. Mr,' he said quickly, before she could highlight his title of 'Sir'.

She hid a smile. 'And that is Clifford. And the spoiled bulldog, Gladstone.'

'How do, folks,' Quilter said genially. 'And what exactly is you doing here?'

She dropped her voice. 'Collectively, we are The Byron Detective Agency. We came up here last night at the telegrammed request of Mr Unwin.'

Quilter removed his helmet and rubbed his jug-like ears. 'So, private investigators you be? That's why you tried to pull the fleece over my eyes in front of the other villagers. I see. Well, I hope you won't play coy over telling me, as the law here, what Mr Unwin wanted you to do for him?'

'I wish we knew,' Eleanor said fervently. 'But we never met him.'

'At least not alive,' Seldon added.

'You see, Constable, when we reached Waketon Court, the gentleman was not at home,' Clifford said.

Quilter shrugged. 'He never was.'

Seldon frowned. 'How do you mean?'

'It were never his home to be in,' Quilter said emphatically. 'If Mr Pritchard had meant it to be, he'd have left Waketon Court to Mr Unwin in his will. Stands to reason.' Grabbing his helmet, he rose stiffly. ''Scuse me a mite, folks, I need to make a telephone call.'

He strode to the door and out into the snow, leaving a puzzled Byron Detective Agency behind him.

10

Left alone, the three of them shared a confused look. Before any of them could speak, Blythe shuffled over in her slippers with a tray. She seemed a subdued version of her previously lighthearted self, her eyes puffy and red.

'Four cups of Christmas Mull and Rocky Bridle to be going on with.'

'Thank you. Both smell delicious,' Eleanor said, delighting in the aromas of clove and cinnamon rising from the generous mug of creamy froth. And the equally tantalising one of roasted nuts and treacle from the dish of intriguingly named treats.

'There's buckets more of both. Just holler,' Blythe called behind her, already leaving them to it.

Eleanor savoured one of the nutty numbers as Clifford thoughtfully covered Quilter's mug with the tray to keep it hot. Despite being alone again, Eleanor gestured to the others to come closer, Gladstone shoving his head under her arm to be part of the huddle.

'At least we can discount the villagers who were at Midnight Mass from being suspects in Unwin's murder,' she whispered.

'You mean Constable Quilter can, Eleanor,' Seldon whispered back. 'Unwin's murder isn't officially our investigation. Yet. In a place this size, we need to play this one carefully. We daren't try and investigate independently without his say-so. But I agree, everyone at that Mass must be in the clear if my initial estimate of time of death was right. And if Unwin was placed on the gravestone when, or soon after, he was killed.'

She nodded. 'Which must have been after the service started otherwise everyone going into the church would have seen him.'

'That would traditionally be at half past ten,' Clifford said. 'Although the service had obviously only just ended when we found the body at one forty-five.'

'Which sounds, in my limited experience, like an unusually long Mass.' Seldon threw up his hands. 'Like anything runs as expected here!' He paused, frowning. 'You know what's really bothering me again, though? The killer obviously wanted the body found.'

She nodded again. 'I thought the same thing.'

As she took a sip of her drink, a warming glow spreading down her throat, Quilter shuffled back through the door, shaking the snow from his clothes. It was only then Eleanor realised he'd braved the weather without his cape, as earlier he'd lain it over Unwin's body.

He dropped into his seat, rubbing some warmth into his hands with a wince. 'Ah! Kind of you to keep me mull warm, thanks.'

'I imagine you're always on duty if you're the only officer in Yorelow, Constable?' Eleanor said sympathetically.

'That I am, madam... ah, m'lady, course it is. But truth be told, 'tis normally quiet around these parts. Bit of fighting or... thieving here and there when folk get a little lively.' He sighed. 'Never had chance to show I could handle more, though. But murder... crumbs!' He rubbed at his reddened fingers again. 'That's why I telephoned to my sergeant in Blackington. Never been more grateful than tonight the powers that be agreed to a special line being put in to my police room. It's the only telephone in the village, you know,' he added proudly.

'And when will an inspector arrive to assist with your investigation?' Seldon said.

'Soon as he can. That being the day after Boxing Day earliest.'

'Not unexpected,' Seldon said pragmatically. 'Christmas is always the worst time of year for a murder.'

'Not that any day's a good 'un for it, sir,' Quilter said ardently. 'Anyway, orders from above is that I'm to do what I can in the meantime.' He stared at his drink, then took a swig. 'Never had a murder to poke about at before, mind. Where to start?'

'Long career in the police force, I imagine, Constable?' Clifford said casually. Eleanor had a hunch he was up to something, however. And quietly, she was hoping he was.

'Three months off retiring, I am, Mr Clifford.'

'Constable, how about a top-up of mull, as I believe you call this delightful Christmas drink?' she said brightly, surreptitiously glancing at Clifford.

'On her ladyship's tab, of course. Like the first one,' he added smoothly. 'Unsurprisingly' – he shot her a mischievous look – 'a top-up of the sweet treats is also needed.'

'Mighty kind.' Quilter picked up the tray and loaded their cups and the near empty plate on it before heading to the bar, calling for either of the sisters.

Seldon tapped the table. 'Come on! What are you two up to? Quick. Before he gets back.'

Clifford tapped his fingertips together. 'Understandably, Constable Quilter seems most reluctant to be the one to take up the investigative mantle. Alone.'

Seldon rolled his eyes. 'Really, my wonderful wife is wily enough without you galloping in as well!'

Clifford tutted. 'As if, sir. Galloping is most undignified.'

Seldon smiled. 'Come on, then. Let's hear your point.'

'It strikes me, sir, that Constable Quilter at this moment will be ruminating on the injustice of life. I mean, after a long-serving career, he will likely be remembered in retirement purely as the officer who failed to solve possibly the one and only murder in Yorelow.'

'If only there was a way we could help him out,' Eleanor said, glancing towards the bar.

Seldon held up his hand. 'I get the idea. So, what about our plans? Eleanor, you've invited Bibby Peach down for Boxing Day, so you could thank her for her help so far in tracing your parents' last trip.'

'I know.' She bit her lip. Bibby was a senior member of staff at the British Library in London. She'd tracked down and arranged for some diaries to be sent from Ceylon. Diaries which, hopefully, would shed a glimmer of light on the mysterious disappearance of Eleanor's parents when she was a child. 'But of all the people who will understand, I think she will. But that still leaves darling Kofi.'

By a twist of fate, Clifford had become guardian to a delightful young Gold Coast boy who currently attended boarding school in England. Kofi had accepted his best friend's invitation to spend the festive holiday with them, but with the caveat that he would spend Christmas Day and Boxing Day itself at Henley Hall.

'Master Kofi would be delighted to join us here, my lady,' Clifford said. 'But there are also the Henley Hall ladies. They will be most disappointed to miss your first married Christmas. Not to mention another agency case.'

Eleanor laughed. 'What our scallywag butler means, Hugh, is that he won't be able to concentrate on the investigation for fear of the mischief the four of them will get up to if left unchecked! Even though, personally, I'd be delighted if we got home in the new year to find them still partaking of Mrs Trotman's home-brewed concoctions. And dancing the can-can around the house in their under—'

'Ahem!' Clifford clapped his hands over his ears.

Seldon's cheeks had coloured too. 'Right. We need Quilter's agreement for us to investigate alongside him. Nothing less.'

She nodded vigorously. 'Yes. And do you really think for one moment he won't leap at the chance of the assistance of a respected detective chief inspector?'

'Ex-chief inspector, remember?'

'Perhaps, sir,' Clifford said. 'But if Constable Quilter were also promised the credit for any progress we made on the case before this other detective arrives from the local town on the day after Boxing Day...'

'That would do it.' Seldon held up his hand. 'All in favour?'

She and Clifford raised their hand in unison.

Seldon slapped the table. 'Motion carried! Now all we need to do is speak to Quilter when he returns.'

Clifford nodded. 'And it seems we are agreed Mr Unwin's murder and whatever he wanted us to solve are almost certainly linked. Perhaps, therefore, we would all feel justified in taking the second three hundred pounds he trustingly left in the desk drawer? Once the case is solved, of course. Unfortunately,' Clifford continued wistfully, 'the agency will now not receive the final three hundred pounds promised, as our client was murdered before we even knew what case we were supposed to be solving.'

'Don't worry,' Eleanor said determinedly. 'We'll know what the case is. Once, with Quilter's help, we've tracked down his murderer!'

11

Eleanor was still deep in discussion with Seldon and Clifford as Quilter reappeared. He set down a refilled tray of drinks, but no sweet treats.

'The Frisham women want to be about their beds as soon as we've supped these. Half the village'll be in here, shouting for their Christmas Day drink before they've had a wink of sleep otherwise.'

Eleanor groaned. She didn't mean to be churlish. The poor sisters must be exhausted. She certainly was after their seven-hour journey. To say nothing of the emotional drain the subsequent events had taken on her. But a man had been murdered. And time was of the essence.

Despite this, she stifled a yawn and nodded. 'They have both been beyond hospitable already. We'll just have to use your rather... intimate-sounding police room, Constable.'

Quilter gaped. 'But Mathilde said you'd arranged to stay here! Besides, I've only a single mattress. And the springs ain't what they should be, I warn you.'

As Seldon coloured, Clifford's brows rose in horror. 'Her

ladyship means only so that this discussion with you might continue, Constable!'

The policeman's relief was clear. 'Ah, I get you now. But tonight? Everything'll wait until morning, surely?'

'It is morning,' Eleanor said. 'However, I appreciate you haven't had any sleep either. And you've a hideous few days ahead, too. What with needing to solve a murder without any assistance. Gracious!' She winced, feeling bad for laying it on so thick.

His already tired face fell further. 'Truth is, I won't get even a half hour in the land of nod for worrying over it. Still, we'd best sup up quick,' he said as Mathilde made a show of damping down the fire while looking pointedly in their direction.

Eleanor grimaced. 'Quickly then, Constable. What would you say to two things? The help of a former detective chief inspector of Scotland Yard. And two associates who have solved a murder or two themselves.'

'For "one or two" read "many"!' Clifford added.

'*Plus*, all the credit for any progress on the investigation until your inspector arrives,' she said firmly.

Seldon nodded at Quilter's raised eyebrows. 'The bottom line is, I have over a decade of experience in murder cases and my wife has a peculiar habit of stumbling across dead bodies.' His gaze roved appreciatively over her face. 'And an even more unlikely, but intuitive, knack of solving how they came to end up so.'

Quilter looked impressed as he turned to Clifford and rubbed his chin. 'And let me guess your part, sir. You're the neat as a pin brains of the whole outfit. Along with keeping the lady out of the worst trouble. Am I close?'

Seldon laughed loudly. 'You're spot on, Constable. So, what do you think?'

Quilter wiped his brow. 'I won't fib. Any credit I could claim, no matter how small, before the inspector shows up would see me retiring the way I'd always dreamed of. And given as Mr Unwin was murdered, I'd be doing him a disservice to say anything but thank the heavens you three are willing to help me catch his killer! You're all far more experienced in these matters than my old uniform buttons could ever think of being. And the throbbing in my left toe is telling me you'll not rest until the one as did for Mr Unwin is sent to swing hisself!'

'Or herself,' Eleanor muttered. The hairs on the back of her neck prickled. She turned to find Mathilde behind her. 'We'll be just five more minutes.'

'Two!' Mathilde said stiffly. 'There's a mountain of preparations I'm going to have to tackle in the morning as it is.'

'Allow me to assist with a few now so there is less to do first thing, Miss Mathilde.' Clifford rose without waiting for an answer and glided after the landlady, making genial conversation.

Grateful he'd bought them a few more minutes, she beckoned Quilter in closer.

'Did Unwin have any enemies in the village? Anyone he'd upset?'

He stroked his chin. 'He weren't a popular newcomer, that's the truth.'

'How "new" was he?' Seldon said.

'Pitched up 'bout five months ago.'

'Constable.' She hesitated. 'Perhaps Yorelow is such a close-knit community that any new arrivals might be received a little... reluctantly?'

Quilter shook his head. 'I see where you're thinking's going with that, m'lady. And the answer's no. Sure, folks here might take a bit of time to warm to a new 'un in their midst. But Unwin were different. He upset folks from the beginning!'

'Now we're getting somewhere,' Seldon said. 'Who did he upset in particular?'

'That Babcock, for starters.'

'The valet at Waketon Court?'

'That's him. He served the late Mr Pritchard while he were alive as loyal as a dog he'd rescued from drowning in the river.' Quilter pulled a face. 'And since, Babcock has let slip on more 'n one occasion or two that he thought Mr Unwin had no right staying at Waketon Court.'

She nodded. 'We got that impression, too. Who else?'

He looked over his shoulder. 'Er, Ned Yearth. But you'll not have met him. He's—'

'Trouble. And delights in being so,' Seldon interrupted.

'Ah! You've had the displeasure of coming across him already then, sir?'

'Twice.' Seldon looked meaningfully at Eleanor. 'The second time was at the grave where we found Mr Unwin's body.'

She shuddered, remembering the look on Yearth's face. Had he returned to the scene of his crime to gloat as murderers sometimes did? 'Why do you mention Ned, Constable?'

'On account of him and Mr Unwin having a bad history.' He scratched his head. 'Right off the bat of Mr Unwin arriving in Yorelow, too.'

'What was the problem?'

'That I, er, don't know exactly.'

'Any other contenders for wanting Unwin dead?' Seldon said hurriedly as Clifford reappeared.

'Loony Luna.' Quilter's hand strayed, as if he was about to cross himself. 'If you found her howling at the moon, I wouldn't be surprised. She's the queerest fish as ever lived in the woods.'

Seldon looked quizzical. 'Literally in the woods?'

Quilter nodded. 'She lives in a... well, a shack, really. Always wrapped in a big hood and cloak all year round.'

Eleanor gasped. 'Goodness! That sounds like the woman who ran in front of the Rolls!'

Quilter tapped his nose. 'Folks here would tell you that if you had run her over, she'd have just got up and gone back to her cauldron on her broomstick.' He shrugged a little sheepishly.

'Why might she be a suspect in Unwin's murder?' Seldon said.

'On account of having a right showdown in public with him, sir. Only a month or so back, I think it was. But to be fair, she's had the same with most everyone in the village at some time.' He scratched his head. 'Not like this, though. Almost came to blows. And she was heard to threaten Mr Unwin that next time she caught him at it, she'd make him pay for sure!'

'At what?'

Quilter shrugged. 'Don't rightly know.'

'And what can you tell us about Unwin himself?'

Quilter looked thoughtful. 'Not much. No one knew Mr Pritchard even had a nephew until he suddenly pitched up. Only bother he gave me was when he got too hot under the collar with Ned.' He shook his head sadly. 'I s'pose he was paying his respects at his uncle's grave when someone did for him.'

Eleanor's stomach clenched. 'You mean that was his uncle's grave we found him on?'

Quilter nodded.

'And his uncle died five years ago?'

'That he did. Fifty-one he was. Contracted pneumonia and a few weeks later, he were gone.'

'How old was Mr Unwin?'

Quilter scratched his head. 'Thirty-five or thereabouts, I think.'

Seldon frowned. 'But how did we miss Pritchard's name, then?'

She threw out her hands. 'Because there is no name on his

gravestone. Just what seemed to be a riddle. Something along the lines of, er...'

'If I may, my lady?'

12

Clifford cleared his throat.

> *"'In an instant. In the twinkling of an eye...*
> *First out of the box, first in if pine.*
> *Created by the hand of man, destroyed by the divine.*
> *Springs into existence in an instant, then burns bright for all time.*
> *Free to own,*
> *Yet costs the sun, the moon and the stars.'"*

Quilter nodded again. 'That it be, m'lady. Mr Augustus Pritchard was as strange a gentleman as you could ever meet. Always talking in riddles, he was. None of the village took any notice of his ramblings after a time. Same with his gravestone. A few folk pondered over it for a week or so after he died. Me too, I admit. But none of us could fathom it and soon forgot about it. But he was definitely the eccentric type. Lived in the past, he did. Wouldn't stand for anything modern. Believed it all to be the work of the devil.'

'Which explains why, in what I presume is the fanciest

house in the village, there is no telephone,' Eleanor said. At Seldon's questioning look, she gestured at the policeman. 'Constable Quilter told us he is the only person in Yorelow with one, Hugh.'

Seldon nodded. 'Of course. That's why there was no telephone number on the telegram either!'

Catching sight of Mathilde stomping their way, Eleanor rose. All three men gallantly rose with her. 'I think we'd better conclude our initial discussion, chaps. Before we retire, though, could I use your telephone, Constable? There are a few arrangements I need to sort for us to be able to stay up here.'

'If as one of these gents will come, too?' Quilter said, looking uneasy.

Eleanor smiled sweetly. 'Constable, I don't bite.'

'That often,' Clifford murmured.

Eleanor laughed. 'Says the vampire amongst us!'

Seldon chuckled. 'I'll come. I wouldn't dream of letting my wife go alone.'

'If I might be excused to stay and let you back in, sir?' Clifford said. 'I feel Master Gladstone may not aid your mission.'

He handed her his slim leather pocketbook with an arched brow. 'The page marked with the black silk ribbon.'

She waved it, trusting whatever he thought she might need it for. 'Shall we, Constable?'

Yorelow's police facility was a tiny, thatched, snow-covered roundhouse twelve people holding hands could easily encircle.

'What an unexpectedly fairy-tale dwelling,' she whispered to Seldon as Quilter unfroze the front door lock by blowing on it.

Inside, nothing quite fitted against the curved walls, which reduced the already modest floor area considerably. A chair with a yellow cushion was behind a small desk with a black telephone occupying pride of place. Next to it was a ledger marked 'Yorelow Police Records'. A diminutive pot-bellied stove and a sink made up the rest of the furnishings. A curtain drawn across one side suggested the constable's sleeping quarters were beyond. What really caught her eye, though, was an array of mediaeval-looking musical instruments in various stages of build or repair on a workbench. And next to them another curtain.

So there is another room, Ellie.

Quilter followed her gaze. 'There's bars behind that. It be the jail. Well, 'tis a single cell.' A groan came from the behind the curtain. 'Occupied at the moment by Mr Pike who kicked off 'is Christmas Eve celebrations a mite too enthusiastically. He's been 'ere since seven this evening and will be till tomorrow morn when he's sobered up.'

'What does he do here, Constable?' Seldon said.

'Mostly drink, sir. Did well for himself to start, he did. Left Yorelow young and became one of them academic types. Should call him "Professor Pike" really. Studied phoney speech, or something up at some fancy university.'

She bit back a smile. She'd ask Clifford to decipher what Quilter meant later. 'How did he end up back in Yorelow?'

'Liked his booze too much. Or the booze liked him. Eitherways, they kicked him out and he came back 'ere.' He flicked a handkerchief over a chair and pulled it around for her to sit on. 'Help yourself to the telephone.'

She winced at the hideously late hour, but resolutely dialled Henley Hall's number.

A few moments later, her housekeeper's voice filtered out of the earpiece. 'Henley Hall.'

'Mrs Butters. It's me,' Eleanor said. 'I'm so sorry to call at this horrible hour.'

'Not a bit, m'lady,' Mrs Butters said cheerily. 'Us aprons haven't been abed yet, anyhow.'

'I truly hope that's because you were partying. Not working. And that you'll tell me all about it when Clifford isn't listening.' She heard giggling. Clearly, all the staff were there. 'Happy Christmas to you all!' she called. 'But I haven't telephoned at rude o'clock just to wish you glad tidings. I'm afraid we three need to change our plans for Christmas.'

'And us and Master Kofi too, perhaps?' Mrs Butters said.

'Absolutely. We need you to come up here for Christmas. But only if you want to?'

'We wouldn't miss Christmas with you, the new master and Mr Clifford. Not for all the world, m'lady.' Mrs Butters' words made Eleanor's heart swell with affection. 'Now, I've a pencil and piece of paper ready.'

Eleanor couldn't hold in her laughter at the meticulous instructions Clifford had written for her in his notebook. She read them out. 'And finally, please send a telegram of apology to Bibby. We'll have to rearrange her visit for after Christmas. Now, this place really is in the middle of nowhere. But when you arrive at the main town, Blackington, you will find there's a telegram waiting for you with instructions on how you're to get from the railway station there to here. Which we'll have worked out by then. I hope,' she muttered.

'Consider it as good as done, m'lady,' Mrs Butters said. 'Young Master Kofi's train is due in first thing this morning, right early. We'll be there to meet him. Don't fret.'

With heartfelt thanks, Eleanor hung up.

'Thank you, Constable,' Seldon said. 'It sounds as though we will definitely be staying.'

Quilter sighed deeply. 'More grateful I couldn't be! Mind, I'll bet you've never had a Christmas like this before.'

Seldon shook his head ruefully. 'If only that were true, Constable!'

13

It was gone three in the morning but Eleanor couldn't sleep. Restlessly, she stared up at the beamed ceiling of the Angel's Summons' attic, wondering what secrets might lie behind Unwin's death.

Next to her, Seldon was having no such problems. His years in the police force had left him able to sink into an instant slumber the moment his head found anything more forgiving than his office desk.

Giving up the unequal struggle, she eased out from under his arm. Sliding out of the bedsheets, she grabbed her clothes and tiptoed towards the door. Gladstone came to and lumbered out of his quilted bed, butting her leg with his nose to make it clear he wasn't going to be left behind. She held a finger to her lips and inched the door open, ushering him out ahead of her.

In the passageway, she shivered in the chilly air. That's what came of being dressed in nothing but one's thigh-length silk night chemise, she mused. Starting with the bottoms before her legs froze solid, she wrestled herself into her clothes as she hurried down the stairs.

'Ahem!'

'Agh!' She clutched one hand over her startled heart as she forced her head through the top of the woollen jumper. 'Merry Christmas, Clifford! Although that was nearly the end of mine before it had begun, you terror!' She looked around the deserted room. 'I'm fully dressed now, so no need to hide and get your starched underthings in a twist!'

With a long-suffering sigh, her butler bobbed up from behind the bar. 'If I might beg to disagree,' he said weakly, hands clamped over his eyes.

Realising the back of the jumper was caught up around her shoulders, she tugged it down. 'While you're there, better pour yourself a brandy after catching a glimpse of a lady's lacy bits! And I've just twigged this is Hugh's pullover. He's going to look quite ridiculous when he comes down in my embroidered mulberry jersey with the frilly cuffs.'

Clifford's lips twitched at the image she had painted. 'Collective indignities aside, merry Christmas to you too, my lady!'

He leant over the bar and patted Gladstone, who was scrabbling up it.

'And to you. But why exactly are you up at stupid o'clock too? The same reason as me, I suspect?'

He nodded.

She smiled affectionately at him. 'Only you haven't snuck out to the graveyard because you hoped I'd join you?'

'Feared,' he corrected drily. Then winked.

With the grace of a cat, he cleared the bar to land noiselessly beside her, the key to the tavern's front door held aloft. He lifted a small festive holly wreath from the wall and slid it over his wrist. 'Your cloak and boots have been warming by the fire. Shall we?'

Outside, the snow had all but stopped. A three-quarter moon hung in the sky, bathing the frozen white-carpeted tableau in a mellow ivory glow. The temperature had plummeted further in the night, leaving lethal but picturesque icicles hanging from the eaves of the tavern and the few cottages nearby. Beneath their boots, ice crystals sparkled like diamonds but made the going slippery. Much to Gladstone's delight as he dived onto his tummy and slid past them.

'Good job you thoughtfully warmed his snug-fitting coat too, Clifford.' Eleanor laughed as her daft bulldog scrabbled back through the thicker snow to take another gleeful slide.

She frowned at his lack of reply. 'What's the matter?'

He sighed. 'Truthfully, my lady? The all-too familiar wish that you had nothing to occupy your thoughts at Christmas but Master Gladstone's antics in this winter wonderland.'

She nudged his arm. 'Nothing can spoil Christmas, Clifford. Not even a murder investigation. That's our rule, remember? Besides, you've finally managed to reconcile two things. The promise you made my beloved late Uncle Byron in his final moments to always look after my safety and happiness. And the recognition that I wasn't made to live life wrapped in cotton wool. And I think Hugh has too.'

He gave her a rare smile and they crunched on in companionable silence to the path into the churchyard. Here, he clipped Gladstone's lead on as she led the way through the graves, her head bowed. Souls were resting here. She could feel them.

Hopefully Unwin's among them, Ellie.

Reaching Pritchard's, she stopped in relief. 'Thankfully, Quilter has had the body removed, as he said he would. I couldn't bear the idea of poor Unwin lying here for too long.' She grimaced. 'Murdered. On Christmas Eve. And on his own uncle's grave too!' She took the holly wreath Clifford had thoughtfully brought along and dropped to her knees in the snow to lay it against the headstone. 'Rest in peace, Mr Unwin,' she murmured.

After a few more words heavenwards, she hunched down,

staring at the gravestone. Even in the pale moonlight, she could make out the inscription.

Having lit the lantern, Clifford joined her. 'My lady?'

She shrugged. 'I couldn't sleep because, perhaps like you, I couldn't stop my thoughts from running over this riddle.' She frowned. 'Or I imagined that was it. But now? Now I'm not so sure.' She sat back on her heels, deep in thought. 'So, Unwin being killed here and his body left on his uncle's gravestone can't be connected with the riddle. Or can it?' They shared an uncertain look. 'Well, something made both of us feel we couldn't wait until daylight to come back here, Clifford.'

Always drawn to stone and the feeling of enduring timelessness it gave her, she pulled off a mitten and reached out. Tracing a finger over the inscription, she mused, 'Quilter said the villagers, including himself, tried to work out what the riddle meant. But they soon gave up and forgot about it. I wonder...'

Clifford cocked his head. 'What, my lady? Why the killer, by placing the body here, would choose to draw attention to this riddle after all these years?'

She nodded. 'Assuming that was their intention? Or, perhaps—'

Gladstone let out a flurry of barks, his hackles raised.

The two of them leaped up. 'Clifford, there's someone else here!' she whispered, the hairs on her neck pricking as if shot through with electricity.

The shadow at the window in Pritchard's study, Ellie?

'We may have been followed,' he murmured gravely. Hastily extinguishing the lantern, he handed it to her. 'Swing it hard if need be!'

He stepped in front of her and pulled out his heavy pocket torch, which doubled as a cosh.

The previously comforting serenity of the churchyard now seemed anything but. Her eyes darted hither and thither, trying to gauge if one of the monumental statues of shrouded figures was actually about to come to life and attack them. Just as Unwin had been attacked on that very spot.

Clifford tapped his ear and shook his head. She did the same. She couldn't hear anything either. Willing her heart not to pound so loudly, she strained her ears again. And her eyes.

Then she caught it. Movement! In the next row of graves on her left.

She let out a sigh of relief. 'It's just a fox out on a scrummage for a bit of supper. Or breakfast, as I suppose it is now.'

'Ah! So it is,' Clifford said, sounding abashed and relieved in the same breath. 'In that case.'

He pulled a bag of Gladstone's liver treats from his coat and tipped them into his hand. Dropping a few to distract her bulldog, he deftly threw the rest over the low wall of the churchyard. After a beat, the fox sniffed the air and shot away to collect its unexpected prize. He slid the bag back into his pocket, relit the lantern, and they both hunched down again to stare at the inscribed words in the yellow beam it cast. But this time, she realised what had really been bothering her.

'Dash it! As I said, I thought I couldn't sleep because my mind was fixating on that riddle. But now I'm here again, I realise I was wrong. It's so obvious.'

He arched a brow in the lantern light. 'Might I be permitted to feel less like the, ahem, "blunt brick" to borrow your oft favoured phrase?'

She tutted teasingly. 'It's not like you to forget to pack your patience, Clifford. Don't you want to try and work it out for yourself?'

'At five-and-twenty past four, on a Christmas morning, in a frozen graveyard where a man was murdered but a few hours before...'

'You have a point.' Without explanation, she shone the torch on nearby gravestones and then back on Pritchard's. 'You see, unlike the others I've just highlighted, this one has only a small amount of moss and lichen growing on it. I realised that's what was bothering me. Not the riddle itself, but why I was able to read it so easily!'

'Commendably astute as always, my lady,' Clifford said appreciatively. 'With Mr Pritchard having passed five years ago, that is more than sufficient time. Certainly for one or more of the close to two thousand species of moss or lichen found in the British Isles to take hold.'

To her confusion, he pulled out his pocket compass and clicked open the lid, turning the instrument slowly. 'Hmm, as I thought.'

She smiled. 'Now who's being infuriatingly mysterious?'

'My lady, in churchyards such as this, traditionally graves are laid east to west, the headstone facing east.'

'Why?'

'It is believed by many Christians that when the Messiah returns, it will be from the east. And that his followers will therefore rise from the afterlife, facing Him.'

'That's fascinating. But let me guess. Here in Yorelow, they're not facing east, is that it?'

'Actually, no, if you will forgive the correction. They are indeed aligned traditionally. Leading one to anticipate a greater rate of growth of lichen than is evident on this one gravestone. Were it to be facing north, and thus exposed to less sunlight, it might explain it somewhat. But here...'

They craned closer to the stone, shoulders almost touching, but for Gladstone having pressed himself between them to see what he was missing. And if it was edible.

'Someone must have—' she muttered.

'Get out of here! Now!' a harsh voice gruffed as a lantern swung in front of her face. 'Or else!'

14

Eleanor and Clifford rose slowly, both turning at the same time.

With the snow having stopped, it was a clear, starry night and silhouetted against it was a figure. The figure held up a lantern, revealing a strapping man with a fearsome scowl in a thick black coat and wool hat. Then, to her surprise, the man's scowl melted into a smile.

'I say, whatever must you think?' The menacing, rough voice had also melted away. To be replaced by a soft, well-educated one.

She glanced questioningly at Clifford.

'My lady, may I introduce the vicar of this delightful church whom I briefly met last night? Reverend, permit me to present Lady Swift.'

The vicar whipped off his woolly hat, leaving his crown of fair hair sticking up at all angles. It was hard to tell in the lantern light and the pale wash of the moon, but he looked only to be thirty at most. 'Pleased to meet you, Lady Swift. I'm Reverend Thaddeus Ansel. Merry Christmas to you, by the way!'

'Merry Christmas to you, too, Reverend!' she said cheerily.

'My season's greetings to you, Reverend,' Clifford added. 'And this is Master Gladstone. With apologies for his disgraceful lack of manners,' he added as the bulldog stretched up the front of the vicar's coat, wagging his tail eagerly.

Ansel's smile broadened as he ruffled Gladstone's head. 'Silly me. I should have recognised this portly fellow from last night. But unfortunately I was distracted...' He glanced at Pritchard's grave. He lowered his voice. 'I realise now, you must be the people Constable Quilter mentioned are going to help him.'

That sounds promising, Ellie. We're trusting Quilter who, in turn, it seems, trusts the vicar.

Ansel shook his head apologetically. 'Goodness, if only I'd known, I would never have challenged you like I did. But I saw your light bobbing about from the vicarage and raced over, thinking that whoever it was must be up to no good. I'm sorry if I startled you. By way of apology, could I entice you to join me in a mug or two of tea to warm up?' His face brightened. 'My elderly aunt sent me something for Christmas. I haven't opened it yet, but it's been a tin of biscuits every previous year.'

Eleanor and Gladstone shared a keen look.

'We'd love to. If it won't put you to too much trouble?'

'On the contrary. I'd really appreciate the company,' Reverend Ansel said fervently. 'This way.' He led them back along the path and up the icy flagstones leading to the church's entrance. 'I must just stop and check everything is properly locked. I'm extra careful about doing so with the way things are nowadays. I left something inside last night I need as well.'

He unlocked the door and hurried through the flint and timber walled vestibule further into the church.

Following him inside, she gasped. 'Gracious, I've never felt so much like I've gone back in time! Even more so than in the Angel's Summons.'

'Indeed, my lady,' Clifford murmured reverently. 'Note the building's overall narrowness and exaggerated height. And the quoins, or corner stones, as well as the pilaster strips. I believe we are privileged to be standing in a genuine Anglo-Saxon church. One dating back to possibly the late six hundreds, at a hasty estimate.'

Reverend Ansel paused on his way past with a ring of long keys. 'Very impressive! St Cuthbert's has served the parishioners here since 697 AD.'

'That makes it well over a thousand years old!' she marvelled, unable to resist running her hand over the pitted-stone pillar beside her.

'Let's hope it lasts at least a few more!' he said sadly. 'Funding for repairs is desperately short. And please excuse the mess after Midnight Mass.' He waved at the spent candles in brass holders, dried flower arrangements and hymn books. Two yellowed tambourines and a tarnished herald's trumpet poked out of a basket, while nearby a simple nativity scene was laid out on a piece of red velvet. 'I shan't keep you long.'

He darted up a narrow winding staircase leading to a tiny choir gallery above.

After a moment, his head of fair hair hung over the carved wood balustrade. 'Actually, will you forgive me for keeping you another few minutes? I really should check the roof. It's on its last legs. And as the extra weight of snow builds up, I'm worried it might cave in.'

He pointed to the vaulted ceiling, where the middle section sagged alarmingly.

'Seems a pleasant chap. Trustworthy too,' she murmured.

Clifford glanced at her mischievously. 'Hmm, perhaps judgement by a certain party has been coloured by the promise of biscuits?'

She rolled her eyes. 'Nothing of the sort. Gladstone wouldn't be so easily swayed!' Her stomach let out an unladylike gurgle, which echoed around the nearby pews. 'Although, I could eat his whole tin right now.'

Clifford tutted quietly. 'And the unusual aspect therein?'

She laughed. 'I shall ignore that remark. What I was saying was,' she lowered her voice, 'I think we can trust the reverend in regard to Unwin's murder.'

He lowered his, too. 'Agreed. Aside from being a man of the cloth, he was delivering the Midnight Mass and would have been missed by the congregation had he left at any point so has a cast-iron alibi for the time of Mr Unwin's death.'

Further discussion was halted by the sound of feet hurrying back down the stairs.

'All alright up there?' she said.

Reverend Ansel nodded. 'As far as I can tell. Now, I hope you're still up for tea?'

As they left the church, Eleanor could just make out a man at the vicarage gate. Reverend Ansel gave him a cheery wave. As the man reached them, he respectfully tugged the brim of his burgundy cap. He was fiftyish, with a long nose and behind his thick-rimmed spectacles, piercing black eyes which seemed at odds with his cloud of russet hair.

'Lady Swift, Mr Clifford, this is Mr Dunstan O'Brien,' Ansel said. 'Dunstan is the churchwarden at St Cuthbert's. And grateful I am, too.'

'It's a pleasure to meet you,' Eleanor said, thinking he would be another good person to ask questions of later. As the churchwarden, he might have seen or heard something. Unless, of course, he'd been helping the reverend with Midnight Mass all evening.

'How do,' Dunstan said.

Reverend Ansel cocked his head. 'I didn't expect to see you today.'

Especially at this hour, surely, Ellie? Dawn has to still be at least two hours away.

Dunstan tugged on his jacket collar. 'You know how it is, Reverend. Being on me own, like, it's good to get out. So, I just came to tidy up the church after last night. If as that suits you?'

'Goodness, yes. Thank you very much, Dunstan!' He passed him the keys he was still carrying. 'I'll come and lend a hand once my visitors have gone.'

The three of them watched the churchwarden hurry inside.

'A most helpful assistant, Reverend,' Clifford said as they tramped towards the vicarage.

Ansel nodded. 'He's proved invaluable since he took up his duties recently. Unfortunately, the only thing he won't do is take responsibility for the church keys, so I have to make sure the place is locked, which is fair enough really with everything else he does.'

'What happened to the previous warden?'

'He left with the last vicar. A particularly loyal old fellow, apparently. Couldn't stomach the idea of serving with a man less than half his age, no doubt,' Ansel said resignedly. 'But I can't complain. Dunstan came to me the day after I arrived and volunteered to take on the churchwarden role. I'd have been lost without him. Now, let's get inside and warm up, shall we? Before we all catch our death of cold.'

Eleanor shivered at his words. There'd been enough death in Yorelow for one Christmas already!

15

To Eleanor's surprise, the snow-encrusted vicarage wasn't behind the church, but across from it, next to Waketon Court.

No wonder Ansel saw the light of our lantern or torch from his window, Ellie.

From the outside, it seemed quite imposing, with its decorative brick chimneys. Like so much of Yorelow, it was timber-framed, albeit painted cream not white between the bowed and twisted oak beams.

Inside, the hallway felt only marginally more like a home than the church had. Mostly because the boot bench was an old pew and the few wall hangings, faded tapestries of religious scenes. And the windows were of a similar design to the church, complete with stained-glass panels. Unusually, there were two staircases, both intricately carved, one with a dove motif, the other fish. Even a modest Christmas tree with minimal decorations would brighten the space, she mused, looking around. The small holly wreath on the hall table, set with a few fir cones, was no substitute.

But the sitting room he showed them into while he excused himself to rustle up tea and biscuits was more homely. An antiquated steamer trunk served as a coffee table between two mismatched armchairs and a worn, and slightly sagging, three-seater settee. On the big, but faded, rug stood another table, stacked with heavy-looking religious tomes and sheets of paper. Two large log baskets were filled with festive greenery, fir cones and candles, making her wonder if Ansel was planning on seasonal decorations after all. If rather late ones. But the fireplace which dominated the back wall made up for any festive shortcomings. It was simply huge, almost rivalling the one at the tavern. And set with a merrily burning fire. Eleanor hid her smile at the shirts and socks drying on a clothes horse in front of it as she went over to warm her frozen hands and feet.

'Well, really!' Clifford tutted, reaching out to remove the clothing.

'Don't you dare!' she whispered. 'You'll only embarrass the poor fellow. He clearly wasn't expecting to entertain visitors at this ridiculous hour. Besides, it could have been worse. He might have been drying his underthings,' she added, much to Clifford's horror.

While they waited, Gladstone explored the room, sniffing in every corner, and trying to wriggle under the furniture in case someone had foolishly left anything edible there.

Ansel reappeared with a tray, bearing three mugs, a large teapot and a brown paper-wrapped parcel. Eleanor hurriedly stepped away from his impromptu washing line and sat in an armchair.

'No silver spoons. Or tea cosy,' he said apologetically as he set the tray down on the trunk.

She laughed, realising only then the teapot was swathed in a red bobble hat. 'I'm sure your parishioners understand when they drop in.'

'They might. If they ever did.' Pouring out three mugs of tea, he sighed. 'It's still taking all my creativity to get some of the villagers to come to the church services.'

Eleanor wondered if his youth was against him. He was so fresh-faced.

'Don't worry, Reverend. You'll get there. With patience, as my wonderful but infuriating butler there repeats often enough that I want to boil his head!'

'For "wonderful", read "beleaguered",' Clifford said ruefully.

Ansel chuckled. 'And I thought I was intrigued before! Would you think me rude if I ask why you're going to assist Constable Quilter?'

Over the rims of their tea mugs, Eleanor and Clifford shared a look of unspoken agreement.

'Not at all,' she said. 'Collectively with my husband, who is still sensibly asleep at the tavern, we are The Byron Detective Agency. We came here to meet with Mr Unwin. But, unfortunately, before we could speak with him...'

'Her ladyship found him dead in your graveyard,' Clifford finished for her.

'On which note.' Ansel put his hands together, Eleanor and Clifford following suit. 'Dear Lord and Father. Eternal rest grant him...' he began. His prayer for Unwin was delivered so tranquilly, it washed over her like a soothing blanket. The three of them sat quietly after he'd finished.

'Life must, and should, go on,' Ansel said, breaking the silence. His brow furrowed. 'A detective agency? So, something wasn't right about the way Mr Unwin died?'

She nodded. 'It seems a definite case of foul play. And because of that, may we ask you a few questions?'

He paused in ripping the brown paper from the parcel. 'By all means.'

'Thank you. Starting then with the graveyard. Have you noticed anything unusual?' She winced. 'Aside from a dead man being found draped over a gravestone?'

He looked thoughtful. 'No, I don't think so. Oh, except a

few weeks ago, I was coming back here late after seeing a parishioner who was unwell.'

'Go on...'

'I intended to cut through the graveyard so I could double-check the church was locked. I told you it's become a habit of mine. But as I got closer, I thought I saw a couple of lights. That's why I dashed out earlier when I noticed yours.'

'And did you see who it was?' Clifford said.

'No. By the time I was near enough, they had gone out. And there was no sign anyone had been there. So perhaps I imagined it?'

Eleanor cut in. 'Possibly. But were the lights at the same grave? Mr Pritchard's?'

He shrugged. 'I'm afraid I couldn't really say.'

He tore the last of the paper off the parcel, much to Clifford's dismay, his ever neat and meticulous sensibilities aghast.

'Ah!' Ansel pulled out a tin and prised off the lid. 'Ginger and almond biscuits. Good old Aunt Esmeralda.'

Eleanor took one gratefully, then several more at his insistence.

'Anything else I might know that's helpful?' he said as they munched, one or two going Gladstone's way from both of them.

'Did anyone leave during your midnight service last night?'

He shook his head. 'Not that I noticed. And given there were only, regrettably, a handful of people there, I think I would have. Would it help you to know who they were?'

'Enormously.'

'And those villagers *not* in attendance would help even more, Reverend,' Clifford added.

Nodding, Ansel took the sheet of paper and fountain pen Clifford held out and, after a minute's thinking and scribbling, handed them back. Clifford passed the paper to her. She scanned it quickly.

Hmm, Ned's name is on the 'not attended', Ellie, interesting! But Quilter's on the 'attended'. Good!

'Thank you, Reverend. Now, this riddle. On Pritchard's grave. A little... unusual, isn't it?'

He nodded. 'I noted it when I first arrived. Curiosity had me trying to solve it. But only briefly. I've had my own challenges since starting here, as I've mentioned.'

'How long have you been in post in Yorelow?' Clifford said.

'Three months. Mr Pritchard had that plot reserved a while before he died, Digger told me. Or "Douglas Dilkes" to give him his proper name.'

She frowned. 'We haven't met him. Who is he?'

'The gravedigger.'

'Mmm. Have you ever seen anyone tend Mr Pritchard's grave, Reverend?'

'No. But honestly, I've been so busy trying to get to know my parishioners that I haven't given the graveyard much attention. To my shame.' He sighed. 'Keeping the church roof from falling down has taken most of my time, too. I'm blessed to have this vicarage but it's so big and I've no money for a housekeeper. It was built for the incumbent rector in 1664, you see. He had nine daughters.'

'What a wonderful treat. A houseful of women! Your favourite thing,' Eleanor teased Clifford.

His lips quirked. 'My posthumous sympathies to the gentleman.'

Ansel laughed. 'That's why there are two staircases. The main house was for the women of the family, while the vicar and his curate had the smaller part. Which I've put up in as the previous vicar did. But even with the larger part half-closed up, it still feels empty.'

She frowned. 'Actually, the rest of my staff are coming up today with my cheeky tomcat, Tomkins. But not Rune, my recently acquired raven. He is staying at Henley Hall with my gardener, Joseph. I was hoping there might be a cottage available for rent. Or someone who lets out rooms at least. The tavern only has two and we've filled those already.'

Ansel shrugged apologetically. 'There's nothing to rent in Yorelow, I'm afraid.'

She raised a finger. 'Perhaps you wouldn't mind putting them up here? I'd happily contribute something towards a new roof for the church.' She winced. 'I'm sorry, that was probably a bit forward of me.'

His face lit up. 'But I say, I'd love to offer them accommodation here at the vicarage.'

Eleanor shook her head. 'Oh goodness, now I think of it, it really is an imposition. I couldn't—'

He held up his hands. 'Lady Swift, you have no idea what a treat it would be to hear a voice other than mine in this mausoleum of a house. Particularly at this time of year. And it is only Christian to offer shelter. Do say yes?'

'Well, it's up to Clifford really,' Eleanor said, not wanting to undermine his position as head of her staff.

Her butler's brow flinched. 'Your four aproned elves staying with a, ahem, young vicar, my lady? Unchaperoned? At Christmas of all times. What could possibly go wrong?' he ended weakly.

Ansel smiled. 'I'm dedicated to my vows, Mr Clifford. You have no need to worry. And the ladies will be in a completely separate part of the rectory.'

'It was most definitely not *your* behaviour which I was questioning, Reverend,' Clifford said hurriedly.

'Oh, don't be concerned about the villagers.' The vicar flapped a dismissive hand, clearly missing Clifford's point it was her mischievous ladies he was thinking of. 'They're already scandalised that I'm not sixty or older. And I think it might actually help them take more notice of me. It's a done deal, to my mind.'

'Reverend, you've saved the day, thank you.' She caught Clifford's concerned look and groaned. 'Ah, no, it won't work, of course.'

'Whatever it is, we can sort it, surely?' Ansel pleaded.

'Thank you, but I don't see how. We need to keep them out of anything to do with the investigation into Mr Unwin's death, you see. Not that they haven't helped out in several previous cases, but this Christmas I promised them a proper carefree holiday. Plus, if the murderer realises they are with us, it might scare them off.'

Ansel's confused look dissipated. 'So, you need to pretend you don't know them, you mean?'

Clifford nodded. 'Most perceptive.'

She shook her head. 'But we don't want to ask you to be complicit in any deceit.'

'I don't consider that you would be,' Ansel said firmly. 'The Bible is very clear about keeping the worthwhile and righteous confidences of another. Take Proverbs in particular. "A man of understanding holds his tongue. A gossip betrays a confidence, but a trustworthy man keeps a secret." See?'

'Ah! In that case, thank you! We'll use Constable Quilter's telephone to send them a telegram.'

'Excellent. If it is alright with you, I'll invite him to Christmas lunch?' At her nod, he continued. 'And do drop me a note when you know what time your ladies will arrive. Just before they get to Yorelow, I'll quietly intercept them and introduce myself and the plan. Deal?'

'Deal,' she said, fighting the urge to hug him.

Clifford shook his hand with a wince. 'I do hope you like pantomime, though, Reverend? And cats of a particularly mischiev—'

Eleanor gave him a look. They had work to do.

'Gladstone?' she called out, realising he hadn't followed them from the sitting room.

After a moment, her bulldog slunk into the hallway, head down.

'Oh no! What have you stolen, you monster?' she cried.

'My slipper!' Reverend Ansel chuckled, tugging it gently out of her bulldog's mouth. 'I've been looking everywhere for that. Thank you, Mr Portly.'

They waved goodbye at the gate with Gladstone woofing. As the vicar disappeared inside, Eleanor turned to Clifford.

'That list of people attending and not attending Midnight Mass should be a great place to start sorting out suspects.'

'Indeed, and...' He whipped a handful of snow from the hedge and held it out to her. '"Nucleation",' he declared in a louder voice, 'is the meteorological term for how snowflakes are formed.'

'Clifford, what are we doing?' she whispered.

'Discreetly watching the gates into Waketon Court, my lady,' he whispered back. 'I thought I saw—'

'A figure slinking behind them! I just caught it too. But who's slipping in there at this hour?'

Her mind went back to Pritchard's study and the churchyard. Was someone shadowing their every move? And if so, who?

'Perhaps it's Babcock? Quilter suggested him as a likely suspect for Unwin's murder.'

'Quite. But where could he possibly have gone to at ten to five in the morning? On Christmas Day too? Well, there's only one way to find out. Let's go wish him a festive return of the day and ask him exactly what he's been up to!'

16

'Not a sound, old chum,' Eleanor whispered in Gladstone's ear as Clifford scooped him up. Taking the lick on her nose as a yes, she darted over to Waketon Court's gates, silently cursing how loud the crunch of snow beneath her boots was. Sensing Clifford's presence behind her, she tapped his wrist. He nodded and pointed. The figure could just be seen flitting in and out of the patchy shadows of the hedge along the short driveway. Whatever they were doing there, it seemed they didn't want anyone to know.

Suddenly, the figure stopped and spun around. Flattening herself against the hedge, she froze, heart pounding. After a minute, the sound of footsteps started up again. She followed. But the more stealthy she tried to be, the louder her own footsteps seemed to become.

Don't just follow in their wake, Ellie. Follow in their actual footsteps!

This was quieter as the snow had already been compacted. But she still couldn't edge close enough to get a clear look. The figure kept too much to the shadows to tell if it was a man or woman, and too hunched to judge how tall they were.

Without warning, the figure vanished into the dark.

'Lost them, dash it!' she whispered, louder than she'd intended. 'We'll have to—'

A stream of light cut across the flagstones only feet away.

'Yes?' a reedy voice called.

Babcock stepped out of the front door.

She frowned. If he was the shadowy figure could he have gone in a side door and appeared around the front that quickly?

She made a loud show of stamping her feet and then strode into the shaft of light. 'Good morning, Babcock. Just clearing the snow from my boots. Merry Christmas!'

He looked down his nose. But not at her, she realised, but at Gladstone, who was sniffing at his slippers.

Did he slip his shoes off because they were covered in mud and snow, Ellie?

'Merry Christmas, Lady Swift,' he said. 'And you, Mr Clifford.'

'You're up with the lark this festive morn.'

He blinked rapidly. 'Naturally. I... I have been so for some time. Engaged in my duties.'

Clifford cleared his throat. 'Which might include inviting her ladyship in out of the cold, Mr Babcock?'

'If you wish. Please step in,' he said stiffly.

In the black-beamed entrance hall, she noticed the Christmas tree had several large crimson velvet bows she hadn't seen on their previous visit. Their added festive cheer seemed odd given Unwin's body had been discovered only a stone's throw away not much more than four hours previously.

As Clifford discreetly stopped Gladstone tugging one of the low-hanging baubles off the tree, she shrugged out of her coat. Babcock took it. She ignored his bemused look at her wearing a man's jumper.

'Very diligent of you, Babcock. Continuing with your duties at a time like this.'

'Christmas Day is no different to any other, m'lady.'

She blinked. Had Quilter not yet told him of Unwin's death?

'Has Constable Quilter been in touch with you?'

'Yes, m'lady. An hour ago. Or nearabouts. He informed me that Mr Unwin had passed away,' he said blandly.

'Anything else?'

His nostrils flared. 'That questions might be asked.'

She clapped her hands. 'Excellent. And being a sharp-witted fellow, you've now worked out that as representatives of The Byron Detective Agency, we are here to ask them. Yes?'

He nodded. 'Do you wish to begin with me, m'lady?'

She frowned. 'You're not alone?'

He shook his head. 'Miss Dora, Mr Pritchard's cleaner, is here.'

Again it struck her that he referred to his long dead master as if he were still living. Although, out of loyal affection, after serving her beloved uncle for more years than she had been alive, Clifford invariably did the same.

'We'll talk to you and Miss Dora together, please. In the study,' she said, wanting to gauge for herself if the pair were in cahoots about anything. Especially Unwin's death.

He led them along the passageway. He bowed his head at the door of the study as he had before. Then held it open for her as she stepped in after an eager Gladstone and ahead of her ever-respectful butler.

Babcock turned to leave. 'I will call Miss Dora, m'lady.'

'Before you do, please tell me why is she here so early on Christmas morning?'

'Because those are her usual hours. She works part-time, three mornings a week. Just as Mr Pritchard directed.'

'And cleaning comprises her only duties?' Clifford said.

'No. She also prepares meals for myself.' His lip curled. 'And for Mr Unwin. Until his recent passing, that is.'

He left, returning almost immediately with a woman in her late forties, Eleanor estimated. Unless the strands of greying hair in her otherwise nut-brown finger waves were signs of premature ageing. Her homespun blue gingham dress seemed a rather summery choice given the bitter cold outside, while the elaborate scallop edging to the neckline was incongruous for a working outfit. Her small lace apron was tied tightly at her waist, as if to emphasise her pretty curves.

Eleanor and Clifford shared a discreet glance.

Dash it, Ellie. He can't tell if one of them was the figure we saw outside, either. Especially as, given the cold, they must have been wearing a thick coat.

'Please take a seat. Dora, is it?' Eleanor said.

The woman bobbed nervously. 'Yes, ma'am. I mean, m'lady. Dora Meath.' She sat stiffly on the edge of the only free chair, while Babcock stood beside her.

'How long have you worked at Waketon Court, Dora?'

'Couldn't say as I've been countin', m'lady, but it's a goodly while.'

'And when did you see Mr Unwin last?'

'It were Monday.'

Eleanor smiled at her, trying to put her at her ease. 'Was Mr Unwin his usual self? By which I mean was he acting oddly at all?'

'Pff! When weren't he!' Dora said with feeling. She bit her lip. 'Apologies. I didn't mean to be rude about the gentleman. Only, I'd never met anyone like him before.'

'What was different about him?'

Dora glanced anxiously at Babcock, but he studied his fingernails, avoiding her gaze. 'The secretiveness always, m'lady. And the staying up in his room all of most every day.'

Eleanor kept a frown off her face. Why would Dora have noticed that if she only worked a handful of mornings each week? She turned her attention to the valet.

'Babcock, when did you last see Mr Unwin?'

'As I told you before, m'lady. I last *saw* him at thirteen minutes past ten yester eve. However, I last *heard* him just before midnight last night.'

'I see. And what did he say then?'

He swallowed hard and glanced at Dora, who was staring at him. 'It's difficult to say, m'lady. What I mean is... it's difficult to say in front of a lady.'

'Then tell me,' Clifford said, striding over to him.

Babcock muttered in Clifford's ear, who tutted, then turned to Eleanor.

'It seems, ahem, the gentleman uttered a... colourful expletive, my lady.'

She hid a smile at the two men's gallantry. 'Then kindly tell me the story minus that... word, or phrase, Babcock.'

He nodded. 'From out in the corridor, I heard Mr Unwin... swear. Which was unusual. I knocked on the study door fearing he'd injured himself, or some such.'

'And when he answered?'

'But that was it. He didn't answer. So after knocking again, I entered. The study was empty.'

'Did you notice anything odd?' Clifford said. 'Except for Mr Unwin being absent?'

'Yes. The French windows were open. Mr Unwin hated fresh air. And a gramophone record was going round and round in its final groove on Mr Unwin's new-fangled recording machine.'

'What did you do?'

'I stopped the machine and placed the record on the late master's desk.'

'Immediately, Mr Babcock?'

'Naturally. I did not listen to it!' he said defensively. 'I would never dream of doing such a thing.' He cleared his throat. 'Then I closed the French windows and left.'

Eleanor remembered the odd noises at the end of the record they'd listened to. Could some of them have been Unwin opening the French windows? She stepped over and tried it herself.

It could be, Ellie. But why would he have interrupted his recording to go out into the garden? And if he had, why did he never return and finish it?

She examined the view. Dawn was peeking over the horizon, bathing the fallen snow in a weak pink-orange glow. It was enough for her to see that any footprints that might have been there yesterday evening would have been covered over with the thick flakes that fell all night. She glanced across at the church, thinking she'd been right before. She could see the study windows from Pritchard's grave.

About to go back inside, a wooden bench caught her eye. It had small wheels at the corners, allowing it to be easily moved from one sunny spot to another.

Or allowing it to be used to transport a body, like an impromptu wheelbarrow, Ellie?

Which meant Unwin might not have died in the graveyard, as they had been assuming. And that the murderer could indeed be a woman. She returned to the study.

'I should like to see Mr Unwin's room.'

'The gentleman's... bedroom?' Babcock said in a scandalised tone.

She smiled sweetly. 'I won't faint. It's not my first time in a strange man's room.'

'Would that were not true!' Clifford murmured.

Babcock's gaze roved over the masculine jumper she was still wearing, his eyebrows raised. 'In that case, m'lady, this way!'

17

The room he showed her, Clifford, and a now even more excited Gladstone into felt cold. Ice cold. Babcock excused himself and closed the door, leaving them to it. She looked around; a four-poster bed replete with drapes was strewn with ripped packing paper, string and well-thumbed magazines. An antiquated wardrobe half-filled the left-hand wall, its panelled doors hanging open, revealing a modest selection of clothing. A dresser stood opposite, boxes, more magazines and newspapers scattered on top. Clifford's horror of the mess was palpable.

'See, the untidiness in my bedroom isn't a patch on this, is it?' she said teasingly.

'Not having the stamina, nor stomach, to ever venture into it, my lady, I am unable to comment.'

She laughed. 'Tsk! And all this time you've pretended it was because you're too chivalrous to step into a lady's bedroom. While it was actually because you knew you couldn't trust the rogue lurking beneath your impeccable butlering togs.'

He rolled his eyes. 'Might we hasten to the less than festive task of searching a murdered man's room on Christmas morning?'

She winced. 'Good call.'

Nodding at his imploring look that she leave the contents of the drawers for his scrutiny, she turned to the boxes on the dresser.

'Gracious! Babcock wasn't exaggerating about Unwin's penchant for purchasing newfangled gadgets. There are things here I've never even heard of; a gentleman's electric shaving contraption, a vibrating plate for mixing cocktails. You could use that, Clifford. Not that your cocktails aren't perfection already. A self-propelling pencil, and press studs which look like buttons on the outside. And a' – she peered at the front of the instruction booklet – 'a polygraph, whatever that is?'

Having finished scouring the bed, Clifford joined her and pursed his lips at the instrument lying in the box. 'Commonly thought an effective lie detector, my lady. Although law enforcement departments in America are working on a true version of such, I read in a Royal Society journal recently. That version, however, is little more than a disgracefully disguised mercury sphygmomanometer, I would conjecture. It measures the systolic blood pressure of a subject. Which is mostly affected by nervousness, agitation and the like which lying might bring on.' He sniffed. 'But so would many other things.'

'Well, what on earth would Unwin have wanted with it?'

'I really can't imagine, my lady.'

She stepped away from the drawers to let him search them. 'I don't suppose you'll sleep for being consumed with horror if I check the pockets of his trousers that are hanging up?'

'Supposition correct! I'll do them.'

Scouring the slim drawer of his bedside table instead only turned up a not exactly laundry-fresh handkerchief and a prick to her finger. 'Ouch!'

'My lady?' Clifford was immediately at her side.

'Oh, it's nothing. Just a scratch from this small pocketknife. He hadn't folded the blade back in the sheath. And no, I don't need... ah!' She grimaced as he swiped one of his own pristine handkerchiefs over the welt before she could pull her hand away. Satisfied it was no longer bleeding, he strode to the wardrobe and began searching there.

Through a narrow archway, she could see a hint of white enamel, suggesting Unwin had at least had en-suite facilities of some kind. But on checking, it was little more than a tiled alcove with a wash stand and a rather basic lavatory. There were no hiding places. She went back to the main room.

'Speak to us, Mr Unwin!' she murmured.

A drop of blood dripped off her finger onto the floor. She tutted and quickly wiped it before Clifford noticed and insisted she went straight to bed. Or hospital!

Wait a moment, though, Ellie...

The bottom of the chest of drawers wasn't quite... right. She grabbed the pocketknife and used the blade she'd pricked herself with to prise the bottom piece of wood away. Behind it lay a small, leather-bound book. She pulled it out and replaced the wood. Whatever it was, it had to be something interesting if Unwin had gone to the trouble of hiding it.

She went over to the window to examine it in the light. It looked like a small journal. Or diary. On the inside page was the name *Augustus Pritchard*. She frowned.

Why was Unwin reading Pritchard's diary? And who was he hiding it from? Babcock? There were several bookmarks sticking up from the pages. They all had the same writing on. '"*The Westminster Gazette*",' she muttered. Opening the page of the first bookmark, she noticed writing on the bottom half, '"Every morning one penny".'

'My lady! Look!' Clifford hissed from the other window.

She closed the book, shoved it in her pocket and hurried over to see a hunched-over figure hurrying out of the front gates.

'The very person we followed and lost, do we suppose?' Clifford said.

And has maybe been shadowing us from the outset, Ellie?

'We certainly do! Quick! If it's Babcock, he won't be downstairs.'

She led the charge, trying to appear nonchalant. Evidently she failed as Dora appeared as she reached the bottom step, looking worried.

'Is there a fire, m'lady?'

'Fire? No, we just have a lot to do today. And... and I have a question for Babcock before we leave.'

'There he is,' Dora said, pointing over her shoulder.

Eleanor turned, her brow furrowing. The valet was emerging from the door under the stairs with a heavy basket of logs.

'Did you need something, m'lady?'

'Er, yes. Why didn't you mention the visitor who was leaving just as we arrived last night?'

'Visitor, m'lady?' He shook his head quickly. 'There were no callers on Christmas Eve.'

She held up a finger. 'Perhaps you'd like to think harder, since I bumped into the gentleman at the front gates.'

Babcock's gaze flicked to Dora, then back. 'With apologies for suggesting otherwise, m'lady, but it could have been anyone passing along the street. They needn't have come from the house unless you actually met them within the grounds?'

'M'lady?'

'Yes?' Eleanor spun around. 'What is it, Dora?'

The cleaner glanced nervously at Babcock, then back at her. 'If you want to know more about Mr Unwin, you're asking the wrong people.'

Was that a warning look Babcock just shot her, Ellie?

'I think as Mr Unwin lived here, Dora, you and Mr Babcock are the people most likely to know about him.'

'Was *staying* here,' Babcock said stiffly. 'He did not live here officially.'

Eleanor ignored the remark. 'Who do you think we should ask, then, Dora?'

'The Frisham sisters!'

Eleanor's thoughts flew back to the wheeled bench outside. Two women could definitely have moved a body. Or was the cleaner just trying to deflect questions from her and Babcock?

Dora darted Babcock another look and retreated to the door. 'I'm sorry, m'lady, but I have to be going.' She turned and hurried away.

Babcock cleared his throat. 'Miss Dora is simply upset about Mr Unwin, m'lady. She doesn't mean anything by her remarks.'

'Perhaps not. But someone *did* kill Mr Unwin.'

He shrugged. 'I really don't know anything except what Constable Quilter told me early this morning.'

'Perhaps. But you know about Mr Unwin's uncle, though? And more pertinently, why you resented Mr Unwin staying here?'

He coloured slightly. 'I didn't... I mean, I might have thought it inappropriate, yes. You see, I've kept Waketon Court going since the master's passing. Fulfilling my duties every day.'

'Why?'

'Out of loyalty and respect for my late master,' he said with unexpected passion. 'And... and to make sure it is in readiness for the rightful inheritor... whenever they wish to claim it.'

She frowned. 'The rightful inheritor? Surely that is Mr Unwin?'

Babcock gritted his teeth. 'No! Otherwise, Mr Pritchard would have left explicit instructions that was the case before his demise. Mr Unwin arrived six months ago, unannounced.' Babcock's fists balled by his sides. 'With the sole intention of stripping the house of its furnishings and selling them! Followed, if he could, by Waketon Court itself. Which he would have succeeded in doing, only over my dead body!'

Unless Unwin died first, Ellie!

18

It took all of Eleanor's resolve to wait until Waketon Court was out of sight.

'Well, what do you make of it, Clif—'

She pitched forward into a pile of fresh snow as Gladstone slid into the back of her legs.

Through the thickly falling snowflakes, her butler's face bobbed down into her eyeline. 'What do I make of what, my lady, since we have uncovered a number of revelations in the last few hours?'

She accepted his elbow to scramble up. Then shook her head at the clothes brush he produced from the seemingly endless depths of his pockets. 'Yes, alright, a fair question, Clifford. Come on! Let's get back to the tavern and rouse my slumbering husband first. We can discuss all this with him.' She brushed down her thick wool overcoat and shook the snow off her mittens and hat. 'For now, let's enjoy this festive weather like a certain bulldog is!'

'Indeed, my lady. But I would lay odds he will already be up. Were I a betting man, that is.'

'Which you're not, of course.' She slowed down as they hit

another section of ice. 'Unless Mrs Trotman throws down the gauntlet during a game of pontoon, hmm?'

He flapped a respectful hand for her to keep her voice down. 'Excuse me reminding you, my lady, but the ladies are supposed to be unknown to us. Hence, using their names now, ahem...'

She glanced over both shoulders, lowering her voice as well. 'My error. You're right. We can't be too careful about being overheard. Especially as I'm not sure whether we've been tailed since we arrived in this forsaken place. But if so, by whom? And why?'

The look on Clifford's face told her they both suspected the same; Unwin's murderer!

As they slid on through the snowy wonderland, she pointed up at the high ridge encircling Yorelow, the sloping sides towering several hundred feet above them.

'Goodness, Clifford! I see why this place is nicknamed the Devil's Porringer now. We really are at the bottom of an enormous cliff-topped bowl. There's even what looks like a ruined castle up on the right there to make it a true fairy-tale setting.' A frisson of awe washed over her. 'All it needs is a giant glass dome placed over it for it to be one of those beautiful decorations that have started appearing this year.'

'A "snow globe", my lady. One encapsulating a sprinkling of the most darling little thatched gingerbread cottages and sugar-dusted fir trees that look positively edible!' he said, mimicking her voice perfectly, another of his endless skills.

She laughed. 'I don't describe everything in terms of food, you monster.'

'Perhaps not.' His expression sobered. 'But such a seasonal snow globe would also cover one most unwelcome person.'

She nodded with a frown. 'Again. Unwin's murderer!'

. . .

At the entrance to the tavern, Clifford's prediction proved correct. Even before she had finished stamping the snow from her boots on the bottom step, the door flew open, bathing her in warm golden light and heat from the fire.

'Eleanor, there you are!'

'Morning, Hugh.' She beamed at him, thinking he looked more handsome than ever. He was dressed uncharacteristically in just shirtsleeves under his black evening jacket, paired incongruously with his cedar twill travelling trousers. She waggled a teasing finger. 'But even though it's Christmas Day, and we're in the seemingly informal setting of Yorelow, appearing in public half-dressed will have Clifford here having kittens!'

Seldon coloured. 'I couldn't find my jumper, blast it! And I only brought a few emergency items in my overnight bag.'

'Then you should have let Clifford pack and play proper valet to you. As he's been itching to do ever since we got married.'

Seldon shrugged apologetically. 'No offence, Clifford. I'm just not used to being fussed over.'

'Neither need you be, sir. If you prefer not.' His brow flinched. 'However, certain... sartorial statements might be best avoided in future, if I might be so bold?'

Eleanor laughed. 'At least Hugh's not actually in his nightwear.'

'Like a certain party still is beneath her pilfered knitwear!' Clifford murmured for her ears only. He glided up the steps. 'If I might be excused to rescue the Frisham ladies from Master Gladstone's overenthusiastic greetings?'

The door closed behind him.

Seldon pulled Eleanor into his chest. 'Happy Christmas, my love! Because it has only just begun, you know?'

She batted his arm. 'As if I'd forgotten!'

He pulled back, a slight frown dogging his handsome face.

'Are you sure you hadn't? Because I was hoping to wake up on our first married Christmas morning... together?'

'Oh, Hugh, I'm sorry.' She reached up and cupped his cheeks. 'I just couldn't sleep. And since you were snoring soundly, I crept out—'

He winced. 'I don't snore! Do I?'

'No, but I've learned after many of Clifford's innumerable tellings-off, the best form of defence is attack.'

Seldon chuckled. 'Poor fellow! I really don't know how he's put up with your wily ways all this time. But I'm very grateful that he has. And for knowing he would be with you while you were up to... what, exactly?'

'Come inside. And I'll tell you over whatever breakfast the Frisham ladies can kindly conjure up.'

As they entered the tavern, only Mathilde seemed to be around. She gave Eleanor a half wave. 'Do you want breakfast?'

Eleanor nodded. 'Yes, please. I'm famished!'

'Make yourselves comfy then,' she called, already halfway through the curtain behind the bar. 'And I'll bring it straight out.'

Eleanor unbuttoned her cloak.

'My jumper!' Seldon cried indignantly. 'Eleanor, you total scamp! I looked everywhere for that.'

'You can't have, silly. It's here. Look.'

She let her cloak slide off into Clifford's hands who had glided back in silently, and twirled around before sitting down. Gladstone launched himself at the bench and wriggled into the space beside her. With a sigh, Seldon joined them.

'Now, Eleanor, perhaps you'll confess where you've been?'

Succinctly, she recounted the morning's events, leaving out only her suspicion they were being shadowed. After all, it was only a suspicion and she didn't need him worrying even more about her. He needed his mind free to concentrate on the solution to Unwin's murder.

They broke off as Mathilde approached with a large tray. Clifford took it off her, this time receiving a slight smile in return.

'Thanks. It's just me here, but there's tea on the way too. And hot toast.'

Eleanor wondered where her sister Blythe was. She really wanted to speak to both of them after Dora's remark. 'I'm sorry we've put you to extra trouble. I hope Blythe isn't feeling unwell?'

'Blythe has just taken the news of... Unwin's death a little hard. She'll be down soon.'

'They were close in a... certain regard, weren't they?' Eleanor added quickly.

Mathilde glared at her. 'That's a rummy conclusion to draw, Lady Swift. I didn't say that's what was troubling her.'

She hadn't, but Eleanor was fishing.

'Not in actual words, no...'

Mathilde pursed her lips. 'If he had caught her eye, it would only have been on account of there being so few unattached menfolk in Yorelow. That are worth having, anyways.'

'Do you take it in turns to run your delightful bar, Miss Frisham?' Clifford said, as if just making conversation. Eleanor knew him too well to know he wasn't, however.

'No point. There's nowhere to go with a few hours off. Not in this backwater!'

'Gracious, but you can't have been here all evening when we arrived so late?' Eleanor said.

'I was. Never left the place.'

Seldon caught her and Clifford's drift. 'And all alone too? Sounds like hard work.'

'Who told you I was alone?' Mathilde glared at him suspiciously.

'No one,' Eleanor said placatingly. 'But when we first

arrived here, asking for directions to Waketon Court, Blythe wasn't here then either. Just you.'

'Oh, I see.' Mathilde picked at her cardigan cuff. 'She just nipped out for a bit. Just so happened it was when you arrived.'

She stalked away.

'So Blythe was out about the time Unwin was murdered,' Seldon whispered. 'Is it possible we've one more we can add to our list of suspects?'

Eleanor nodded. Which meant they might very well be staying under the murderer's roof!

19

As Clifford returned with the second tray, Eleanor surveyed the food with glee. 'Not bad for a Christmas breakfast in such an out-of-the-way hamlet. Heaps for me, please!'

Gladstone woofed keenly in agreement. Clifford glanced at Seldon, who was flicking through his notebook.

'Whatever for me, thanks,' he said distractedly.

Clifford tutted. 'Without even being introduced, sir?'

Eleanor nudged Seldon, who looked up. 'Oh, sorry.' He placed his notebook down and sat up straighter. 'I'm all ears.'

Clifford half bowed. 'If I may present creamed oat confection for starters. Followed by golden batter kingdoms; kidney slices enrobed in a piquant soufflé with a side of diced roast potatoes. Turkey rissoles infused with wild sage and heritage onion. Plus a modest accompaniment of cold cuts, comprising mustard-baked tongue and black pudding slices. Along with soda bread toast and carrot or beetroot jam.' He picked up a metal dish from the tray, lifted Eleanor's bulldog from the bench, and set him down next to it. 'You have not been forgotten either this Christmas morn, Master Gladstone.

Sausage medallions and crunchy croutons in dripping gravy for you.'

'Now, hopefully can we get any talk of murder out of the way and salvage at least some of Christmas Day?' Seldon said over the sound of her bulldog's eager munching.

Eleanor nodded, busy savouring the creamy egg combined with the rich gamey flavour of the kidney. Clifford, meanwhile, whipped out his slim leather pocketbook and Eleanor's trusty crime-solving notebook.

Absent-mindedly spearing a rissole with his fork, Seldon swallowed it. 'Delicious! Right. We're pretty sure Unwin was killed between eleven forty-five p.m. and twelve forty-five or thereabouts. Babcock's statement that he heard Unwin just before midnight fits in with that estimate. Victim was killed by a single blow to the head. Murder weapon, unknown and unfound so far. Unless?' He looked up hopefully.

Clifford paused in pouring tea for Eleanor. 'No news on that to our knowledge, sir. But had the murder weapon come to light, I'm sure Constable Quilter would have rushed straight here with the news.'

'Speaking of Quilter, he gave us three names.' She wrote them down as she spoke. 'Babcock, the loyal-even-in-death Waketon Court valet. Ned, seemingly the village troublemaker. And "Loony" Luna, as the locals call her, the wild woman of the woods.'

Seldon frowned. 'What happened to being objective in investigations?'

'That's your thing, Hugh. It's nothing personal to these people. It's just that my brain works differently to yours.'

'You don't say!'

She gave a mock huff at the look of shared amusement that passed between him and Clifford. 'So, you'll want to see...' She rummaged in her skirt pockets. 'Dash it! Where is it?'

'Ahem.' Clifford slid a sheet of paper across to her.

Seldon craned over to read the first heading. 'A list of villagers who were at Midnight Mass. Amazingly helpful!'

'And those who weren't are listed below.'

'Doubly helpful! But how?'

'Reverend Ansel, the vicar, sir.'

Eleanor nodded. 'He's a real top egg and is helping us more than we could ever have dared hope.'

She filled him in on the vicar's offer to accommodate her ladies and Kofi.

'We'll have to find a way to thank him,' Seldon said emphatically. He tapped the list. 'Let's focus on those *not* at Midnight Mass first, starting with Ned. He's already got motive and opportunity. We all heard him threaten Unwin. And—'

'He was busy gloating over Unwin's body in front of us!'

Seldon grimaced. 'Although we don't yet know exactly why he had it in for Unwin. So, we need to talk to Mr Yearth as soon as possible.' He turned back to the list. 'Hmm, Babcock's name is here as not attending Mass, either. Although we knew that as well, of course, because we were at Waketon Court around half past midnight and he met us. Now, Constable Quilter suggested Babcock resented Unwin. And we three definitely got that impression too. But resenting him moving in uninvited doesn't seem motive enough to kill him to me.'

Eleanor and Clifford shared a look. 'This morning, Babcock told us he believes Unwin was planning to strip Waketon Court of all its furnishings, Hugh. And then to sell the house itself, if he could.'

Seldon nodded slowly. 'That's more like it.'

'And even more interesting, Babcock is adamant Unwin couldn't, not being the rightful heir.'

'Interesting. Who is the rightful heir?'

'He wouldn't elaborate.'

'We need to find that out.' He looked thoughtful. 'You said something about a cleaner there as well?'

'A Miss Dora Meath, sir.'

'Hmm, Constable Quilter didn't mention her?'

Eleanor tapped his page. 'No, Hugh. But if Unwin did sell Waketon Court, she would almost certainly have lost her job. And there can't be many others available in Yorelow. If any.'

'Bit weak as a motive for murder, though.'

'On its own, yes. But I got the feeling there's something going on either between her and Babcock, or the man I bumped into outside the gates when we first arrived.'

Seldon rubbed his chin. 'I suppose she and Babcock had the house to themselves until Unwin turned up unannounced.'

'Behind closed doors and all that,' Eleanor said with a coquettish wiggle.

Clifford stiffened in horror. 'If I might suggest focusing on identifying the mystery man you encountered, my lady? Since we both subsequently followed a furtive figure entering Waketon grounds. And saw them leave again.'

'But we don't know if it was the same person,' she said. 'We do know it wasn't Babcock, however. We proved that by racing down the stairs to try and catch him out.'

'Literally!' Clifford glanced disapprovingly at her. 'Any hint of elegance abandoned as usual!'

She tutted. 'It's true, Hugh. You should have seen Clifford, suit tails akimbo, charging down the stairs!'

Seldon chuckled. 'No, he didn't, Eleanor.'

'Thank you, sir.' Clifford threw her a muted look of triumph.

Seldon coughed. 'So, onto the third name Constable Quilter gave us. "Loony Luna". Also not in attendance at Mass, according to our vicar.'

Eleanor nodded. 'Quilter seemed to have no idea why she and Unwin were at each other's throats.'

'Also a priority to interview then.' Seldon regarded the paper. 'So, the rest of the names on the vicar's list of non-attendees... ah!' He lowered his voice. 'The Frisham sisters, Mathilde and Blythe. According to the former, the latter seemingly had the opportunity.'

'And possibly partly the means. Certainly of moving the body.' Eleanor recounted her theory about the wheeled bench in the garden. 'We've all just assumed so far that Unwin was killed on Pritchard's gravestone. Which you can see from the study, by the way, so it's not far.'

Seldon gave her an appreciative smile. 'Very, if infuriatingly, astute of you.'

'Thank you. Although, feel free to leave out the infuriating part next time.'

'Couldn't possibly. Too long on the police force. I'm sworn to being entirely factual.'

'You rotter! Anyway.' She lowered her voice further. 'Dora told Clifford and me we should be asking the Frisham sisters about Unwin, not Babcock and her.'

'Perhaps Constable Quilter knows more on that point?' Clifford said. 'I am reminded of how awkward he seemed in imparting the news of Mr Unwin's death to the Frisham ladies.'

'Excellent!' Seldon jotted down a note and looked up. 'Right, any other thoughts?'

'Reverend Ansel said he thought he saw a light in the graveyard late one night.' Eleanor tapped a name on the paper. 'This man, Douglas Dilkes, is the gravedigger. He might know about any unusual goings on there.'

'Given the riddle on Mr Pritchard's gravestone, the stonemason who made it also springs to mind to speak to,' Clifford added.

'What's his name?'

'I shall endeavour to find out, sir.' Clifford rose and glided away to the bar with the teapot.

Eleanor tucked into another of the moreish rissoles while

slathering two slices of toast with the surprisingly delicious beetroot and carrot jams.

Clifford returned a few moments later with a refilled pot of tea. 'Mr Jarrett Maystone is the stonemason.'

'Good. We'll speak to him too then,' Seldon said. 'Mmm. His is one of the only other two names we haven't mentioned on the reverend's list as not having been at Midnight Mass. The other is Peter Pike. We'll have to find out—' He broke off as Clifford cleared his throat.

'Miss Mathilde told me Professor Pike was arrested at six o'clock yesterday evening by Constable Quilter. Apparently, he was detained in Yorelow's police cell until this morning in order to sleep off the worst of his festive overindulgence.'

Eleanor nodded. 'He was there when we went over, remember, Hugh?' She sighed. 'Well, at least in all of this, we've identified one person who couldn't possibly have killed Unwin. Professor Pike.'

'And another,' Seldon said, tapping a name on his notebook, 'who had motive and opportunity enough to do just that. Ned!'

20

Upstairs in their bedroom, Seldon pulled her to his chest. 'Eleanor, promise me we'll still have a proper Christmas? Despite—'

She pressed a finger to his lips. 'I promise, Hugh. And it'll be an easy promise to keep too. The ladies and darling Kofi will be here soon enough. And as you know, to my absolute delight, even Clifford can't rein them in once they've got the festive bug.'

She kissed his chin. 'Now, it's lovely that you came up here for a snatched Christmas cuddle, but we really should crack on with the case, you know.'

'Actually, Eleanor, I came to change as well after what Clifford said about my outfit. But murder solving has to come first, I know.'

'Doesn't mean we can't have a little fun in between, though!' She slapped his arm. 'And speaking of Clifford, race you!'

They were still playfully jostling each other as they shot down the stairs to the bar, side by side.

'Who won, Clifford?' she said keenly, twirling to hide she

was doing up the last button on her fern tweed suit jacket and matching skirt.

Seldon tugged on his hastily knotted tie.

Clifford looked them both over thoughtfully. 'A close-run finish. However, I am forced to say, the winner is... your ladyship.'

'What?' Seldon said.

She groaned. 'No, Hugh. He's right. Dash it! I fell into his devious trap of doing exactly what he's been angling for since we arrived. Dressing like a lady and being quick about it, too!'

Outside the tavern, Eleanor slipped on her trusty mittens and glanced up at the glacial blue sky. Wisps of white cirrus clouds, or 'angel's hair', trailed high above her, the air crisp with anticipation.

Seldon pulled his woollen overcoat tighter around him and looked up and down the road. 'How are we going to find this Ned character then?'

Clifford pointed left. Trusting his judgement, Eleanor slid her arm into Seldon's and started off the way he'd indicated.

'I believe, Hugh, that, in the few brief minutes you and I were changing, the wizard who masquerades as our butler braved the snow to Quilter's to find out where Ned lives.'

Clifford nodded. 'Along with how to find Miss Luna's woodland shack, my lady. Plus, telephoning the telegraph office to arrange for a telegram to be waiting at the last train station for the ladies and Master Kofi. To inform them of the final arrangements.'

'Excellent! Thank you, Clifford,' Seldon said. 'Now, let's go speak to Ned!'

At the rough patch of snow-shrouded grass that masqueraded as the village green, Clifford turned right instead of heading towards the church. And then led them down the second of the two unmarked turnings they had discovered on their arrival in Yorelow.

Gracious, was that really only late last night, Ellie?

To their collective amusement, Gladstone seemed filled with extra Christmas joy. He pounced gustily on every deep snowdrift they passed, often disappearing entirely. When he emerged, the powdery frosting left clinging to him made him look increasingly like a portly snowman.

'Hardly in keeping with The Byron Detective Agency's professional image, Master Gladstone,' Clifford said fondly, trying to wipe the excited bulldog's face while dodging the wildly flailing tongue.

Eleanor smiled. If only the four of them had nothing else to do but frolic in this beautiful white wonderland. She took a deep breath and rallied her thoughts.

'Is Ned's house much further, Clifford?'

'"His room", my lady. If you will forgive the correction. Mr Yearth takes board and lodgings. And no, I believe it is close by.' He stopped and pointed. 'There, in fact.'

'That! Gracious, the entire upstairs is so lopsided it looks as if it's about to collapse.'

Clifford tutted. 'A consequence of insufficiently seasoned timber being used in the construction. Hence the top floor twisting as it dried out.'

She stared at the timber-framed cottage that had once been painted a shade of ruddy earth before it had faded to a muddier hue and the forest of ivy taken hold.

'Right,' Seldon said. 'How are we going to play it with Ned?'

Eleanor shrugged. 'Same as always, Hugh.'

'Meaning what? I wasn't part of "always" before I quit the police.'

'Lucky you, sir,' Clifford said in martyred tones. 'Suffice to say, extemporising does not begin to cover her ladyship's favoured modus operandi.'

Seldon stared at him. 'What does that even mean?'

Clifford's lips pursed. '"Winging it", sir.'

She nodded. 'Flying by the seat of our—'

'Wits!' Clifford interrupted hurriedly.

Seldon rubbed his forehead. 'If I ask nicely, Scotland Yard will probably still take me back.'

At the shoulder-height door, Eleanor gave the knocker a genial rap and threw on a smile, determined to give Ned a fair crack at playing nice this time. After the sound of a bolt being drawn back, a very different face poked out.

'What you want?' The woman in her mid-sixties staring out blinked thoughtfully behind her rimless spectacles. She was so petite, she did not need to duck her head of greying wisps to stand straight under the diminutive door frame. But there was something about her that made Eleanor think whatever she lacked in height, she made up for in spirit.

'Merry Christmas,' Eleanor said brightly. 'Please excuse us disturbing you, but we wish to speak to Mr Yearth.'

The woman frowned. 'You mean Ned?'

'Is there another?'

The woman rolled her watery blue eyes. 'Cor, one's enough!'

One of their agency's calling cards appeared over Eleanor's shoulder. She held it out. 'Perhaps you can let him know we are here, Mrs...?'

The woman doubled over, wheezing. 'Mrs, indeed! Me! Chance'd be a fine thing. Lummy, there's been better fish at the bottom of the lake yonder than any man as ever were born here in Yorelow.' Her tone turned serious. 'In truth, the war took most of the good 'uns.' Just as quickly, she regained her frothy festive manner, waving a bony finger at Eleanor. 'So, it's "miss". But folk calls me Ada.'

'A charming name it is, dear lady,' Clifford said silkily,

wading in to help Eleanor with this unpredictable, but irrepressible woman.

Ada flapped her apron at him, eyes bright with delight. 'If yer fancy cracking the ice on the lake yonder and taking a dip in it, I'll snag Ned's rod and hook yer out. I reckon you'd be a fine catch!'

To his credit, Clifford hid his shudder well.

Having recovered from another fit of laughter, she shook her head. 'Shame yer've wetted yer boots for nothing, mind.'

Seldon frowned. 'Are you saying Ned is not at home?'

'That I am. He ain't been back hereaways since last night.' She clucked her tongue. 'Waste of the hot bottle I set to warming his bed.'

'Do you have many boarders lodging with you?' Eleanor said, thinking Ned's housemates might know more about his movements.

'Nope. House is too small for more 'n just Ned.'

At the sound of a crash at the end of the hall, Seldon stared accusingly at Ada. 'It is extremely important we speak to him,' he said, in a steelier tone.

Ada placed her hands on her hips and stared back. 'Well, course it is. Why else would yer be calling on Christmas morn?'

'If it wasn't Ned making that noise, then—' Seldon broke off as a streak of black and white fur shot past, followed by a blur of every conceivable colour of feline in between.

Gladstone growled, then backed hastily behind Clifford's legs as the pack of cats skidded to a stop to casually size him up, tails poised and twitching.

Eleanor shook her head in wonder. 'Seven! That's quite the collection.'

'The others'll be about somewhere,' Ada said contentedly. 'Probably gone for a walk with me goose.'

Seldon paled. He'd had a couple of run-ins with hissy geese

in Little Buckford. Personally, Eleanor knew he'd rather face an armed thug. 'Do you know when Ned will be back?'

'*If*, yer mean.'

Seldon stiffened. 'Why would you think he may not come back?'

'I never said he wouldn't,' Ada said defensively. 'But if yer had looked in a ditch along yer way here, yer might have found him. Wouldn't be the first time for him to sleep it off in one when he's got proper worse for wear. But' – she shook her head vigorously – 'that's his business. Not mine. Nor yours.'

'Actually, it is ours.' Seldon took the business card Eleanor was still holding and gave it to Ada. 'We are assisting Constable Quilter in looking into the death of Mr Inigo Unwin.'

The landlady nodded blandly and slid the card into her apron pocket without glancing at it. 'Thought as much.'

'As Ned isn't here, we'd like to ask you a few questions,' Eleanor said.

Ada folded her arms. 'Try. See what yer can get from me.'

'Cooperation, I trust,' Seldon said. 'Because Mr Unwin's death is being treated as suspicious.'

'Well, that's tinker's news!' Ada scoffed. 'Meaning course it's fishy. What man of only thirty-summat ups and pops his fancy city boots on a gravestone on Christmas Eve night? But coming after Ned over it just 'cos he's been in trouble before, that's not fair.'

Eleanor shook her head. 'That isn't the reason we need to speak to him.'

'He was very... vocal about Mr Unwin in front of us, you see, Miss Ada,' Clifford said.

'Menacingly so,' Seldon added firmly.

Ada snorted dismissively. 'That's just Ned's way of talking. But it's true he thought that Unwin was the most troublesome cur ever to foist himself on Yorelow.'

'Why?' Eleanor said.

Ada sighed. 'Because Mr Unwin caught Ned helping hisself to some bits out of the back of the delivery cart as always calls on the Angel's Summons. Unwin told old Quilter. And Ned was in a right lather of trouble over it.'

Eleanor and Seldon shared a concerned look.

Why hadn't Quilter mentioned that to us, Ellie?

'Is that what Ned and Mr Unwin argued about recently?' Eleanor said.

Ada shrugged. 'Expect so.'

'How well did you know Mr Unwin?' Seldon said.

'Me?' She rolled her eyes. 'Aside from knowing his face, not at all. The very idea of me having any doings with the likes of him! I'm too busy trying to keep body and soul together and a roof over me head to be hobnobbing with the folks in the fancy house.'

'So you didn't know his uncle, Mr Pritchard, either then?' Eleanor couldn't help asking, still intrigued by the riddle on the grave they had found Unwin draped over.

'Ah, well! He were a very different kettle of frogs. Not uppity like that Unwin man. But Mr Pritchard, he was less right upstairs' – she tapped her forehead, then pointed at the second floor of her house – 'than even my old timbers!'

'What time did you last see Mr Yearth yesterday?' Seldon said.

Ada scrunched her face up. 'Truthfully, I couldn't say. I don't keep a clock in me house. And Ned does as he fancies. So, I make his meals when it suits me. And he eats 'em when it suits him.'

'That sounds the perfect arrangement.' Eleanor glanced teasingly at Clifford, who, she knew, was coursing with horror at the idea of living without a precise schedule for meals.

Ada looked up at the sky. 'Course, the bells!'

'The church bells?' Clifford said.

Ada tapped her ear. 'That's 'em. Gave us decent folk yester

evenin' the nod it was time to start wrapping warm to go to Midnight Mass.'

Seldon smiled weakly. 'I see. So just before ten thirty, I presume? And that's when you last saw Mr Yearth?'

Ada poked him in the arm. 'I never said that. He'd been gone a good half hour before they started. Yer need to listen better, sonny!'

21

Eleanor turned to Seldon as they continued down the lane towards the woodland shack where the mysterious Luna lived. 'Interesting woman, Ada, wasn't she?'

He grimaced. 'Exasperating! Blast it, is there no sense of urgency at all in these country people?'

'"Folk", Hugh,' she said teasingly.

Clifford's lips twitched. 'Father Time obviously has yet to find his way down the only track in, and out of, Yorelow, sir.'

Seldon chuckled. Eleanor too, more grateful than ever for her butler's infallible knack of knowing just what to say to lighten the mood.

'Seriously though,' Seldon said. 'I'm concerned Constable Quilter didn't mention he knew the reason why Ned held a grudge against Unwin.'

Before she could agree, Clifford paused. 'This division was not mentioned?'

The track they were on split into three; two footpaths and what looked like a way through the undergrowth made by animals. Clifford rescued Gladstone's enthusiastic bulk from yet another unexpectedly deep snowdrift while they pondered which one to take. Untamed snow-capped hedgerows abounded. And beyond, the thick and ancient woods of Yorelow ran up the steep slopes of the punchbowl as if hemming the hamlet in.

A rustling behind the brambles on her right caught her attention. She cocked her head. 'A pair of deer, Hugh?' she whispered loudly. That would make for a magical sight on Christmas morning. Seldon shrugged, while Clifford scooped a bemused Gladstone into his arms and gently cupped the bulldog's muzzle. She was about to investigate when a voice hissed,

'Per'aps, it is. Per'aps, it isn't!'

She flinched. Where had she heard those words, and that voice, before?

The man I bumped into outside Waketon Court, Ellie.

She guessed the voice had come from the other side of the hedge. Glancing left and right, she looked for a gap. Finding none, she put her head down to shove a way through. Before she could, Seldon tugged her shoulder. Behind him, Clifford was pinching the bridge of his nose. And behind him was a man staring at them.

'Ah! Merry Christmas,' she said brightly, noting he was gentlemanly enough to take off his cap. Stepping over to him, she realised in daylight he wasn't as wizened as she thought in the eerie yellow glow of his lantern. More weathered-looking, with rugged lines around his striking grey-blue eyes, his lean jaw and frame suggested he'd led a life of manual labour. She estimated he had maybe just rolled into his fifties. And that in his day, he had probably been rather easy on the eye.

She smiled. 'I'm Lady Swift. I didn't have a chance to introduce myself last night. Nor, earlier this morning, actually.'

He stared back at her, then rubbed his hand over his mouth. 'I don't follow you, miss. But Yuletide greetings to you too.'

Clifford's brow flinched. 'Perhaps you missed the lady's title, Mr...?'

'Dilkes. Douglas Dilkes,' he said genially. 'And no, I didn't.'

She ignored the remark. 'I believe everyone calls you "Digger" because you dig the graves in St Cuthbert's churchyard? Is that so?'

He tugged on his jacket collar. 'I don't mean to sound churlish, but you been following me?'

She blinked. Or was it the aptly named Digger who had been following them since they'd arrived?

'Why would you think we'd want to?' Seldon said casually.

'Because folk is saying you're three nosy beaks from foreign parts!' He winced. 'Only, that may have not come out best word-ways. Apologies, miss.'

She flapped a hand. 'Not at all. In fact, we "three nosy beaks" are private detectives.'

'Looking into the suspicious circumstances surrounding Mr Unwin's death,' Seldon added.

Digger looked away, kneading his left shoulder as if it was aching. 'Isn't that the police's job? Aren't you likely to get yourselves into trouble digging around in other people's... business?'

Was that a veiled threat, Ellie?

Eleanor raised her hand. 'Mr Dilkes. We just have a few questions you can help us with. As St Cuthbert's gravedigger, perhaps you have noticed some unusual activity around the church?'

He shrugged. 'Bit odd that Mr Unwin being done for on that gravestone, I suppose.'

'Something other than the poor fellow ending up as he did, I mean. For instance, Reverend Ansel told us he saw some late-night activity in the churchyard and—' She broke off at Digger's vehement headshake.

'That's the trouble with those who come in from outside of the Devil's Porringer. Not meaning to be rude about the reverend, but whatever he says strikes me as a fair bit fanciful. Things here in Yorelow are... different, that's all.'

'Different in what way?' Seldon said.

'How should I know what outsiders are used to? I'm a Yorelow man!'

Eleanor took a shot in the dark. 'Why were you coming out of Waketon Court at almost midnight last night?'

He frowned. 'Me? Says who?'

'I do. You and I collided outside.'

He massaged his shoulder again. 'That's right. Outside being the word, miss.'

'But you'd just come through the gates from the house,' she bluffed.

He tipped his head at her and muttered to Clifford, 'See what I said about those who ain't from Yorelow? Always seeing things as isn't the case.'

Seldon's jaw tightened. 'Then what were you doing outside the Waketon Court gates at that very late hour on Christmas Eve?'

His genial demeanour evaporated. 'Nothing that needs be told to strangers. Especially as it's not to do with Mr Unwin having died!'

'Been murdered,' Seldon corrected crisply.

Digger swallowed hard, but didn't reply. Neither did he make his excuses and leave, Eleanor noted. Was he hanging around to see if he could pick up on what they'd learned elsewhere? If so, out of curiosity? Or necessity, as the murderer? Figuring they wouldn't get anything more from him following the same line of questioning, she switched tack.

'We'd like to speak to Mr Maystone. I assume you know him as he's the stonemason for the village?'

Digger gave her a politely pitying look. 'There's only a few handfuls of folk in Yorelow. Course I know Jarrett. I know everyone.'

'Any idea where he might be at this time of day?'

'Seeing as it's Christmas morn, he'd normally be in the

Angel's Summons by now for a pint. Only I happened to see him still in his workshop a few minutes ago. Backaways from the tavern but off to the right before old Quilter's hut.'

She had to bite her lip to hide a smile at his description of the local police station. It was far too apt for the delightfully quaint thatched roundhouse.

He doffed his cap to her, then nodded to Seldon and Clifford. 'I need be about my own Christmas morn now. Good day, all.' He turned on his heel.

'One more question.' Seldon stepped around to face him. 'Where were you between eleven last night and one thirty this morning?'

'Easy,' Digger said, making a point of stepping around Seldon. 'After I bumped into the lady there, I went home to me bed.' He folded his arms. 'And stayed there, before you ask.' He ambled away.

'Enjoy your day off,' Eleanor called after him. 'I assume you have one or two, seeing as it's Christmas?'

He turned back around. 'I do, miss. Just the one. Which suits me fine.' His eyes lit up. 'Because I'm sure looking forward to burying that Mr Unwin!'

22

As the Angel's Summons disappeared from view, Seldon shook his head. 'Blast it!'

Eleanor slid her arm into his. 'What is it, Hugh?'

'Ah! I didn't mean for that to come out aloud.' He sighed. 'I know I was the one who insisted we'd get back to celebrating Christmas after our next two calls. But it would be unethical not to let Constable Quilter know what progress we've made.'

'Of course. But he'll be coming to Christmas lunch. We can update him then.'

Kofi and the four ladies who made up the female staff at Henley Hall would hopefully arrive at the rectory in time for lunch too. Unless they were already there, of course.

Following Digger's directions to the stonemason's workshop, they soon arrived at a set of open iron gates with a small yard, and an ancient-looking barn beyond. The yard was peppered with boulders of grey rock and slabs of sandy-coloured stone to one side, and gravestones on the other, all peeking out from a blanket of snow. A continuous rumble and a 'thud chink', 'thud chink' came from the direction of the barn. As they approached, the source of the rumbling turned out to be a slowly spinning barrel, from which an arc of water flew out with every revolution. Nearby on a long bench, stone statues in various stages of completion were surrounded with all manner of tools.

She couldn't resist whipping off a mitten and running her fingers over the uncut rocks. Stones of any sort had always attracted her. They gave her a comforting, grounded feeling. Even now, a pretty pebble, or even flint, she spotted out on a walk often ended up in her pocket.

'You wouldn't think someone could make a living just making gravestones in a hamlet like this!' Seldon muttered.

She grimaced.

Let's hope that doesn't prove the case during our investigation, Ellie. One body to bury is enough.

'I imagine you cannot, sir,' Clifford said to her relief. 'However, the local stonemason in such a place as Yorelow would also repair buildings and other stone-based structures. Hence the materials over there.' He pointed at several sacks and containers in the other corner. 'The basis for mortar; pitch, asphalt and clay, I believe. The term "mortar" derives from the Latin "mortarium", meaning "crushed". I believe there may also be other materials such as sand involved sometimes.'

She realised the hammering had stopped. Was the stonemason watching them?

'Shop?' Seldon called.

A brawny-chested man wearing a bib-topped leather apron over his collarless shirt stepped into view. He had close-cropped black hair and matching dark eyes. He held a formidable-looking hammer in one hand and an equally formidable-looking chisel in the other. His sleeves were rolled back to his elbows, revealing bare forearms so sculpted they looked like an artist's anatomical study of muscles and sinews. He tugged down the strip of wool wrapped across the lower half of his face and eyed them suspiciously.

'I can't fathom what strangers want from a stonemason on Christmas mornin', but welcome ye be.'

'This is my wife, Lady Swift. I'm Hugh Seldon. And this is Clifford,' Seldon said. 'Collectively, we are The Byron Detective Agency.'

'And what of it?'

Jarrett's indifferent response wasn't matched by the wary look in his eyes. With the toe of his boot, he kicked a lever on the frame holding the rotating barrel. The rumble slowed and stopped. He strode over to another barrel, whacked the ice on top with the hammer and plunged his face into the water. Eleanor shivered. That had to be freezing cold.

Her gaze roamed to the bench and the profusion of tools scattered along it, many of which ended in a sharp-looking blade. The fatal wound she'd spotted on Unwin's temple swam horribly into her mind.

Oh gracious, Ellie! The murder weapon could be lying among those tools, right in front of us.

Taking advantage of Jarrett now drying his face on a length of rough sacking, she scoured them, Seldon and Clifford joining her. She gestured urgently at a thick brass hook on a long wooden handle.

Clifford shook his head and drew a distinctive curve in his gloved palm. She sighed. He was right. There were plenty of chisels, but, like that gauge's hooked end, none of them had the right curve to have made the gash to Unwin's head.

Jarrett strode back over. 'You can get yourself hurt messing around with things you know nothing about.'

'And festive tidings to you, Mr Maystone,' she said. 'Now, we just have a few questions relating to Mr Unwin's death. We came up here at his request, you see.'

He looked between the three of them. 'Names Jarrett to all folk. And makes a bit more sense then. You pokin' about in things that have nothing to do with you.' He wiped his hands on the back of his trousers. 'But you can still get yourselves burned.'

Was that another threat, Ellie?

They were racking them up today.

'Really?' she said nonchalantly. 'What we wanted to ask you, however, was not about Mr Unwin to start with, but about his uncle, Mr Pritchard. Or more specifically, his gravestone. I assume it is your work as the only stonemason in Yorelow?'

Jarrett nodded slowly. 'That Mr Pritchard was the strangest bird I ever met. He commissioned it well before he died, he did. Had his inscription all written out.'

'Did he acknowledge you might think the actual wording... unusual?'

'No. And I weren't going to question it. A job's a job, after all. But' – he rubbed a rough-skinned hand over his chin – 'after we'd gone over it a few times, he shortened it to make sure it fitted. And as I remember, he muttered something about hoping it would still make sense to someone one day. Complete nonsense it was, if you ask me.'

'Everybody wants to be remembered after they're gone,' she murmured sadly.

'Did you have any dealings with his nephew, Mr Unwin?' Clifford said.

Jarrett shrugged. 'Saw him around now and then. Seemed an alright enough sort to me. Not that I had any dealin's with him personally.'

Eleanor noticed Seldon had stiffened almost imperceptibly during the last few exchanges.

'Just one last question, Jarrett. Purely routine. We're asking everyone to try and get a picture of what happened last night.'

She caught it then. A slight twitch in Jarrett's left eye.

'Where were you between eleven and one this morning?'

'I was up there, to start.' He jerked a thumb over his shoulder.

'On the roof?' Seldon said.

'No. In me rooms. They're in the attic of the old barn.'

'And then?'

'Well, after a wash and brush-up, I went off to Midnight Mass, along with the other folk.'

Eleanor fought to keep her expression neutral. Perhaps she hadn't managed it, she thought ruefully, as Jarrett scrutinised her face. 'Just like a cat,' he muttered.

'What is?' Seldon said with a slight frown.

'Your missus' eyes. So green.'

He reached into a metal pail and dropped a stone in her hand.

Her breath caught. It was an exquisite polished oval of vibrant emerald, patterned with an intricate concentric swirl which pulled her gaze to its centre. She felt she was looking into another world.

'Malachite. And local, perhaps?' Clifford said.

Jarrett nodded. 'I tumble stones and polish 'em as a sideline for extra money. Never know what proper gem might turn up. Leastways, I keep hopin'.'

'It's extraordinarily beautiful. I must pay you for it.'

He shook his head. 'That one 'taint worth much. Keep it.'

Thank you,' she said genuinely. 'And thank you too for your time.'

He shrugged. 'Welcome, I'm sure. You'll be wantin' to get on, like me. Anywhere you need a steer to find next?' he added casually, but his tone betrayed his interest.

'We're heading to where the lady called Luna lives,' Seldon said. 'But we have directions.'

He sucked in his teeth. 'Not right in the head, she is. I did the gravestones for her parents. Bad business.' He shook his head as if expunging a memory. 'Anyways, Merry Christmas, all.' He spun on his heel, kicked the rotating barrel back into life, and disappeared into the gloom of the barn.

. . .

'A penny for them?' she said once outside the gates.

Seldon rubbed his chin. 'Jarrett was relaxed enough while we were talking about Unwin. It was only when we switched the conversation to Pritchard that he seemed to tense up.'

'Maybe that led him into a lie?' she said.

He nodded. 'About being at Midnight Mass. He's not on the list of attendees you got from the vicar.'

'Neither was he among the group who flocked out of the church and over to gawp at poor Unwin's body, as far as I can recall. But, to be fair, I could easily have missed him. But what stopped you grilling him about that just now, Hugh?'

'Because Jarrett wasn't even a suspect until just now. And it was his relationship or dealings with Pritchard that seemed to make him nervous, so he possibly still isn't. And letting someone think they've got away with fooling you sometimes works best, I learned. The hard way. By being beaten to the punch once by a certain unorthodox titled lady and her dubiously skilled butler.'

'Dubiously. Tsk!' Clifford tutted with mock affront. His lips twitched. 'I believe, however, it was actually twice, sir.'

They soon reached the end of town and after another five minutes, took an unmarked turning into the snowy woods, the densely packed trees punctuated by outcrops of the grey rock they'd seen in Jarrett's yard. Gladstone amused himself catching the clumps of snow in his mouth as they fell from the branches and then shaking his head violently at how cold they were.

The going soon got harder.

'I hadn't realised everything would be so steeply uphill,' she panted.

'According to Constable Quilter's directions, it is not far now,' Clifford said, brushing snow from his trousers. 'Or we are hopelessly lost.'

Spotting the twinkle in his eye, she threw a snowball at him, which he ducked easily. Before she could throw another, he pointed ahead.

'In fact, I believe we have arrived at the lady's dwelling.'

In a small clearing stood a log-timbered cabin on toadstool-shaped stone stilts, fronted by a narrow veranda. The snow-blanketed roof came down almost to the ground. Along with a quaint arched door, she thought it had a delightful hint of the fairy tale about it.

Evidently not to Seldon. 'A poacher's hideout,' he said gruffly.

Clifford raised an eyebrow. 'If you will forgive the correction, sir, more a former woodsman's abode, I would suggest. Given its skilful interlocking joinery construction.'

They crunched up to the steps, which Eleanor noted had been cleared of snow and ice. Gladstone's nose twitched furiously as he raced ahead and sniffed along the small gap at the bottom of the door.

Seldon knocked.

Silence.

After a moment, he knocked again, more loudly. 'Hello?'

Nothing stirred until a bird shot out of the nearest tree with a screech of alarm.

Clifford stepped to the window. Averting his eyes, he tapped on the glass. 'Miss Luna, we are not here to cause trouble, I assure you.'

'Fibber! We're here to question her about Unwin's murder,' Eleanor whispered as she rejoined them, having had no more success at the side window.

A prickle ran down her spine.

You're being watched, Ellie.

She had no idea how she was so sure. Inexplicably, she was also sure the watcher meant them no harm. Unlike the previous occasions she'd felt they were being scrutinised. She scoured the trees. No one.

Seldon cleared his throat. 'Clifford, it's shameful of me to ask, but have you brought...'

'I don't know what you mean, sir,' Clifford said, tapping his coat front with a nod.

As he produced his picklocks and bent towards the door lock, the frisson she was feeling increased. The memory of the woman darting perilously in front of the Rolls flooded back. That stare!

'Chaps!' she murmured. 'We shouldn't.'

Seldon took her gently by the shoulders. 'Eleanor, I realise I'm usually the one to harp on about sticking within the law, but—'

She nodded. 'I know. Normally, I'm the one dragging poor Clifford into a spot of breaking and entering. All in the name of catching a killer, of course. But this time it's different.' At Seldon's bewildered look, she shook her head. 'I honestly can't explain why, but' – she held his gaze – 'we *really* shouldn't.'

He ran his hand through his snow-damp chestnut curls. 'We've trekked all the way out here. It's madness to just leave without scouting around inside.'

She grimaced. 'I know, Hugh. But my—'

'Intuition?'

Clifford cleared his throat. 'To paraphrase the eminent Charles Darwin, sir, "The very essence of intuition is that it's followed independently of reason."'

At her nod, he held his hands up. 'Whatever the baffling beast that is your intuition is telling you, I trust it. Let's go.'

'Back to Yorelow, Master Gladstone,' Clifford said, trying to coax the bulldog who had collapsed on the veranda back onto his feet.

'Come on, Mr Lazy Bones!' She bent down to give him a hand. 'Oh my!'

Seldon strode over. 'What?'

She picked up a sodden scrap of paper and handed it to

him. Clifford produced his pocket magnifying glass, but she waved it away. 'We don't need that, Clifford. I know exactly where we last saw something like this! "Every morning, one penny!" And look!' She pointed a little further along the veranda. 'There's—'

A knife embedded itself in the wooden plank inches from her hand.

23

To Eleanor, when they had first arrived in Yorelow it had seemed like a frozen festive scene in a snow globe. Now, as she, Seldon and Clifford left the Angel's Summons, the snow swirling around them like a dervish reminded her more of a frantic *danse macabre*. As if a giant, devilish hand had given the globe an extra brutal shake. The three of them fought their way against the wind down the winding high street to the church and then to the back of the vicarage.

As they approached, she turned to the two men. 'Now, we promised we wouldn't involve the ladies, or Kofi, in this investigation. They deserve their Christmas. We searched for whoever threw that knife with no luck, I know, so they're still out there. Somewhere. At liberty. But even you have to admit it was a clumsy throw.' She looked pleadingly at Clifford. 'Wasn't it?'

He nodded. 'Indeed, my lady. The knife was already losing momentum and height before it reached the veranda. Hence ending up embedded in one of the steps.'

And not in me, Ellie.

Seldon shook his head. 'It was still way too close to you, Eleanor!'

She looked to Clifford for support again.

'Indeed, it was, sir. However, it hardly penetrated the relatively rotten wood. Had it, heavens forbid, struck her ladyship, it would have inflicted no more than a light—'

'Clifford!' Seldon raised his hand. 'Enough! I agreed when we set up the agency I would no longer mollycoddle my wife. But there are limits. And unknown persons throwing knives at her are it!'

She nodded vigorously. 'I agree.'

He stared at her suspiciously. 'You do?'

'Yes, Hugh. And unknown persons throwing knives at my fellow agency members is the limit for me too!'

A smile played around the corners of Clifford's mouth. 'I apologise for saying so, sir, but her ladyship is correct. That knife could have been intended to hit any of the three of us. Although, I personally believe it was intended to hit none of us. It was merely a crude attempt to scare us off.'

'Yes! By Loony Luna!'

'No, Hugh!' she said firmly. 'Think about it. We had already abandoned trying to break in. If it was Luna who had thrown that knife, she'd have done it when we first arrived and it was obvious we were about to break in. Someone else threw that knife. Whoever it is has been our shadow since we arrived here.'

Seldon threw his hands up in surrender. 'Alright. I admit it doesn't make sense it was her. And yes, the knife could have been for any of us. Or, as Clifford said, more likely none. And to save you saying it, Eleanor, yes again!'

She stared at him. 'Yes what?'

'Yes, it's going to take a lot more than one sloppy knife thrower to stop us hunting down Unwin's killer. Now, let's put on our festive faces and party Lady Swift style!'

Eleanor flung her arms around him. 'You know, Hugh, I really do think I love you more every day!'

She turned towards the back door of the vicarage and stopped. Something caught her eye. Something different...

At that moment Ansel opened the door and a ribbon of fur shot out. Gladstone slipped his lead and bounded forward to meet his friend, who was already pawing at Eleanor's skirt.

'Hello, Tomkins!' she whispered. 'We're trying to be discreet.' But remonstrating with the excited tomcat was fruitless. Ansel beckoned them all in and shut the door behind them.

'Happy Christmas!' cheered the ladies and Kofi, lined up in the kitchen, which was decorated with holly garlands, replete with red berries, silvery spruce, and gold and green ribbon.

'And Happy Christmas to you!' she, Seldon and Clifford chorused back.

Gladstone wriggled along the line, his stumpy tail wagging furiously as he was petted and made a fuss of.

Mrs Butters bustled over. 'Oh, m'lady! 'Tis such a treat for us all to be here together. I hope you're ready for some proper Christmas celebrations?'

Eleanor's head nodded as keenly as Gladstone's tail wagged. 'Absolutely!' She turned to Ansel. 'Happy Christmas to you again, Reverend. And thank you once more.'

He beamed. 'What better day to be united as one than on Christmas Day!'

'Although we almost never did!' Polly said.

Ansel nodded. 'I intercepted them as arranged at the top of the punchbowl. Then loaded them and their luggage into a pony and trap I borrowed from one of my few loyal parishioners. But the road in was treacherously slippery already. Even for a sure-footed animal.'

'Aye! And definitely for Mrs Trotman,' Lizzie said, holding back her laughter.

Mrs Trotman tried to look stern but failed. ''Tis true, m'lady. I came a right cropper and fell on me—'

Clifford's vigorous hand clap rang around the kitchen.

'Ladies, we can talk more over lunch. Speaking of which, I imagine you still have much to prepare, Mrs Trotman?'

'We do that, Mr Clifford. Although a lot we brought with us will have to be served as cold cuts and the like as we weren't sure of the cooking facilities, so played safe.'

'Whatever you conjure up, ladies, will be utterly delicious as usual, I'm certain,' Seldon said.

As the ladies continued with preparations overseen by Clifford and his now right-hand helper, Kofi, Eleanor and Seldon brought Ansel up to speed on their investigation so far.

When they'd finished, he stroked his chin. 'Well, you've certainly made progress. Unfortunately, I can't really add anything that might help. I've never noticed any unusual comings and goings from Waketon Court. And none of the characters you mentioned are regular churchgoers, so I've had no chance to really get to know them.'

'And you didn't notice Digger or Jarrett hanging around the graveyard before the service, perhaps?' Eleanor said.

He shook his head. 'Although, I do now recall Dunstan had to deal with a slight disturbance just as I was finishing my sermon. Someone came in late, I think. But I didn't see who. You'd have to ask him.'

So it could have been Jarrett, Ellie?

A knock on the back door interrupted their discussion. Ansel opened it, revealing what looked like a snowman. Quilter shuffled in, shedding layers of snow as he did so. Behind him through the door, Eleanor could see it was now almost a whiteout.

'Blimey!' He looked around at the ladies and Kofi. 'Happy Christmas to you all. I didn't thinks as how you'd have made it. Must have got through just before this lot started proper. Road out, and in, is impassable for sure. As saying goes, "You can check in to Yorelow, but you can't check out till the snow says so!"'

Or maybe a murderer, Ellie!

She noticed he was carrying a large bag.

'It's my hurdy-gurdy,' Quilter said. 'Normally, we has some song and dance after Christmas lunch around these parts. Although it's nigh on time for Christmas dinner!'

Her eyebrows rose. 'A what?'

'A hurdy-gurdy, my lady,' Clifford said as he passed with Kofi, both of them balancing a stack of plates. 'A mediaeval stringed instrument. The strings are played by turning a wheel, producing a single drone note, the pitch of which is then altered by using a small keyboard.'

She threw out her hands. 'Well, Constable, given the raging storm of white outside at the moment, I think an indoor activity after lunch would be a fine idea. But first...'

She and Seldon shared a look.

'Let me arrange a hot drink to warm you up, Constable,' Clifford said, taking the policeman's coat and gliding away.

'And while he does, we'll quickly update you on progress,' Eleanor added. 'Then we can all enjoy Christmas lunch without talk of murder!'

Seldon filled Quilter in on what they'd learned since they'd last spoken. Quilter listened intently until he'd finished. 'You don't hang around, I'll say that for you, sir.'

'Thank you, Constable. Is there anything you can tell us about this Jarrett character?'

Quilter scratched his chin. 'Well, his family 'as been stonemasons in Yorelow for generations. Jarrett inherited the business from his father, but I've always got the impression his heart were never really in it. Always dragging his feet over jobs, as if he'd rather be doing something else. Never really made a go of it and consequently had a bit of trouble with debt around the village. He's sometimes got a bit of a hot temper and has had the occasional run-in when he's drunk a little too much. But nothing you wouldn't expect in a small town.'

'I see,' Seldon said. 'Moving on, we did go to Luna's cabin as I said, but we didn't search it... It was locked, and we would have needed you present before gaining access.' At Quilter's disbelieving expression, he hurried on. 'Anyway, we found an item outside that seems to suggest Unwin may have gone to Luna's for round two of their argument.'

He showed Quilter the bottom half of *The Westminster Gazette* bookmark she'd found on Luna's veranda, 'Every morning one penny' written on it. 'We're sure this came from Mr Pritchard's diary that Mr Unwin was reading. So maybe, out of public view this time, their argument became even more heated. To the point she decided Unwin had to be dealt with, perhaps?' He shrugged. 'This is all speculation, of course.'

'Do you have any background information on Luna that might be helpful? Anything that would allow us to understand her, and her possible motives, more?' Eleanor asked.

Quilter scratched his chin as he gratefully took the cup of steaming tea Clifford passed him. 'Well, m'lady, I'd best start at the beginning. I knew Luna when she weren't no bigger than a newborn lamb. Lived up at the castle yonder.'

Eleanor gasped. 'The ruined one on the hill as you come into town?'

Quilter nodded. 'Lyndseer Castle. That's her full name, Luna Lyndseer, but as I said, folks call her Loony...' He cleared his throat. 'Well, her folks had lived around here for generations. But time weren't kind to Yorelow. It got left behind as everything, and everyone, went south. Or north. The railways and roads they built weren't nowhere near the village neither. Over the years, most of the family left. By the time Luna were born, only her mother and father lived in the castle with just a couple of old retainers. But like all entitled folk, despite their hard times, they still saw themselves as...' He glanced hurriedly at Eleanor. 'Not meaning—'

She raised her hand. 'Constable. I inherited my title and

wealth from my uncle only a few years ago. But I know what you mean. It's difficult to forget past glories and adjust.'

He grimaced. 'Well, they never did. And in some ways, they were right. They had no money, but they still lived in a castle. Though it were built as a house originally. Then just made to look like a castle.' He cleared his throat again. 'Sorry, I'm rambling here.' He took a swig of tea and continued. 'Luna was a strange child. Her parents wouldn't let her mix with the other children, so she grew up on her own. They schooled her in the castle as well. She hardly ever left. Awkward child she was the few times I saw her. But somehow, one day she met Mr Pritchard.'

Eleanor's breath caught. 'They didn't?'

He nodded. 'Fall in love? They did, m'lady. And hard. The rest no one knows exactly. But she kept it a secret, knowing her father would never agree to her marrying someone from Yorelow, even if he had a little money. Well, finally I take it Pritchard decided it couldn't go on like that. Turned up at the castle unannounced one evening, so the story goes. Luna came back to find her father throwing him out by the scruff of his neck, vowing if he came near his daughter again, he'd have him slapped in jail.' Quilter paused, looking uncomfortable.

Eleanor felt a chill in the pit of her stomach. 'What happened then?'

'No one quite knows, m'lady. But there was speculation. Long and short of it is, that night the castle burned down. Both Luna's parents were found in the ashes in the morning.'

'And Luna?'

'She'd disappeared, m'lady. Was found wandering in the woods days later.'

Eleanor bit her lip. 'You mentioned some speculation?'

He shuffled his feet. 'That's right. There were talk, rumours really, that Luna had set the fire. There weren't no evidence, but somehow them stories took hold.'

'What about Pritchard?' Seldon said.

'Well, sir, I interviewed him with Luna there and asked if he'd had anything to do with the fire? He denied it. So I asks Luna, who denies it too. Then she turns to Pritchard and asks if he believes her.' Quilter shook his head sadly. 'He didn't say nothing, but you could tell from his face that he had a suspicion she might have.' He shrugged. 'Anyways, Luna stares at him, then lets out a screech like a wounded wolf! Sent the shivers right through me, I got to confess. Then she ran from the room back to the woods. And she's been living in them woods ever since.'

So that's why she's an outcast, Ellie. And why she won't speak to anyone.

A thought struck her. And immediately vanished. She frowned, trying hard to recall it. Somehow she felt as if she'd lost something important she'd never had.

'Did Mr Pritchard try to persuade Miss Luna to return, Constable?' Clifford said.

Quilter shrugged. 'I don't know, Mr Clifford. He never talked of it. And I never saw them together from that day forth.'

While Eleanor was digesting the story, what she felt about it, and how it might tie into the investigation, Seldon pulled a handkerchief from his pocket.

'I have further evidence, however, that Luna definitely had more dealings with Mr Pritchard's nephew.' He unwrapped it and showed Quilter what Eleanor had just pointed out to him before the knife landed on Luna's veranda.

Quilter whistled softly. 'Them's the same as you found near Mr Unwin's body.'

Seldon nodded. 'Do you know what they are?'

'I do now, sir. They is fragments of a clay pipe.'

For some reason, Eleanor dreaded asking the next question. 'And do you know where they come from?'

'That I do. They be from Miss Luna. Explains why you found them on her veranda as well.'

'But they could be from another clay pipe, Constable?' Clifford said.

Quilter shook his head. 'Miss Luna is the only one what still uses them. A lot of folks used to have them before the war, but now them what do smoke, smoke cigarettes or them briar pipes.'

Eleanor's brow furrowed in puzzlement. 'Why does Luna smoke a pipe?'

He chuckled. 'Does seem a bit odd, granted. I mean some women smoke nowadays, and a few like them fem—' He coloured. 'Er, sorry, m'lady, what I was saying was as a child, Luna used to grind her teeth something terrible. Her parents tried everything but couldn't cure her of it. She wouldn't have nothing the doctor gave her neither. Then somehow, one day, she got hold of an old clay pipe. Well, instead of grinding her teeth down, she ground the stem down and ever since she's kept it up.'

The thing we found in the Rolls's grille was from her pipe, Ellie.

'Never actually smokes 'em,' Quilter continued. 'And when they became hard to get after the war, she started making her own out in that shack of hers. Plenty of clay around these parts. And that, as they says, is all I knows.'

Mrs Butters appeared in front of them. 'Lunch is ready, m'lady.'

'Splendid,' Eleanor cheered. 'Let the festive feasting begin!'

24

As they all sat, Mrs Trotman and Mrs Butters set down two plates of golden pastries, wafting mouth-watering hints of sausage meat and sage. The table was beautifully but simply set with the same green and red holly, silvery spruce and golden ribbon as the rest of the kitchen. The place settings also included a linen napkin expertly starched and folded into the shape of an angel.

The women bumped hips and giggled. Clifford shook his head.

'I fear, my lady, before we arrived, your staff may already have had a small dose of festive spirit of the bottled variety!'

Eleanor leaned over and whispered loudly, 'Tell me, Clifford. Just how do you intend to keep order among the staff when we are already witnessing such disgraceful behaviour?'

Over the table's laughter, he said in a long-suffering tone, 'I fear, my lady, the answer is I shall not. However, what must the reverend think?'

Ansel smiled as he looked around the table. 'I think, Mr Clifford, that Christmas comes but once a year. And as it says in

Psalm 118:24, "This is the day that the Lord has made; let us rejoice and be glad in it."'

Delighted that he was enjoying himself as much as everyone else, she gasped as the ladies left and returned with even more plates of delicious-smelling fayre. Catching Mrs Butters' eye, Clifford made a show of removing his pristine white butler gloves. Eleanor smiled to herself as the ladies nudged each other.

Ah, Ellie, now they can all truly relax and enjoy themselves.

Clifford strode over to a spare table that had been reserved for the drinks. His hand hovered over the bottles. 'Mrs Trotman. Would you care to suggest where we start among your home-made concoctions?'

The cook turned to Ansel. 'Before we do, Reverend, the truth is all them distillations is my non-alcoholic alternatives. I brought them as her ladyship told us we would be celebrating in the local vicarage and you, yourself, was being so kind as to put us up.'

Ansel laughed. 'That was very thoughtful of you. And in which case, include me in whatever you serve.'

'Actually,' Eleanor said, 'I must just address the Henley Hall tradition of presents on Boxing Day. Unfortunately, this year they will have to be delayed until our return.'

'Which hopefully won't be long,' Seldon added.

They shared a look.

He doubts it as much as I do, Ellie. We seem to have got nowhere so far.

Reminding herself it was still early days, and more importantly Christmas lunch, she banished the subject of murder from her mind. Almost.

'Right. Clifford, I believe you and Mrs Trotters were sorting out the drinks?'

After everyone's glass had been filled with home-made

rosehip and pear press, Seldon dinged his with a spoon and waved it around the table.

'I'm not the best at giving speeches, so I'll keep it short. I just wanted to thank the reverend for making it possible for us all to celebrate this special day together. And to apologise for any unseemly behaviour later.'

Everyone laughed, including Ansel.

Eleanor stood up next. 'I second that. Thanking the reverend, that is! As you know, we were hoping to spend Christmas Day at Henley Hall this year. But, in all honesty, this feels just as special. So, I want to thank you, ladies, from the bottom of my heart, for giving up your usual Christmas to come here. And for all the wonderful ways you make my life easier every day, whether back at the Hall or not. And always without drama or complaint. Merry Christmas!'

As everyone clinked glasses, she noticed Kofi shoot Clifford a glance and Clifford nod back. The young boy stood up. 'I do not have a fine speech like Lady Swift. But I am wishing to say in my country we celebrate Christmas by eating two to five times a day. And many snacks in between, so I think she would like this very much.'

Eleanor slapped Seldon on the arm as he roared with laughter. Even Clifford's eyes twinkled. Kofi raised his glass. 'And the way to say "Merry Christmas" in my country is "Afishapa!"'

"Afishapa!" everyone chorused back as they clinked glasses.

As Eleanor drained her glass, next to her, Gladstone barked in excitement, his tongue hanging out like a slice of ham. She cupped his wrinkled jowls. 'You and Tomkins can be as unruly as you want today, my old chum. I'll even turn a blind eye to a little begging for titbits under the table. It is Christmas and you need to eat, drink and party, too!'

Gladstone woofed agreement while Tomkins meowed his consent.

Clifford eyed her sideways.

She tutted. 'It's no good relaxing your precious rules just for the ladies today, Clifford. You'll have to include our four-footed contingent as well. And speaking of relaxing, are you actually going to let your hair down a little on this oh-so special day?'

He half bowed. 'As my mistress wishes.'

With her plate loaded, she tucked into a Christmas lunch of sausage rolls, cold meats, relish and stuffing, with gusto.

Seasonal chatter flowed back and forth across the table, the two young maids joining in as fully as the adults, to Eleanor's delight. As usual Mrs Trotman's cheeky humour had everyone in stitches. Even Clifford allowed his amusement to show, keeping up his promise to her to relax. Well, as much as he ever did.

In fact, she was the least talkative of the table. Instead, she sat back in her chair and just soaked up the warm festive feelings floating around the room. She'd spent many years wandering the world, from her childhood onwards. First on her parents' sailing boat. Then on a bicycle. And finally, working for a luxury tour operator as far afield as South Africa. Now the feeling of being at home surrounded by family and friends celebrating together was almost too much. And the cherry on the icing on this festive cake was that her husband was sitting next to her. Under the table, she squeezed his hand.

'Happy Christmas, Hugh,' she murmured.

Without a word, he swept her into a kiss to a rousing cheer from the assembled company.

Rather than admonish the ladies, Clifford looked away, adjusting his cuffs. 'Apologies, Reverend,' he said. 'But you were warned about unseemly behaviour. Although I expected it to come from another quarter!'

Once everyone had eaten their fill, the plates were whisked away, the lights turned down, and dessert served; Christmas pudding or mince pies in custard, minus the brandy in deference to the reverend again. While dessert was eaten, Lizzie placed three glass jars wrapped in red, green or gold tinsel on the table, the lit candle in each making the tinsel glitter. Then the table was cleared in a trice and everyone retired to the lounge, which was decorated with home-made bunting the ladies had intended for Henley Hall. The bunting all bore seasonal messages and shimmered as Ansel closed the curtains to keep prying eyes out. It was dark outside by now, so wouldn't seem odd to anyone, anyway.

As the ladies, with Clifford and Kofi's help, were setting up for the second part of the Christmas Day festivities, Seldon drew Quilter to one side. She joined them.

'Just a quick word. I understand this is your investigation, Constable,' Seldon said evenly. 'But if we are to assist to the full, we need you to feed us any local information you may have.'

Quilter frowned. 'Of course, sir. Can't be no other way.'

'Then would you please explain why you told us you didn't know why Ned had a grudge against Unwin?'

Quilter held up his hands. 'Fair play, sir. I should have owned up. Trouble is, Yorelow is a place unto itself as it were. People sort out their own problems and the police only get involved if they 'ave to. That's how it's been since before I was born, let alone put on a uniform. And the Frisham sisters agreed if Ned replaced the stuff he'd taken, they wouldn't press charges.'

'And you, Constable?'

'I warned Ned if he committed one more offence, I'd make sure he was prosecuted fully for it.'

Seldon looked him in the eye. 'Is there anything else we should know?'

Quilter nodded. 'Ned is my nephew. Of sorts.' He held his hands up. 'In a place like this, most everyone is related to everyone else.'

Eleanor noticed Polly hovering a few feet away. 'Yes, Polly?'

'Mrs Butters said to tell you everything is ready for the dancing, your ladyship.'

'Excellent!'

As Polly scurried off, she turned to Quilter.

'One more thing, can you tell us anything about Mathilde and Blythe's relationship with Unwin?'

Quilter scratched his head. 'There was some talk of Blythe having been sweet on Mr Unwin, but I haven't seen it meself.'

'What about this matter of the "rightful heir" to Waketon Court?'

'Well now, everyone knows there's some legal wrangle going on, but Babcock ain't never elaborated on it. All I knows is, Babcock wanted Mr Unwin out of Waketon Court. And Mr Unwin wanted Babcock out, but couldn't 'cos he didn't own the house. Babcock is the officially appointed guardian of the place, I think, until the wrangle is settled.'

Seldon sighed. 'Well, there's no hope until after Christmas of finding out who Unwin was in dispute with over ownership of Waketon Court. One thing's for certain though, with what we know now, Ned is looking like our number one suspect for Unwin's murder.'

Followed closely by Luna, Ellie.

Mrs Butters appeared. 'Will you be long, my lady? Only I fear if the young 'uns don't get to let off some of their energy soon—'

'We'll be no more than a minute, I promise.'

As she left, Ansel waved Eleanor, Seldon and Quilter closer. 'I overheard the last part of your discussion concerning Ned. I'm reluctant to divulge something, but it wasn't told to me in sacred trust, so I feel I should.'

Eleanor's pulse quickened. 'What is it, Reverend?'

'One of my few, but loyal, parishioners, let slip a rumour Ned is actually Pritchard's illegitimate son.'

Quilter's eyebrows rose. 'That's news to me! How did they come by that bit of information, Reverend?'

'I'm afraid I'm not at liberty to reveal.'

Eleanor frowned. 'But that's not a motive for Ned to have killed Unwin, is it? As he was illegitimate, even with Unwin dead, he still wouldn't have inherited anything from Pritchard's estate.'

'No,' Seldon said thoughtfully. 'Greed might not be a motive, but jealousy could be. Ned has to scrape by, all the while seeing his father living in one of the grandest houses in Yorelow. And then, when he's dead, Unwin turns up and claims the lot and does exactly the same. Maybe it was too much for Ned and he decided to act and make sure no one inherited it?'

Quilter nodded. 'I'm with you, sir.'

'Good, Constable. First thing in the morning, we'll confront Yearth and then, as our second-placed suspect, return to Luna's cabin.' He turned to Eleanor. 'And I'm sorry, but on this occasion, if she's there or not, we'll have to enter.'

Ansel clapped his hands. 'As you said, all that is for tomorrow. This evening it is time to eat, dance and be merry!'

Eleanor's eyes widened in surprise as Quilter took the hurdy-gurdy out of its bag and turned the handle. A long, almost cello-like sound emerged. Then he played the built-in mini keyboard and she was transported to the Great Hall in an English mediaeval mansion.

She clamped her hand over Gladstone's snout as he started howling, his stumpy tail wagging furiously.

'A sarabande, my lady,' Clifford said as he passed with Kofi. 'Originally originating from Latin America, it was banned by the Spanish Inquisition in the sixteenth century for raising the passions. In the seventeenth, however, it became popular in France and lost its lascivious character.'

'Shame!' Eleanor pouted, her foot tapping to the tune.

'But still worth twirling a lady to!' Seldon took her hand and led her on to the impromptu dance floor.

Soon they were joined by the ladies, Mrs Trotman dancing with Mrs Butters and Lizzie with Polly. At the second dance, another stately affair, Kofi joined them with Clifford. Over the next hour, everyone danced with everyone else as the tunes Quilter rattled off became livelier and livelier. Finally, Mrs Butters, Mrs Trotman and Ansel left the young 'uns to it, Kofi, Polly and Lizzie dancing in a circle, while Eleanor and Seldon danced arm in arm.

As she was swept around the room by her dreamy husband, she let her eyes close and wished Christmas Day would never end.

And that if it did, they wouldn't still have a vicious killer to catch in the morning.

25

As a particularly hectic jig came to a close, Mrs Butters insisted Quilter have a refreshment break. Gladstone decided he also needed a break, but of another sort, as he pawed at the door.

'I'll take him out,' Eleanor said as Seldon rose. 'We won't be long. It's properly dark by now, so no one will see us. You catch your breath for round three!'

Quickly she shepherded Gladstone down to the kitchen. Slipping into her coat, she helped the wriggly bulldog into his and clicked his lead on. Checking she had a torch in her pocket, she unlocked the door and peered out. The snow had almost stopped. Coast clear, she stepped out into a magical moonlight night.

'Come on, Gladstone, we want to be back having fun as quickly as possible!'

The only problem was, there was no path, only a thick, pristine blanket of snow over everything. However, the white-topped gravestones poking through showed her where the path should be and they set off, Gladstone shouldering his way through the powdery snow. Once clear of the churchyard, she started towards the nearest trees on the edge of the wood.

Suddenly the bulldog stopped. He stood stiffly, head raised, eyes alert.

Eleanor crouched down beside him. 'What have you seen or smelt, boy?'

Unease crept up her spine. Snow dropped off a clump of trees further into the woods.

There's no wind and it can't be melting, Ellie, it's freezing. Birds?

Another clump fell from a tree slightly further away. Then another.

Someone's there, Ellie.

Her head told her to turn around and make for the safety of the vicarage, but her heart...

Her head won.

Having retreated to the churchyard and then the vicarage, she halted. She was certain someone was behind her. She spun around. At the edge of the woods stood the woman they'd almost run down in the Rolls. From a distance, she seemed to be about Eleanor's height and build, although the long, black cloak she still wore made it hard to be sure. Her features were difficult to make out as well, as they were partly hidden by the cloak's oversized hood. She could make out her piercing eyes, though. She was staring at Eleanor, but... differently. Almost... beseechingly? As Eleanor's hand reached for the kitchen door, the woman stepped back into the woods and... vanished.

Before she could turn the handle, the door swung open.

'Your ladyship,' Polly said, giggling. 'You're missing the dancing! Mrs T—'

Eleanor thrust Gladstone's lead into the surprised girl's hand. 'Polly. Tell Hugh I'm fine. I... I have to go somewhere. I can't explain, but tell him I'll be back soon and to save the last dance for me!'

. . .

For the third time, she shone the torch on her watch. She'd been following Luna through the woods for twenty minutes or more now. She shook her head to herself. How was the woman finding her way? Small pockets of moonlight penetrated the trees here and there, but otherwise it was black as coal underneath the canopy. She hadn't even seen a beam of torchlight ahead.

Shivering despite her thick coat and stout boots, she brushed as much snow as she could off, and stumbled on, Luna always keeping just in sight.

Another five minutes later and she emerged onto a dirt road, bathed in moonlight. To her left, it curved steeply upward along the side of the river. The other way must lead back into Yorelow, she figured. An owl hooted. In front of her was a mediaeval-looking stone bridge she'd never seen before. She glimpsed Luna already halfway across.

Where is she taking you now, Ellie? And why?

Wrapping her coat tighter, her feet like frozen blocks of ice, she trudged over the bridge. On the other side, a small path snaked up the hill, then turned sharply right.

Then she saw it. The ruined castle! She shivered. Not at the cold this time, but at the memory of Quilter's tale. Why had Luna brought her here, of all places?

And where was Luna?

With no option, Eleanor carried on up the path and under the main stone archway into the grounds, any wooden or metal gates having long gone. She stopped once inside, imagining what the place must have been like when it was a home. Luna's home. Childish laughter floating down the corridors. The murmur of conversation over the dinner table. The bustle of downstairs as the servants hurried hither and thither keeping a grand home running like clockwork. At least, she hoped it had been something like that.

She took a step forward and gasped, her hand flying to her

chest. A few yards in front of her, bathed in a ring of mercurial moonlight, lay a body.

For a moment she stood frozen to the spot. Then recognition dawned.

'Ned—'

'Yearth, my lady.'

She spun around. 'Clifford! How?'

The answer came as a snorting, snuffling Gladstone scrabbled around the corner, followed by Seldon.

'Never underestimate a bulldog looking for his mistress, my lady. Especially when she probably still has the aroma of liver treats, if not the actual item, on her coat. A bulldog may have a shorter "snout" than a traditional scent hound, such as a bloodhound, but their noses are still ten to a hundred thousand times more sensitive than a human's.'

'And,' Seldon added glancing grimly at the body, 'I've quickly learned never to underestimate how much more sensitive your "snout" is for sniffing out trouble. And,' he added, striding over to the body, 'usually with a capital "T".' He knelt down and felt for a pulse. 'Nothing.'

She nodded. 'Not surprising given that red spreading stain from the back of his head.'

He grimaced. 'Déjà vu.'

Clifford knelt on the other side of the body. 'From first observation of the injury, I would hazard the same weapon "as did for" Mr Unwin, as Constable Quilter would undoubtedly put it.'

She felt something alight on her nose.

A snowflake.

'Given the weather's turning, I suggest we examine the body and search the area for the murder weapon and any other evidence before the snow returns with a vengeance and buries everything.'

For a moment, she wished they could just let the snow

gently lay a shroud of pure white over the bloody scene as if nothing had ever disturbed the peace of the place.

Instead she left Seldon with the body that used to be Ned and in the milky moonlight, scoured the area, accompanied by Clifford and a subdued bulldog.

The part of the house-cum-castle Ned's body lay in obviously used to be the grand hallway. In the fire, the wooden roof must have collapsed. Charred remains of timbers still lay piled up around the blackened stone walls. The floor must have been marble at one time too, but it had all been pilfered long ago, leaving just rough vegetation.

And among the vegetation, fragments of—

'Clay, my lady,' Clifford murmured, shining his torch on it.

She bit her lip, not wanting to articulate what she, and she imagined he, was thinking.

Luna, Ellie. But was she just the finder of Ned's body? Or also—

'The perpetrator?'

She glanced up to see Seldon standing behind her. He shrugged. 'A little of that mind-reading of Clifford's must be rubbing off on me. That's what you were both thinking, wasn't it?' He nodded towards the body. 'I'm afraid Clifford was right. The evidence suggests the same instrument was used to kill Yearth as killed Unwin.' He raised his hand as she opened her mouth. 'Which doesn't mean Luna was responsible. But tell me, Eleanor. How did you get here?'

She sighed, her breath crystallising in the freezing air. 'Yes, Hugh. It was Luna. She led me here.'

He nodded. 'I thought it had to be.' He glanced around. 'And now she is?'

'Gone. I don't know where.'

He sighed. 'Since we've arrived in Yorelow, there's some... connection between you two. Some sort of bond I don't understand.' He shrugged. 'Maybe you're both just free spirits.'

She stood up, her mouth set. 'Well, if we don't find out who really killed Ned, and Unwin, Luna won't be a free spirit much longer. And no, I don't know why, but she didn't do this, Hugh.' She waved at the body. 'She wouldn't. Not here.'

He nodded. 'For the moment, that's all I need to hear. Clifford, I know I said I promised not to cotton wool my wife once we started the agency, but that doesn't include her roaming around a murder scene at night on her own. Please continue to search the rest of the grounds clockwise, but keep her within sight. I'll search anticlockwise and I assume we'll meet up again somewhere.'

Before she could protest, he disappeared through a partially collapsed archway. Clifford indicated the other collapsed archway on the side of what was once the grand entrance hall and together they stepped through into the burnt-out shell of what had once been a—

'Ballroom,' she breathed in awe. Stone arches two storeys high ran fifty to sixty feet down one wall. She knew from her own ballroom back at Henley Hall, there would have been floor-to-ceiling windows, arching up to an imposing painted ceiling. Only now they arched up to the star-sprinkled sky, the lack of a roof allowing the moon to flood the ballroom with a ghostly light. While in a macabre wintery waltz, the sighing wind whirled snowflakes around a bloodied angel's trumpet lying in the middle of the dance floor.

26

Eleanor slipped out of the Angel's Summons and hurried down the road as fast as the icy conditions would allow. Even though it was Boxing Day morning and the myriad icicles hanging from the buildings glinted in the early sun like jewels, she had no eyes for them. She'd slept fitfully, finally rising as dawn broke. As arranged, she, Seldon and Clifford had met Quilter on the doorstep of the tavern. The three men had then left for Luna's cabin, while she'd walked in the opposite direction, a sleepy Gladstone in tow.

Leaving the high street, she carried on down an alley before doubling back. She had no reason to think she was being followed, but after yesterday and the knife at Luna's cabin, she was taking no chances. The stakes had risen. Their leading suspect was dead. And they were now investigating two murders.

Slipping around to the back of the vicarage, she was about to tap on the door, when it was opened by a beaming face.

'There you are, m'lady. I was expecting you. I've got the kettle on and some Boxing Day muffins with home-made damson jam on the go.'

'Thank you, Mrs Butters. Are the others up yet?'

Her housekeeper shook her head. 'No. It were a late night as you know, m'lady, and there's precious little to be done until later, not being at the Hall. So I've let them sleep in. It's just you and me. I don't think the reverend is stirring yet either.'

As Eleanor sat down at the kitchen table Gladstone wandered over to Tomkins, who was lying in his bed by the range, tail twitching. The two rubbed noses. Then Gladstone lumbered in next to his friend and plopped down.

'So.' Mrs Butters bustled around the kitchen, getting the tea ready. 'The Master and Mr Clifford have gone a-huntin'?'

Eleanor grimaced. 'Yes. With Constable Quilter for Luna.'

Mrs Butters set the teapot on the table. 'But you don't think as how she is responsible, do you, m'lady?'

Eleanor shook her head. 'No. I don't. I know the evidence is against her. Especially as we found more clay fragments up at the castle. And Clifford found the weapon we believe killed Unwin and Ned. It was the herald trumpet Clifford and I spotted in the church the morning after Unwin was killed.'

Eleanor was transported back to standing outside the church listening to 'Hark the Herald Angels Sing', not knowing the musical instrument being blown would soon be an instrument of death.

In fact, Ellie, given Unwin must have been murdered before the end of Mass, it would already have been used to kill him!

'Apparently, the reverend borrowed it from the Frisham sisters. It is part of their tavern sign. Hence the name "Angel's Summons". Clifford examined the trumpet with his magnifying glass and spotted a hair caught in the nick where it's badly folded. It doesn't match Ned's, but it does Unwin's, which is why we're pretty sure, along with the actual wounds inflicted, it is the weapon used in both killings.' She sighed. 'Quilter's sure when it's tested, they'll find Luna's fingerprints on it. He reckons Ned knew she was up there and was trying to bring her down to claim some kind of reward. But she surprised him and bashed him on the head, same as Unwin.'

Mrs Butters frowned. 'Seems a bit rummy to me. There weren't no actual reward offered, was there?'

'No. Quilter hadn't really enough evidence to arrest Luna for Unwin's murder before. He only wanted to question her. But now she's led me to Ned's body and he found more clay fragments, it's a different story. And if Ned was Pritchard's illegitimate son, there's a link between both murders; they were both relatives of Pritchard. So maybe that's what Ned was actually doing up there when he was killed.'

'And Miss Luna was in love with Mr Pritchard?' Mrs Butters's frown deepened. 'You don't think—'

Eleanor grimaced. 'I did at first. But apart from anything else, Ned's age is all wrong. Luna can't have been his mother. But if she had killed Ned, why on earth would she lead me, one of the agency working with Quilter, to Ned's body? She knows those woods so well, I'm sure she could have hidden the body and it would never have been found.'

'Or dropped it into that there river you crossed to get to the castle, m'lady.' She poured them both a cup of tea and stoked the range.

'Exactly!' Eleanor took a sip, the hot liquid instantly warming her. 'I believe she either came across Ned's body or saw him being killed and knows who the murderer is.'

Mrs Butters paused in getting the muffins. 'Which means she may be in danger if the killer saw her too?'

Eleanor nodded grimly. 'That's why I wanted Hugh and Clifford to go with Quilter, really. And, just to reiterate, no one is in danger here in the vicarage. Even though the weapon that killed Ned, and we think Unwin, was last seen in the church, the reverend has a cast-iron alibi for both deaths.'

Mrs Butters passed her a plate of hot muffins with lashings of butter and jam, having first put down Tomkins and Gladstone's breakfasts. 'Oh, I know that, m'lady. But if that there trumpet came from the Angel's Summons, maybe there's a mite of suspicion on them sisters too, then?'

Eleanor nodded. 'It's possible. One of them, Blythe we think, was sweet on Unwin so we need to interview both of them again to try and find out just how sweet.' She shook her head. 'Love can turn to hate all too swiftly.' She took another bite of muffin and a swig of tea. 'Speaking of suspects, as I've no idea how long Hugh and Clifford will be, perhaps— Ah! Mrs Trotman, just in time.'

'Morning, m'lady,' her cook said. 'Here's me still in me bed things and you up and dressed, eating muffins no less.'

'Well, I'm sure there's more to go around. I was just about to have a quick review of where we're up to with all these recent developments. All input welcome.'

Mrs Trotman pulled up a chair as Mrs Butters poured another tea and slid a muffin her way. 'Be delighted, m'lady. The young 'uns are still asleep and three heads are better than one.'

Mrs Butters brought Mrs Trotman up to speed on developments while they cleared the breakfast plates away. Eleanor meanwhile made sure the two furry friends had full bellies and were curled up snoozing soundly by the stove. Then Mrs Butters produced her and Mrs Trotman's agency notebooks. Eleanor already had hers at the ready, open at a blank page.

'Right. Let us ladies see if we can have a breakthrough before the men get back. Or at least figure out if we're missing something obvious. We'll start with a quick recap now our leading suspect has himself become a victim! Ned could still have killed Unwin. However, given the same weapon seems to have been used in both killings, Quilter agrees we're probably looking for a single killer. And until we find out otherwise, we'll proceed on that assumption. Agreed?'

The other two ladies nodded.

'So,' Mrs Trotters said, 'did any of them suspects for Mr Unwin's murder also have a reason to wants to kill that Ned?'

Eleanor grimaced. 'Unfortunately, not that we know of at the moment. In fact, we have no known links between Ned and any of our other suspects. Except perhaps Luna, as we said.'

'And that Mathilde, though. You mentioned as how she'd had him banned?'

'That's right! And she was definitely more upset about him barging into the tavern that first night than she let on.' She slapped her head. 'And I've just remembered something she said then. "There's one more thing I needs do tonight as won't wait. And it was due longaways back!" or something similar. Maybe she was referring to Unwin? Although, it was more likely Ned thinking about it, so she's definitely on our reinterview list. In fact, we need to reinterview all our other suspects for Unwin's murder too; Jarrett, Dunstan, Digger, Dora and Babcock. To see who had a motive for wanting Ned dead. And who hasn't got an alibi for the time of his death. Without speaking to Luna, Hugh could only guess Ned hadn't been dead for more than an hour or two before we got there. So somewhere between five thirty and seven thirty yesterday.' She sighed. 'Hopefully someone will slip up or point the finger. Now, what about another cup of tea?'

Mrs Butters rose to replenish the pot. 'What about that riddle what was on Mr Pritchard's grave? You said as there might be a link with Mr Unwin's death. So if you thinks the same person did for that Ned as Mr Unwin, then perhaps there's a link from that there riddle to Ned's death too, m'lady?'

Eleanor nodded eagerly. 'Yes! Unwin was placed so deliberately there, I'm sure there's a connection between it and his murder. And, therefore, maybe Ned's.' She flicked back a couple of pages. 'Here it is:

"In an instant, in the twinkling of an eye...

First out of the box, first in if pine.
Created by the hand of man, destroyed by the divine.
Springs into existence in an instant, then burns bright for all time.
Free to own,
Yet costs the sun, the moon and the stars."'

Mrs Trotman frowned. 'My, that is quite the riddle, m'lady.'

'"At the last trumpet: for the trumpet shall sound, and the dead shall rise again incorruptible: and we shall be changed!"'

The three ladies spun around.

'Oh! Good morning, Reverend,' Eleanor said. 'You gave us a start there.'

Ansel smiled. 'I'm sorry if I startled you, but that line. The moment I saw it when I first arrived in the village, I recognised it. It's from 1 Corinthians 15:52. 2. "In an instant, in the twinkling of an eye, at the last trumpet: for the trumpet shall sound, and the dead shall rise again incorruptible: and we shall be changed."' He shrugged. 'But that's about as far as I got with the riddle.'

Mrs Butters set down a new pot of tea. 'Well, I'll make some more muffins and you can earn your Boxing Day breakfast helping us unravel the rest.'

'A splendid exchange, Mrs Butters!' He turned to Eleanor. 'The one thing I did notice was that the first line was engraved in a different script or font. So perhaps it is meant to be the title, or heading and separate from the rest of the riddle?'

She nodded. 'You're right. Oh, my! Of course! The last—'

'Trumpet! The weapon that was used to kill both men,' Ansel said thoughtfully.

Eleanor tapped her page. 'So we seem to have a direct link between the title, or opening line, of the riddle, and both murders?'

'But Mr Pritchard can't have written it knowing this was

going to happen, can he, m'lady?' Mrs Trotman said incredulously.

Ansel shook his head. 'I can't see how myself. Unless he intended to come back from the dead and commit both murders. The whole thing is just too fanciful.'

'I agree.' Eleanor frowned. 'It seems much more likely the other way around. The killer took his cue from the opening lines of the riddle.'

'But why?'

'I've no idea,' she said grimly, 'but together we'll find out!'

The kitchen door swung open. Seldon strode in, followed by Clifford.

She tried to read his expression. 'Luna, Hugh?'

He held his hands up. 'Nothing! It's like she's disappeared off the face of the earth!'

Which now in Quilter's eyes, Ellie, will make her look doubly guilty.

27

Despite being Boxing Day, Eleanor, Seldon and Clifford wasted no time in heading out to reinterview their remaining suspects. They promised the ladies and Kofi they would be back for lunch. And then there would be a proper festive treat to follow courtesy of Ansel! They abandoned the reverend surrounded by Kofi, Polly and Lizzie begging to know what it was, and snuck out into the crisp winter morning. Eleanor was wrapped up in her thickest cable-knit jumper and heavy green woollen coat in an attempt to keep Jack Frost at bay.

Seldon had agreed with Eleanor if they could uncover a motive for Ned's murder, they'd be halfway to solving Unwin's. With the snow overnight having obliterated any more potential clues up at the castle, and with no hope of outside help, it was down to the three of them. They had to make a breakthrough soon.

'And Constable Quilter, sir,' Clifford said as they navigated the main road, which was now more like an ice rink.

Seldon nodded. 'Granted, he's a good man. But he has to live here after this investigation is over. We don't,' he added grimly. 'So let's go rattle some cages.'

Eleanor gasped. 'I think you have my script, Hugh.'

Clifford tutted. 'I very much fear, my lady, it is a case of rampant rhinoceritis!'

Seldon laughed. 'It is still our Christmas. And I must say I'm as keen as the "young 'uns", as Mrs Trotman calls them, to see what the reverend has planned after lunch.'

'Me too,' she said as the Angel's Summons came into view. 'So let's find our first target as quickly as possible.'

Clifford pointed down the road. 'I believe, my lady, the game may be coming to us.'

As they watched, Jarrett reached the tavern and entered.

'Let's go!' Eleanor muttered.

Seldon nodded. 'Now, remember. No one outside of our circle knows we found Ned's body last night. And I'm sure Luna, wherever she is, hasn't told anyone. So let's see if we can get one of our suspects to slip up.'

A chill ran through her.

Let's hope wherever Luna is, she's safe, Ellie.

Inside, Jarrett was just sitting down in a corner seat with Dunstan, Ansel's churchwarden, two pints of porter on the table.

Two suspects for the price of one, Ellie.

They all three strode straight over. Without waiting to be asked, she pulled up a chair and sat down, waving regally.

'No, please, gentlemen, do not get up. I'm already sitting, as you can see. Now, we don't want to waste any more of your Boxing Day time than you want to waste ours.'

Jarrett scowled at her. 'I warned you what would happen if you stuck your nose into matters that didn't concern you!'

She stiffened.

Is he referring to Ned's murder, Ellie?

'Perhaps you'd refresh our memories, Jarrett?'

He smirked. 'I said you'd be back here asking more pointless questions.'

'Very droll,' Seldon said, rolling his eyes and remaining standing. 'Now you've had your little joke, would you mind explaining why you lied to us about attending Midnight Mass the night of Mr Unwin's murder?'

Jarrett's eyes bulged. 'Who told you... I mean, that's not true!'

Seldon waved him down. 'There's no point in denying it. We have it from an impeccable source.'

'You can't have! I was there.'

'From the beginning of the Mass, Jarrett?'

Dunstan slapped his tankard down. 'Look. I can confirm that Jarrett was at Mass. It's true he came in a little late, but once there, he stayed until the end.'

Jarrett looked daggers at him. 'Why you—'

Dunstan raised a placating hand. 'They obviously already knew. This isn't a joke. A man is dead and someone's going down for it. So, it's best to make a clean break of it, if you ask me.'

'Well, no one did!' Jarrett snapped.

'Gentlemen, please!' Eleanor scolded. 'Everyone else is trying to enjoy a quiet Boxing Day drink. Now, Jarrett, no more games.'

Jarrett scowled, but nodded resignedly. 'Alright. I did arrive late for Mass. I had... other business to attend to first.'

'What business? And with who? Ned?'

Even though she'd purposefully dropped the now deceased Ned's name into the conversation, she hadn't expected to get quite such a reaction from one of them. Jarrett turned positively pale.

'How did you... I mean—'

Dunstan leaned across the table. 'You see! They know already. Don't be a fool. Tell them the truth, man!'

She tried to keep her expression neutral. Was Jarrett about to confess to Ned's murder?

He slumped in his chair. 'Yes, I went to see Ned with... with Digger. He wanted me to... back him up.'

Eleanor held her tongue. If they asked anything now, he might clam up again. After a moment, he reluctantly continued.

'Digger's sweet on Dora, you see.'

So that's what Digger was doing coming out of Waketon Court the first night you bumped into him, Ellie. And he was probably the shadowy figure you and Clifford saw the second time.

'What has that got to do with Ned, Jarrett?' Seldon said blandly. He flashed her a look. They needed to run with this.

Jarrett took a sip of his drink. 'Ned is sweet on Dora as well.'

'More like obsessed!' Dunstan muttered.

Jarrett shrugged. 'Either way, she'd told him she wasn't interested and that should have been that. But Ned would never take no for an answer.'

'We've seen that ourselves,' she said, glancing at Seldon and Clifford. From what Jarrett had just told them, Digger now had the motive to kill Ned they'd come looking for.

The only question, Ellie, is did he? Or is Jarrett desperately trying to throw suspicion off himself for Ned's murder?

Jarrett waved his tankard. 'Well, there you go then. Me and Digger went round to Ned's to knock some... I mean, to reason with him to leave the girl alone. He knew she was sweet on Digger, too.'

'So did you "knock some sense" into him, Jarrett?' Seldon said smoothly.

Jarrett shook his head quickly. 'No. He weren't there. So Digger went off to see Dora, and I hotfooted it to Mass.'

She sighed inwardly.

Okay, Ellie. No confession.

She hid her frown.

Clifford cleared his throat quietly. She stiffened again. That usually meant he was up to something. 'You are obviously aware, Dunstan, that the duties of a churchwarden are laid down by the Canons of the Church of England? Including maintaining order and decency in the church and churchyard. Particularly while a service, like the Christmas Midnight Mass, is running?'

Dunstan eyed him suspiciously, while Jarrett sat back, looking pleased the spotlight was firmly off him for the moment. 'Y-e-s? What of it?'

'Dunstan. Did Jarrett finally arrive at Mass before, during, or after Reverend Ansel had delivered the sermon?'

She struggled again to keep her face neutral. Clifford was obviously now probing around Unwin's murder. What had he spotted?

Dunstan took a long sip of his porter. Too long.

'Before, I think. Yes, that's right.'

Ansel told us the person had entered just after his sermon, Ellie. A lapse of memory? Or is Dunstan covering for Jarrett? And if so, why?

'Have you been a churchwarden before, Dunstan?' Clifford said.

'Not as such. I've helped out now and then in other churches.'

Seldon frowned. 'There are no other churches in Yorelow that I'm aware of.'

Dunstan huffed. 'I mean in other places I've lived.'

'I see. And when did you come to Yorelow?'

'About two years ago.'

'From where?'

'Birmingham.'

Seldon's eyebrows rose. 'Yorelow is quite a change from the big city. What prompted the move?'

Dunstan shrugged. 'Age-old story. I had an affair. Wife found out and left. I started drinking when I should have been minding the business. My life, and business, went down the drain. Anyway, I drifted from crap job to crap job for a while until I ended up as a delivery driver. I covered a lot of Warwickshire, Worcestershire and Staffordshire. And one of the places I delivered to was Yorelow. It was the furthest you could get from my old life, so I rented a room from the Frisham sisters to begin with, then moved out. And here I am.' He took a swig of porter. 'Anything else you want to know about my life history?'

Eleanor's mind was racing. 'Was it your van that had items stolen from it when you were delivering to the Angel's Summons?'

Dunstan's eyes narrowed. 'I didn't know anyone else knew about that.'

Seldon's look confirmed he was thinking the same thing. It gave Dunstan a connection to the two dead men. Ned had been the thief, and Unwin the one who had reported him.

Coincidence, Ellie? Or was there more to the story than they'd been told?

'So,' Clifford continued, 'as the canon also covers churchyards, I assume you can shed some light on the goings-on there too?'

Dunstan rolled his eyes. 'Has the reverend been telling you that story again? About seeing lights at night around the gravestones? I reckon it was just a couple of drunks looking for a quiet spot to drown their sorrows. I used to.'

'And lastly, Dunstan, that same canon—'

Dunstan looked in disbelief at Eleanor. She shrugged. 'I know. I have to put up with this all day, every day. You, Dunstan, just need to answer the question truthfully so we can all get on with our Boxing Day. Now, Clifford, you were saying?'

'I was saying that Dunstan's duties as churchwarden also include responsibility for the church's chattels, or non-fixed possessions. Therefore, you must have been aware of the unexpected addition of a certain herald, or angel trumpet?'

Dunstan leaned back in his chair. 'You'd better ask the reverend about that. It were his idea to borrow it from the tavern. I just noted it down as not being part of the' – he glanced at Clifford –'church's chattels.'

'Did anyone at anytime during the midnight service go into the area it was stored in?' Seldon said. 'Excluding yourself and the vicar, of course?'

Dunstan shrugged. 'Not that I know of. But the rear door of the church wasn't locked. I suppose anyone could have come in. But they didn't, did they? Because the reverend played the thing at the end of the serv—' His eyes widened. 'Is that what did for Unwin?'

'Thank you for your time,' Seldon said firmly. 'Just one last question. Where were both of you between five thirty and seven thirty yesterday evening?'

Jarrett looked at Dunstan and then Seldon in puzzlement. 'What has that got to do with Unwin's—'

'Kindly just answer the question, gentlemen,' she said amiably, but with a hint of steel in her eyes.

Jarrett shrugged. 'I finished a few things up in me workshop. Then Dunstan turned up around four, I think it was, and helped me out for an hour or two. Then we cracked open a few drinks upstairs in me place to celebrate the festive season.'

Dunstan nodded. 'Only it might have been more than a few in the end. I crashed there for the night as I have no work today and the reverend doesn't need me until tomorrow.'

Convenient, Ellie. Both of them alibiing each other for Ned's murder? Or maybe it was just two friends celebrating Christmas together?

She sighed inwardly. That was the trouble with always investigating murders. It made you so cynical!

Seldon rose. 'Enjoy the rest of your Boxing Day, gentlemen.'

. . .

'Well done,' Eleanor cheered once they were outside. 'We've established a motive for Digger wanting Ned dead and a connection between Dunstan, Unwin and Ned. And it seems Dunstan was prepared to lie to cover Jarrett's actions.'

Seldon nodded, but grimaced at the same time. 'True. But for a moment I hoped we'd surprised one of them into betraying they already knew Ned was dead. Still, on to our next suspect. Maybe, if we're lucky, they'll do just that!'

28

'Constable!' Eleanor called, waving enthusiastically.

For once, neither Clifford nor Seldon admonished her for her less than ladylike behaviour in public. They were as keen as she was to speak to the local bobby.

Quilter crossed the still icy road and doffed his helmet. 'Thank you again for yesterday, m'lady. I had a splendid time. Although, I must say, them ladies of yours are a high-spirited bunch and no mistake!'

Clifford shuddered. 'Perhaps a veil is best drawn over the last hour or so of the evening, Constable?'

Quilter winked. 'I won't tell if you don't, Mr Clifford. But it were Christmas Day, and it comes but once a year as me old mum used to say, bless 'er. Now, I don't imagine her ladyship called me over so lively like just to pass the time of day?'

'Most astute, Constable,' she said. 'Actually, we have an update for you. And perhaps you have one for us?'

He shook his head. 'Still not a hair or hide of 'er, m'lady. She's gone to ground good and proper. Would take an army to find 'er in them woods, she knows them that well.'

Let's hope so, Ellie.

Seldon quickly filled Quilter in on what they'd learned.

He whistled softly. 'I can see why as you're so keen to talk to Digger, sir.'

'Exactly, Constable. If what we were told is true, he is our number one suspect for Ned's murder at the moment. Obviously after Luna,' he added hurriedly at the bobby's look. 'And we were hoping you might know where we could find him?'

'The Angel's Summons, most likely.'

Eleanor shook her head. 'We've just come from there.'

He scratched his head. 'Ah! Well then, you wants to be trying the graveyard.'

Seldon looked at Quilter with incredulity. 'What would he be doing there on Boxing Day?'

'Well, he'll be working, I reckon. There ain't usually no call for burying people today, true, but Digger likes to get them graves ready nice and early, no matter how hard the ground.'

She shivered, remembering Digger's remark about looking forward to burying Unwin.

Thanking Quilter, and assuring him it was better if he didn't come as well, Eleanor set off with Seldon and Clifford for the church. And sure enough, at one end of the graveyard they came across Digger shovelling dirt. He tipped his cap.

"Ow do, folks. Happy Boxing Day.'

'The same to you, Mr Dilkes,' she said. 'Who are you digging this for?' She indicated the hole, which was only a few feet deep.

He paused and leaned on his shovel. 'It be for Mr Unwin. You heard of anyone else what needs a grave a-diggin'?'

She blanched, then scoured the man's face. Did he know about Ned? Or was it genuinely just a throwaway remark?

'No, but maybe you can think of someone else you might like to dig a hole for?'

Digger half-smiled. 'You mean that Ned?'

The man's matter-of-fact tone made her freeze. Was he playing with them?

'You weren't a great fan of his, were you? I believe he was... pestering your girl?'

He regarded her blankly. 'I ain't got a girl.'

'Oh, come now!' Seldon grunted. 'We know you have been paying visits to Miss Dora Meath at Waketon Court. And Ned was also hitting on the girl. You and Jarrett went around to warn him to stay away. Did things get out of hand, Mr Dilkes?'

Digger regarded Seldon coolly. 'Ain't sure why you're askin'. Thought you were only interested in the dead 'uns.'

Something in his tone made her mind up. Whether he was stringing them along or not, they weren't going to find out any more about Ned like this.

'We are. And it's refreshing to see a man who is so dedicated that he'll work on Boxing Day. Or is it just that you're making an exception for Mr Unwin?'

Digger's tone remained casual, but his eyes narrowed. 'And why should I be treating the likes of him any different?'

'Because, like many people, you were not a fan of Mr Unwin's either, were you? But it went deeper than that, didn't it? You were enemies.'

Digger regarded her impassively. 'And why would that be?'

She smiled sweetly. 'I don't know exactly, Mr Dilkes. But perhaps Dora might?'

Catching on, Seldon nodded. 'In fact, I think we might get Constable Quilter to—'

Digger moved with surprising speed. Brandishing his spade, he stepped up to Seldon. 'You leave her alone. Or else—'

'Or else, what, Mr Dilkes?' Seldon said, standing his ground. 'You'll deal with me the same way you dealt with Unwin?'

And maybe, Ned, Ellie?

She winced. There was definitely more tension in the air

now they were reinterviewing suspects. It was as if their suspects had decided the stakes had risen as well.

Digger hesitated, then stepped back, thrusting the spade into the freshly dug earth. 'Alright. I'll come clean. But only if you leave Dora out of this. Otherwise, I'm not saying a word.'

'Well, you have my word, Mr Dilkes, that we'll only speak to her to corroborate anything you tell us. Nothing more.'

She mentally crossed her fingers.

And possibly ask about her and Babcock's involvement in Unwin's murder, Ellie.

He nodded slowly. 'Then I'll tell thee. I didn't kill Unwin, but I ain't grieving now he's gone, neither. He almost cost me me job. And more.'

'And how exactly did he do that, Mr Dilkes?' Clifford said.

He scowled. 'By accusing me of grave-robbing! Threatened to report me to the reverend and then Quilter!'

She held her breath. If Unwin had told both Ansel and Quilter why hadn't either of them passed the information on?

'And did he?'

To her relief, he shook his head. 'No. He didn't get the chance, did he? Someone up and did for him. But it weren't me, as I already said.'

She frowned. When they'd spoken to Jarrett and Dunstan, she had been convinced Digger had been coming from seeing Dora at Waketon Court the night Unwin died. But what if he'd been coming from the graveyard instead? Maybe that's what Unwin had seen from his study window while recording the message for the agency? Digger robbing Pritchard's grave? She shuddered. When she'd bumped into him, had he fresh blood on his hands?

She tried to keep her features neutral, but Seldon was obviously thinking along the same lines.

'Thank you for your cooperation, Mr Dilkes. We'll speak to

you again soon, I'm sure. Enjoy your...' He waved at the half-dug grave.

'Just one more question before we go,' she said sweetly. 'If you want us to keep Constable Quilter away from Dora. Where were you between five thirty and seven thirty yesterday evening?'

Digger's brow furrowed. 'I... I can't remember. Walkin', I imagine.'

'Where?'

He shrugged. 'Around. Just around.'

As the three of them walked away, she turned to Seldon and Clifford.

'Did you believe him? About any of it?'

Clifford raised an eyebrow. 'I think the jury is out, on my part. Certainly until we speak to Miss Meath. Which is where I assume we are going now?'

Seldon nodded. 'We need to check his story as much as we can. I'm pretty sure he was with her whether he was "walking around" or not. But something's off. It's true Digger seems to have had a reason to kill both Unwin and Ned, but—'

'But it isn't the same reason?'

He grimaced. 'Exactly, Eleanor. That doesn't quite sit right. I'm not convinced we've really uncovered why Ned died up at that castle last night. Yet. Which means...'

Clifford nodded grimly. 'Tensions are rising. One can't rule out the possibility of there being another killing!'

Or another flying knife coming our way, Ellie.

29

As Clifford swung the rusted iron gate open and stood to one side to let her and Seldon pass, a light clicked off, leaving Waketon Court in darkness. Her eyes narrowed. She was in no mood for playing games. She should have been spending Boxing Day wrapped in the arms of her husband back in Henley Hall with nothing to do but relax and have fun. Not investigating a double murder. But after speaking to Digger, it was obvious Dora knew a lot more than she'd told. And that she, Digger and Babcock were forming an unholy trinity in her mind. The three of them were obviously in cahoots about something and each of them had a connection with the two dead men. Dora with both.

As she reached the wide front door, she gave it an especially hearty rap of the knocker.

Silence.

Seldon, whose mood seemed to match hers, rapped even harder.

Nothing.

'Right!'

She set off around the side of the house, peering in every

window. As she peeked through the kitchen one, she saw the tail end of a skirt whip into the scullery.

She tried the door. It was open. Marching in, she called out, 'Good day, Dora! Is Babcock lurking in there with you, too?'

She looked around. All three chairs at the table had been pushed back. In contrast to the rest of the spotless surfaces, the table had traces of tea, sugar and... was that cake? After a moment, Dora shuffled out. She was wearing another homespun dress, this one covered with pretty dark flowers and tiny shiny buttons. Again, Eleanor thought it too nice to be working in. ''Tis just me here, m'lady.'

In the depths of the house, she heard the faint sound of footsteps.

And a ghost, apparently, Ellie.

She smiled sweetly. 'In that case, we might as well talk here.' She sat down at the table.

Dora gasped. 'In the kitchen?'

'Her ladyship's favoured place for most everything,' Clifford murmured, gliding in behind Seldon, who grunted in amused consent.

'In that case, m'lady, I'd better put the kettle on.'

Eleanor leaned forward. 'For someone who only works, what is it, three mornings a week, it's amazing you're always here when we pop around?'

Dora fiddled with the hem of her apron. 'Thing is—'

'Dora!'

The woman jumped at Eleanor's sharp tone.

'Er, yes, m'lady?'

'I didn't come here to make idle chit-chat. I came here because he needs your help!'

Dora frowned. 'Who, m'lady?'

'Digger, of course.' She shrugged. 'It may already be too late.'

Seldon nodded. 'Constable Quilter might be leading him off in handcuffs as we speak.'

Eleanor half rose. 'Maybe it was a waste of time coming here, anyway.'

Dora lunged forward and grabbed her wrist. 'Please don't go!' Staring at her hand in horror, she let go of Eleanor. 'I'm so sorry, m'lady, but...'

Eleanor sat back down. No one had specified what Digger might have been arrested for, but from Dora's reaction, it was obvious she thought it was something very serious indeed.

Maybe Ned's murder, Ellie?

'Listen, Dora. You have one chance to save him. Tell me the truth. What went on between you, Digger and Ned?'

Dora started. 'Ned? I thought you were investigating Mr Unwin's...' Her hand flew to her mouth. 'You don't mean...?'

Eleanor hesitated, then nodded grimly. 'Ned is dead. And Digger—'

'No! No, my Digger would never hurt nobody!'

'Then why did he and Jarrett go around to teach Ned a lesson?' Seldon said coolly. 'He wasn't in, was he? So they what? Returned last night for a second go? And perhaps things got out of hand?'

Dora looked at Eleanor beseechingly. 'Oh, m'lady, you must believe me. I went out with Ned once it were true. But I soon realised he was a wrong 'un and broke it off.'

'Let me guess, Miss Meath,' Seldon said. 'He wasn't having any of it?'

Dora nodded. 'He told me I'd always be his. And he'd... kill,' she whispered, 'any man who made eyes at me.'

'Which Mr Dilkes did?' Clifford said.

Dora nodded again. 'But not like Ned. Digger's a gentleman. He was here the first time you called, m'lady, but he was leaving 'cos he wouldn't stay the night.' She wiped her eyes with her apron. 'Anyway, that's why Digger was trying to see me without anyone knowing. But Ned followed me and found out anyway.'

'So, he confronted Digger,' Seldon said. 'There was an argument, and Digger kill—'

'No!' Dora cried. 'It's not true. Digger was with me the night Mr Unwin got done in. And all yesterday afternoon and evening, if that's when Ned...'

Eleanor changed tack. 'Babcock must really like Digger. He seems quite happy to... how would you put it, Clifford?'

'To facilitate Miss Dora's... arrangement with Mr Dilkes, my lady.'

'It weren't like that!' Dora said defensively. 'He never stayed the night or nothing like that, as I told you. That's why you spotted him in the bushes the following morning. He was returning, having left the night before.'

'Was he with you between five thirty and seven thirty yesterday evening?'

She half nodded, but stopped, her eyes wide.

'Was Babcock also with you the whole time?' Eleanor said.

'Let's ask the gentleman.' Clifford whipped back the door from the kitchen to the hall. Babcock was standing on the other side.

Eleanor beckoned him in. 'Come in. We've been waiting to speak to you. Been there long?'

'Long enough to confirm everything that Dora has told you, m'lady,' he said unabashedly. 'Specifically, that I was with both Miss Dora and Mr Dilkes between the hours you mentioned.'

Beyond convenient again, Ellie.

'Tell me. Didn't you feel a little like a gooseberry?'

'I beg your pardon, m'lady?'

'Granted. Now, why are you so keen to help Dora and Digger?'

'It is what my late master would have wanted.'

She did a double-take. When Babcock spoke about

Pritchard like that, it reminded her so much of Clifford's way of speaking about her late uncle.

'However,' Babcock continued, 'Mr Yearth turned up here and threatened me if I did not stop them meeting here.'

'And what did you do?'

'I sent him away with a flea in his ear, naturally.'

'Is that all?' Seldon said. 'You didn't happen to follow him and cave his head in?'

Babcock's left eye twitched. 'No, sir. Is that what has happened to the gentleman?'

His dispassionate tone made her certain if Babcock hadn't killed Ned, he was definitely capable of doing so.

'I'm sure you know the rumours about Ned being Mr Pritchard's illegitimate son?'

Babcock nodded. 'However, I have no comment to make on the matter, m'lady.'

She kept a close eye on his face again. 'Did your dispute with Mr Unwin concerning the future of Waketon Court have anything to do with Ned?'

He looked genuinely confused. 'No, m'lady.' He hesitated, then seemed to decide. 'Mr Pritchard stipulated in his will, his house, money and possessions should pass to his legal heir. If they had not stepped forward to claim them within five years of him dying, then it was all to go to the next in line.'

'Mr Unwin?'

'Yes, m'lady. The five-year period expires in one month's time. Mr Unwin initially challenged the ruling and tried to get the time shortened. But the ruling was upheld.'

'And,' Seldon said, 'I suppose there's no use in asking you to divulge who the legal heir is? Or whether they are still alive even?'

Babcock's left eye twitched. 'I am sorry, but I am not at liberty to say, sir.'

They all exchanged a glance. It was obvious that was his last word on the subject. As she rose, Eleanor remembered something.

'Babcock. The last time we were here, Dora told us to talk to the Frisham sisters if we wanted to find out more about Unwin. Should we do so if we also want to find out more about... Ned?'

And perhaps his murder, Ellie?

He shrugged. She obviously wasn't going to get any more out of him unless she changed tack.

'Perhaps, if we wanted to find out more about certain items allegedly taken from a delivery van?'

He gave her an almost grateful look. 'Again, I cannot comment, my lady. However, I assume you have already talked to the two ladies about the incident? In which case, did it not strike you as strange that Mr Unwin's public-spirited behaviour seems to have failed to make him... beloved of the Frisham sisters?'

Out in the cold, crisp air, Eleanor shook her head. 'Here we go again. Now Babcock seems to have a motive for both murders. But...'

'Not the same one for both?'

She nodded vigorously. 'Just like Digger!'

Seldon rubbed his chin. 'Perhaps Babcock couldn't find this legal heir. And with time running out...'

'Did away with Unwin? And maybe framed Luna for it? If everyone in Yorelow believed she'd basically killed her parents, they'd happily believe she killed Unwin. And to be fair, I think most do.'

Clifford held up a finger. 'Perhaps you have hit on it, my lady. Perhaps the "Ned problem" was unrelated to Mr Unwin's death. But it escalated suddenly and Babcock had to act. And he realised he already had the perfect fall guy set up. Or in this case, woman.'

Seldon slapped his forehead. 'Of course. If everyone believed Luna had killed her parents and Unwin, then they'd need little persuasion or evidence to believe she'd killed again!' His eyes narrowed. 'Or, by Jove, perhaps she had!'

Eleanor kept quiet. Her head couldn't argue with the logic. But her heart, that was a different matter. But both of them couldn't deny the noose was slipping tighter and tighter around Luna's neck.

30

As Eleanor, Clifford and Seldon entered the Angel's Summons, the mood was tense. Despite learning a lot of new information, they'd failed to get the breakthrough they'd been looking for and the consensus was this was their last chance. The Frisham sisters and their tavern were at the heart of village life. And it seemed the secrets they were harbouring connected both the dead men with not only themselves, but Dunstan as well. And Babcock's cryptic remark about the incident added fuel to the idea that perhaps the sisters might be the missing link between both deaths. It was time to take the gloves off.

Inside, the tavern was deserted except for Mathilde and Blythe behind the bar. They were arguing so furiously they failed to notice The Byron Detective Agency entering in full force. As they approached, Eleanor's sharp hearing caught the words 'That Ned needs to—'

Then they spotted her, Clifford and Seldon and clammed up.

'Please, ladies, don't stop on account of us,' she called. 'Actually, we've come to discuss the same thing.'

Both sisters exchanged a worried look.

'What's that, then?' Blythe said innocently.

'Ned.'

Mathilde snorted. 'If he comes in here again, I'll give him more than a piece of my mind!'

If they do know Ned is dead, Ellie, they are certainly putting on a convincing show of innocence.

Eleanor nodded. 'Really? Like you did the first time? Or was that just for our benefit?'

Mathilde put her hands on her hips. 'That Ned is banned and—'

'And as I said,' Eleanor interrupted brightly, 'that's exactly what I've come to discuss. Now, I seem to remember at the time, Ned suggested it was Mr Unwin who should have been banned, not him. Maybe he was right? After all, Ned was only carrying out his part of the deal. It wasn't his fault Unwin stuck his nose in and spoiled it for everyone. But obviously you had to keep up appearances and fake outrage. Including banning Ned. But' – she tapped her chin – 'if the attempted robbery was genuine, why did you tell Constable Quilter that you didn't want to press charges?'

Blythe shuffled uncomfortably. 'You can't go around upsetting people in a small place like Yorelow. It's not like the fancy sort of town you come from where no one knows nobody!'

Eleanor hid a smile. In Little Buckford, the 'fancy sort of town' she came from, everyone knew everyone else's business. And hers, often before she knew it herself!

'Quite. But you did upset someone, didn't you? Ned. He was unhappy about being banned and about having to take the rap from Quilter for your little scheme. Did he threaten to tell the brewery?'

Blythe snorted. 'Don't be daft! How could he without admitting—'

'Be quiet, you fool!' Mathilde rounded on her sister. 'That mouth of yours will get us into trouble if—'

Eleanor raised her voice. 'Ladies! It's too late to worry about whatever trouble you might get into for what you did. That is nothing compared to the trouble you're definitely going to get into for the murder of Inigo Unwin. *And Ned!*'

For a moment, there was no reaction. Then the two sisters stared at each other in disbelief. Mathilde was the first to recover.

'Ned? Dead?'

The shock in her voice sounded genuine. But was it? Seldon stepped forward.

'I strongly suggest you come clean about any dealings you had with either of the deceased.'

'Not only because otherwise you are a possible accessory, ladies,' Clifford added. 'But also because the killer has already eliminated two people associated with yourselves. Who knows who may be next?'

They all three looked pointedly at the sisters.

Blythe clamped her hands to her temples. 'I can't stand this any longer. Everything's got so out of hand.'

Mathilde scowled at her. 'If you dare say a word, I swear I'll—'

'Do nothing, Miss Frisham,' Seldon said firmly, stepping between them. 'Except stand there quietly and let your sister speak.'

She stood seething but silent while Blythe did just that.

'It was all Mathilde's idea. We're tied to the brewery, you see? We have to order everything through them, not just drinks. And by the time we've paid their inflated prices, there's nothing left for us. Basically, we're just selling their stuff for them for free!' She shot her sister a scared look but continued. 'So, Mathilde got talking to Dunstan who works for them as one of their drivers. We got to know him when he lodged here. Together, they cooked up the scheme to steal our own delivery before it got here. Dunstan told us the stuff was the brewery's responsibility until we took it off him and their insurance would pay or they'd have to take the loss.'

'So let me guess,' Eleanor said. 'You got the bad boy of Yorelow, Ned, to do the dirty work?'

Mathilde shrugged. 'He was happy to get a cut. And knew how to do it, so it looked genuine. Only that nosy Unwin came out of nowhere.'

Blythe nodded. 'He had Dunstan bundle Ned into the van and drive to Quilter's place. Ned were apoplectic! Insisted as how Dunstan could have made sure he got away. Said Unwin hadn't even recognised him. Dunstan had a right go back, too.'

So Dunstan and Ned had bad blood between them too, Ellie?

Mathilde shrugged. 'And that's all we know. But nothing Ned, or Unwin, did warrants them being... *murdered*.'

Eleanor glanced at Blythe, who was surreptitiously wiping a tear from her eye.

At the reminder of Unwin's demise, Ellie?

The woman looked at her defiantly. 'So what? Maybe I *was* sweet on Inigo. He was a better man than any of them born in Yorelow!'

Without a word, Mathilde stepped past Seldon and snaked her arm around her sister's waist. 'Now, if there's nothing more you wants, we've got an establishment to run. Together!'

Having ordered a round of drinks, they sat in a quiet corner by the crackling fire and supped in silence for a moment. The thick burgundy velvet of the bench seat was a welcome rest for Eleanor's tired legs. How she wished she was back at Henley Hall curled up in the corner of her own settee. She took a sip of the unusual local ale, then grimaced. Seldon put his tankard down, shaking his head. Clifford followed suit, nodding.

'I agree, sir. The somewhat muddied woody notes are not really complemented by the persistent bitterness of the hop—'

Seldon gave him a look. 'I wasn't shaking my head at' – he regarded his drink – 'whatever this is.' He paused. 'But actually, it's a good example of what's wrong with this case!'

Eleanor leaned forward eagerly. 'We're all ears, Hugh. Explain?'

He glanced around. Satisfied they couldn't be overheard, he continued. 'It seems like we've made progress on both murders. We've found out some of the ingredients that might have gone into the lead-up, and the death itself, of both victims.'

'A recipe for murder, as it were, sir?'

Seldon nodded. 'Yes. But a poor one at the moment. Like this ale, the ingredients we do have just don't sit well with each other in my gut. Let's start with Unwin's murder and with Ned. He was our leading suspect for it. But now he himself is a victim.'

'And Babcock, our next top suspect, Hugh, I'm not convinced about for some reason.'

It was Clifford's turn to nod. 'I agree, my lady. I am not saying he couldn't have killed Mr Unwin, but again, it doesn't sit right. Mr Babcock, if I might be so bold as to say, is one of the old school of butlers and valets.'

'Much like yourself, Clifford,' Eleanor said. 'Unwaveringly loyal to your master, even' – she swallowed a small lump in her throat – 'even after death.'

Seldon see-sawed his head. 'You may be old school, Clifford, but you have some very new-age skills I haven't encountered in any traditional butler before!'

Clifford half bowed. 'Thank you, sir. And thank you, my lady. My point is, however, that Mr Babcock, in my estimation, might show a little... unprofessional disdain to anyone who, in his eyes, disrespected his late master and his wishes. And would, I am sure, try his level best to thwart that gentleman. But to murder him? One must not forget that Mr Unwin was a relative of Mr Pritchard, and Babcock's loyalty to the Pritchard family would extend to some extent to Mr Unwin.'

'I think I agree with you,' Seldon said. 'I find it hard to imagine Babcock going to those lengths. Unless there's another ingredient in the mix we don't know about yet. But until we do, let's move on to this Luna woman. All we've really got to go on for her is a second-hand account of two people having sharp words and almost coming to blows, followed by a few threats. If every argument like that led to murder, the streets would be littered with bodies!'

Even though the subject was serious, his words made Eleanor laugh. 'I do agree. Now Dora...' She sighed. 'To be honest, I know I put the idea forward, but having thought about it again, I can't see her killing Unwin just in case her job was under threat, either. I mean, she didn't even live in. So had Unwin sold Waketon Court, she would have been jobless, perhaps, but not homeless.'

Seldon let out a deep breath. 'True. And we don't really have a solid motive for our remaining suspects Jarrett and Dunstan yet.'

'Although, Hugh, we do for the Frisham sisters.' She grimaced. 'Well, we know Blythe was romantically attached to Unwin, so there could have been some kind of lovers' quarrel. And from her attitude, I am wondering if Mathilde was jealous of her sister's...' She tailed off at Seldon's pained expression. 'I know, Hugh. No real solid facts to go on there either.'

Seldon took a sip of his drink. 'The really puzzling thing is that we have more motives for Ned's death, even though we haven't worked out how it's connected to Unwin's yet. Which is a first. Often, there's very little to go on with a second murder like this.' He counted out on his fingers. 'Dora, Digger, Jarrett and Babcock have a motive because of Ned's involvement with Dora and his subsequent threats. And Dunstan and the

Frisham sisters because of Ned's involvement with their bungled "robbery" and his possible later threats also.'

'Oddly,' she jumped in, 'the only suspect who doesn't have a relatively clear-cut motive for killing Ned is the very one Quilter is out at this very moment trying to arrest!'

Seldon pushed his tankard away with disgust. 'This whole episode so far has been one long...' He looked up sharply. 'Riddle!'

31

'That's it!' Eleanor slapped her hardly touched drink down. 'The riddle on Pritchard's gravestone. The ladies, the reverend and I had a look at it this morning while you were out with Quilter.'

Seldon scratched the back of his head. 'I still can't figure out how it can have anything to do with recent developments. It was set in stone five years ago. On the other hand, everything in this case is a riddle. Why Unwin asked us down to start with and what he wanted us to investigate to begin with! So, possibly, even if it isn't related, it might throw up an oblique clue or two.' He threw his hands up. 'After all, beggars can't be choosers. And no offence to the ladies or the reverend, but I'm not sure they are quite a match for Clifford's—'

'Encyclopaedic knowledge and infuriating logicality?'

Seldon laughed. 'I wouldn't put it like that, Eleanor, but in essence, yes.'

'If you would rather I left you to it, sir?' Clifford half rose, but his eyes twinkled.

'Sit down!' Eleanor said. 'We need your giant cranium for this, you know that.'

He did as requested. 'Actually, my lady, that may not be the case. You are assuming that Mr Pritchard was a gentleman of ordered thought who constructed his riddle logically.'

Seldon grunted. 'He's right. Pritchard might have had the disordered brain of a complete lunatic!'

Clifford shot her a glance. 'In which case, sir, we will be fine.'

She folded her arms. 'Why, you cheeky—'

He held up his pocket watch. 'We are due back at the vicarage in twenty-three minutes. If we are to make any significant progress, may I suggest we start forthwith?'

She hid a smile and opened her notebook where she'd jotted down the riddle on the gravestone and her attempt to unravel it with the ladies' and reverend's help that morning.

She read out the first line: '"In an instant. In the twinkling of an eye..." The reverend confirmed that is a straight quote from the Bible, Corinthians: The next line is "and the trumpet shall sound".' She tapped the page. 'Obviously, we believe Unwin and Ned were both killed with the same type of trumpet angels are depicted blowing! The only thing I wondered was if the first line is actually not part of the poem, but a heading? On the gravestone itself it was inscribed in a different font. The reverend noticed it as well.'

Clifford looked thoughtful. 'I also recall that, my lady. However, if I may offer a contrary opinion, I felt it was done to draw extra attention to it. So, it may in fact be a refrain, a line that comes back at the end, perhaps, but there was simply no room to repeat it.'

'Actually,' Seldon said, 'Jarrett did tell us Pritchard had to alter the riddle a couple of times to get it to fit on the gravestone.'

'Which is why I believe there is no heading, or title, sir. And I think, reading it again now, that had space been no problem,

Mr Pritchard might very well have entitled the riddle "What am I?"'

She and Seldon skimmed it again with 'What am I?' added at the top.

Seldon nodded slowly. 'You're right. It does seem to fit. But' – he waved at the words in her notebook – 'we need to remember we are only interested in it in so far as it helps us solve one, or both murders.'

'Perhaps, therefore,' Clifford said, 'it might be profitable to consider why Mr Pritchard would have left this riddle on his gravestone in the first place, and how it can possibly have led to two deaths five years later?'

'Mmm.' Seldon rubbed his chin. 'Perhaps he had something of value that he'd hidden before he died and he knew others wanted?'

Eleanor nodded eagerly. 'Brilliant, Hugh! Everyone in the village seems to think Pritchard was—'

'Eccentric, my lady?'

She shrugged. 'I was going to say something else, but yes, that would be more polite. So, it fits in with his character and love of riddling, if that's even a word.'

'It is, my lady,' Clifford said. 'Interestingly, it is also the process, invented by Madame Clicquot around 1818, of rotating a bottle of champagne a quarter of a turn while upside down to facilitate the removal of sediment. The bottle, not the lady, of course.'

Seldon rolled his eyes. 'When I suggested that the ladies and the reverend were no match for Clifford's "encyclopaedic knowledge" as you put it, Eleanor, this is not quite what I meant.'

'Apologies for sidetracking the conversation, sir,' Clifford said. 'But by the very nature of riddles, approaching them from oblique angles can often produce the best results.'

Seldon held his hands up. 'Granted. But back to what Pritchard might have hidden. And don't say champagne!'

Eleanor bit back her laugh. 'The next riddle, within this riddle, is if Pritchard did hide something, how did Unwin know about it? Did he know before Pritchard died? Or did he only find out when he saw his uncle's gravestone? In fact, was he even at Pritchard's funeral?'

'All good questions,' Seldon said. 'Unfortunately, all without answers.'

Clifford cleared his throat. 'Actually, sir, not wishing to—'

'Clifford, you have my express permission to offer any contrary opinions for the rest of this conversation. In fact, the rest of the investigation. Okay?'

He nodded, 'Thank you, sir. We do know that Mr Unwin was not at Mr Pritchard's funeral because Constable Quilter informed us that when Mr Unwin arrived here, no one knew him.'

'Ah!' Eleanor said. 'I forgot to add on to "encyclopaedic knowledge and infuriating logicality", the memory of an elephant.'

Seldon slapped the table. 'So, maybe we're getting somewhere. Pritchard hides something of value and Unwin either turns up looking for it or works it out after arriving. But he's not the only one looking for it. Someone else knows Pritchard's dying secret. Unwin's killer!'

'Exactly, Hugh. It all fits.'

'Then let's try the second line with that in mind. 'What am I? "First out of the box, first in if pine,"' she read out. 'I've no idea what the first part refers to. What box?'

'I am not sure, my lady,' Clifford said. 'But I would suggest the second half of the line refers to a coffin.'

Seldon grimaced. 'Mmm. "Pine box". Seems fair enough. So what would you put in a coffin first?'

'A body,' she said grimly.

Clifford frowned. 'Possibly, my lady. But if the answer to "What am I?" is a body, then how does that fit the next line? "Created by the hand of man?"'

'A murderer "creates" bodies?'

'And then the "divine" destroys them at the last trumpet by changing them?'

All three looked at each other and shook their heads.

'Too much of a stretch,' Seldon said. 'And let's not lose sight of the fact that this was written by Pritchard five years ago. He can hardly be our killer! Let's tackle the second to last line. "Springs into existence in an instant, then burns bright for all time."'

'Love,' Eleanor murmured without hesitation.

Seldon squeezed her hand under the table.

Clifford nodded. 'A very creative suggestion, my lady.' He scanned the poem. 'It could fit with certain lines, but ones like this "Created by the hand of man, destroyed by the divine ", I am not so sure about.'

She bit her lip. 'Me, neither. So, where have we got to?'

Seldon pursed his lips. 'My feeling is that the killer took his inspiration, for want of a better word, from it. Hence the link in the first lines and in both murders, to angels' trumpets. Why the killer did that, however, is another question. Either just to confuse, or...'

'For symbolic purposes, sir?'

Eleanor nodded. 'I thought there was something of the theatrical about the way Unwin had been draped in full view over his uncle's grave.'

Seldon frowned. 'Which seems more... personal... more *macabre*. And certainly doesn't fit in with Unwin, or Ned, being murdered because of some thievery from the back of a van.'

'Or because of some rivalry over the local beauty, even.' Eleanor shook her head. 'This last line, "costs the sun, the moon and the stars", I assume means costs you everything you have, or hold dear? Whatever it is, it may have cost Unwin, and Ned, their lives!' She rubbed her face with her hands. 'If only... Clifford? What is it?'

Out of the corner of her eye she had seen his usually inscrutable expression waver.

Seldon exchanged a look with her. 'Come on, man. What have you worked out?'

Clifford hesitated. 'I hope I am wrong, but I believe I know what the second line is referring to.'

Seldon frowned. 'Don't be ridiculous, man. Any breakthrough at the moment is welcome. What has that unusually large cranium of yours figured out?'

Eleanor leaned forward eagerly.

'I believe, sir, that "First out of the box" may refer to Pandora's box.'

Eleanor gasped, remembering a line from a childhood book of Greek fables she'd read many years ago; *as Pandora opened the lid of the box, all the evils of the world escaped to plague mankind for a thousand years to come.*

A chill crept up her spine.

For once, she desperately hoped her infallible butler was wrong.

32

'Where on earth did they come from?'

Ansel held up his hands. 'I have no idea. They were here when I arrived. I can't imagine my rather elderly and...'

'Curmudgeonly, Reverend?' Mrs Trotman said innocently.

He fought a smile. 'I might have chosen a more... Christian word. Anyway, I cannot picture my predecessor actually using them.'

'But there is a whole cupboard of them, your reverend,' Polly said in awe.

'Aye, and all sizes,' Lizzie added, staring in awe at the assembled ice skates in the front hall of the vicarage.

Ansel clapped his hands. 'Well, let's say Providence arranged for them to be here. And I believe Mr Clifford knows exactly where we can use them.'

Seldon grimaced. 'I'm as keen as anyone here to have a break from the murder and mayhem that's dogged our Christmas in Yorelow so far. And I'd love to have a few hours with nothing to do but...' He glanced at Eleanor and blushed. 'But it's just that we can't all be seen together, remember?'

She nodded. 'When we first arrived here, I'd have agreed, Hugh. In fact, I think I suggested it. But back then, I thought we might scare off the killer.' She shook her head grimly. 'But now...'

'I second that. I do not think our killer is the retiring kind,' Clifford said drily.

'And besides, Hugh,' she added brightly. 'We can still keep up the pretence, if you prefer. We can go the back way. I'm sure Clifford somehow knows all the devious routes to get to the lake.'

'Actually, my lady, I have the information from Constable Quilter.'

'There you go, then. And as an extra precaution, ladies, the story is we met up only this morning. You invited us along because you felt safer after all the goings-on to have a couple more men around. No offence, Reverend.'

Ansel laughed. 'None taken. Shall we?'

Clifford led the party out of the back of the vicarage and quickly across the lawn to the nearest trees. Eleanor's heart skipped. This was where she'd first seen Luna the evening she'd led her to Ned's body. But Clifford then turned the opposite way into the woods, following what seemed no more than an animal track.

It was still bitterly cold, the temperature hovering a few degrees below freezing. The snow had crystallised on everything, like a permanent, glittering covering. Everyone was dressed in their thickest coats, hats and scarves, with their stoutest boots. And the mystery of why Gladstone and Tomkins had not been adorned in Christmas jumpers as normal had been solved. They hadn't been ready before the change of plans had forced them all up to Yorelow. Mrs Butters had finished them this morning. And now the daft duo were decked out in matching festive red and green winter coats.

After a few minutes, they emerged onto what looked like an old forestry track. This made the going easier, arms swinging vigorously to warm up, the women chatted with the men, while the young girls giggled together. And everyone smiled at the antics of Tomkins, who was skittering on ahead and then returning to skip back and forth over the ambling bulldog, using his back as a springboard.

Fifteen minutes later as the woods thinned, Eleanor stepped out of the tree line, her eyes widening.

'It's the lake we ended up at when we took the wrong turning the night we arrived!'

After almost running Luna down, Ellie.

Despite the gathering clouds, the weak sun shone onto the frozen surface like a celestial spotlight.

'Indeed it is, my lady,' Clifford said. 'Perfect for' – he opened the bag he was carrying, revealing several sets of ice skates – 'the inaugural joint Henley Hall/Byron Detective Agency Boxing Day Skating Challenge!' He turned to Ansel. 'Apologies, Reverend. The joint Henley Hall/Byron Detective Agency and St Cuthbert's Skating Challenge. Once, that is, we have tested the thickness of the ice.'

Seldon and Ansel joined Clifford, Ansel carrying what looked like part of an old church weathervane. Marching to the edge of the lake, they hacked a hole in the ice. Clifford produced a tape measure from who knew where and measured the ice's thickness. They repeated this, venturing further on to the frozen water each time while Eleanor, Kofi and the ladies put on the skates Ansel had inherited along with the vicarage.

As she stood up rather unsteadily on hers, the three men returned to land, Seldon sticking the impromptu ice-breaking tool in the earth.

'I declare this lake safe to skate on!' he announced to a rousing cheer from the ladies.

As the men changed into their skates, Eleanor led the

charge on to the ice. She'd spent most of her childhood in the tropics, then boarding school, neither a haven for skating. However, her natural sense of balance meant she had no difficulty in staying upright.

Mrs Butters and Mrs Trotman had definitely not spent their childhood in the tropics or at boarding school, judging by the way they sedately but confidently skated on to the lake. But it was Lizzie who drew all eyes as she set off at a fast pace on a short sprint, ending in a graceful pirouette.

'Wherever did you learn to skate like that, Lizzie?' Eleanor gasped.

'Scotland, m'lady. We had a fair bit o' snow and ice at Castle Ranburgh, nae doubt about it. The loch never froze, but the wee lochans did.'

'Of course! Maybe you'd better show poor Polly how to do it, Lizzie.'

'Aye, m'lady. She'll catch on quicker than a midge in summer!'

Eleanor doubted it as the girl glided back to the edge of the lake to help her friend, who was struggling to stand. Polly had found her feet in many ways over the last year, growing visibly in confidence. But in other ways she was still the gangly, uncoordinated thirteen-year-old Eleanor had got to know when she'd first inherited Henley Hall and its staff. And she loved both sides of the young girl's personality equally. Her heart swelled with almost motherly love for her other maid, Lizzie, too. Even though she hadn't been with her as long as the other staff, her outgoing manner and can-do attitude had immediately endeared her to everyone.

And her kindness, Eleanor thought, as rather than show off her obvious prowess on the ice, she took Polly's hands and patiently showed her how to stand without falling over. And then how to slide slowly forward like a proper skater.

She was so engrossed in watching the two girls that she

gasped as her hand was firmly taken and she was whisked away. As they gently glided to the far side of the lake, Seldon snaked his arm around her waist.

'Merry Christmas, darling,' he whispered in her ear. Spinning her to a stop, he kissed her.

She sighed. 'It is rather magical, isn't it?'

He burst out laughing.

She gaped. 'Hugh Seldon! Here I am being all romantic and—'

Before she could finish, she caught sight of it, too. The terrible two had obviously ventured down to the ice and Gladstone was sliding across it on his well-padded tummy with Tomkins perched on his back. As the duo slid to a graceful stop, Lizzie and Polly skated up behind and pushed them off again, much to the amusement of Mrs Butters and Mrs Trotman, too.

She glanced around the lake to see Clifford, Kofi and Ansel, hands behind their backs, skating along, deep in conversation. She wondered where Kofi had learned to skate so well.

'Hugh. This really is the perfect way to spend Boxing Day! No talk of mur—'

His lips, pressed to hers, made sure of it.

Inevitably, after half an hour of elegant and effortless skating, someone suggested a competition. A relay race across the lake and back in pairs. And to make it fair, the fastest had to team up with the slowest. Lizzie stayed with Polly, Eleanor teamed with Mrs Butters and her dodgy hip, while she insisted Seldon team up with Mrs Trotman. Cunningly, on the understanding her husband could skate reasonably fast, but her cook would be far too distracted to concentrate. That left Clifford with Kofi, Ansel having retired early to attend to his Boxing Day rounds visiting the sick and elderly.

The racing started orderly enough, with Lizzie setting a blistering time, and Polly not so. Eleanor put all she had into her run, but Mrs Butters' hip decided it had put up with this nonsense for long enough and refused to cooperate. Next, Clifford set a measured pace, equalled by Kofi. With Lizzie and Polly's times being tied with Eleanor's and Mrs Butters, it was down to Seldon and Mrs Trotman. Eleanor watched without surprise as her husband put in a quick run, and then in amazement as her cook did too, to win. She slapped her forehead. She'd completely forgotten how competitive her cook was whenever they all played cards together in the kitchen.

Clifford was just handing them their prize – the impromptu ice-thickness measurer – when a prickle ran down her spine. She spun around, scouring the perimeter of the lake. Someone was—

A commotion at the edge of the woods attracted her eye. A moment later, her breath caught as Luna walked out into the clearing.

She was about to call out. But the words died on her lips as Quilter stepped out behind Luna and clicked a pair of handcuffs on her wrists!

Back at the vicarage, Eleanor, Seldon and Clifford left the ladies and hurried over to the police house.

''Ow, do, folks!' Quilter called as they entered. 'Take a seat.'

They all three sat at the small table.

'Constable?' Eleanor lowered her voice. 'I take it...' She nodded towards the single tiny cell hidden behind the curtain in the far corner of the room.

Quilter nodded back.

Seldon frowned. 'How did you...'

'Know she would show up, sir? I didn't. 'Twere a guess. The minute as Mr Clifford asked me for directions, I thought to meself, that's where you almost ran Loony, er, Miss Luna down.'

'Very astute, Constable,' Clifford said.

'Thank you, Mr Clifford. And I reckon she'd been watching you three. You knew it when you were thinking of... entering her shack. Which is the real reason why you were none too keen to do so, perhaps?'

Seldon smiled wryly. 'I have to give it to you, Constable. I think you may already be more of a detective than you give yourself credit for.'

Quilter's chest swelled. 'Coming from you, sir, that ain't no empty compliment. Anyways, I set meself up in the woods a while before you arrived and watched. Then Miss Luna turned up, and I nabbed her.'

Eleanor winced. 'Did she put up a fight?'

Quilter shook his head. 'Came as quiet as a lamb. Almost resigned to it, I'd say. I've rung me boss, and he's well pleased. Now, that fancy detective what is coming down first thing tomorrow can just take custody of the prisoner and all's dandy.'

A puzzled look crossed Eleanor's face. Quilter should have been ecstatic, but somehow, despite his words, his tone wasn't.

'Congratulations are in order, Constable. After all, now you'll be able to retire the way you dreamed of. As the man who captured Yorelow's one and only double murderer.'

Quilter rubbed his chin. 'I suppose I will, m'lady.'

Seldon glanced at her, a puzzled look in his eyes too. 'You did your job, Constable. It was your case in the end. And you made the arrest. The only course of action that made sense given the evidence available at the time.'

Quilter nodded, looking a little happier. 'And I'll warrant, as I says before, that there weapon what was used for both murders will have her fingerprints on it, proving beyond doubt she—'

'Actually, that's where you're wrong, Constable.'

Eleanor turned in surprise at the sound of a familiar voice. Even Clifford raised an eyebrow.

'And why would that be, Mr Babcock?' Quilter grunted.

Standing in the doorway, the valet shrugged. 'Because the fingerprints on that... item aren't hers. I'll vouch for it.'

The four of them exchanged baffled glances.

'And how exactly, would you be knowing that, Mr Babcock?' Quilter said.

'Because, Constable, they are mine!'

33

'Well, mercy be, m'lady. I never saw that one coming!'

'I know, Mrs Trotman, none of us did!'

Eleanor, Seldon and Clifford were back at the vicarage, Mrs Butters serving tea, with Polly and Lizzie helping. It was probably time for pre-dinner drinks rather than tea, but all normality had gone out of the window at two such unexpected twists in one day.

'It is all very... unsettling in its way,' Ansel said, accepting a cup of tea from Lizzie. 'No sooner is Miss Luna under lock and key, than in walks Mr Babcock out of the blue and, well, all but confesses to both murders!'

Seldon scratched the back of his head. 'I know, Reverend. I've never come across anything quite like it in all my years policing. I mean, I thought at first that Babcock was lying. To protect Miss Luna.'

Polly put her hand up, then quickly lowered it. 'Begging your pardon, sir. But Mr Babcock were, weren't he? The policeman arrested Miss Luna and then Mr Babcock said it were him, so the policeman would let her go?'

Eleanor nodded. 'Yes, Polly. Luna was under arrest and I

assume, now, isn't. But if Babcock was just trying to protect her, then saying it was his fingerprints on the murder weapon, not hers, wouldn't make sense.'

'Ah!' Understanding dawned in the young girl's eyes. ''Cos the minute it was checked, and them fingerprints was found to be the lady's not his, the policeman would just arrest the lady again?'

'Exactly, Polly,' Seldon said. 'So I assume they *must* be Babcock's fingerprints.' He held up a finger. 'And Babcock knew what the murder weapon was. That news wasn't public knowledge. If you add that to the fact that he openly wanted Unwin out of the way and had no alibi as he wasn't at Midnight Mass, then, well.' He held his hands out and shrugged.

Eleanor bit her lip. 'You were equally sure it was Luna before, Hugh.'

He see-sawed his head. 'To be fair, once Ned was out of the picture, Babcock was always my favoured suspect. But the evidence against Luna was too compelling to ignore as well. If I'm honest, however, it never felt quite as... solid.'

She nodded. 'I get the feeling Quilter felt the same. He should have been so pleased with himself when he arrested her, but somehow, wasn't.'

'I also thought the same, my lady,' Clifford said. 'It does seem, however, as if the correct culprit has now been apprehended.'

'Hardly apprehended. He gave himself up.'

'Not quite such a feather in Quilter's cap. But that's why I like the man,' Seldon said with sudden animation. 'He'd rather forgo a lot of the glory for peace of mind, knowing the right man's going down for the crime. I respect that!'

'"The mind is never right but when it is at peace within itself," as Seneca the Younger said, I believe, sir.' Clifford threw her a look. 'However, my lady, I feel that you are still not happy with the outcome.'

Seldon looked at her quizzically.

She winced. 'Can I never hide what I'm thinking from you, Clifford?'

'Perhaps not, my lady. But your thoughts are not an open book to all.' He glanced pointedly at Seldon. 'Yet, that is, sir. And my sincere condolences to you when they are!'

Seldon laughed at her look of mock outrage. She shook her head.

'I'll deal with you later, Clifford.' Her tone became more serious. 'But you are dead right, as usual.' She winced again at her bad choice of words. 'It's not that I necessarily doubt Babcock is guilty. It's that he confessed. And gave himself up. He obviously did it for Luna and... well, it just reminded me of the times both of you have tried to protect me.' Unexpectedly, she felt her eyes watering. She surreptitiously wiped them. 'Anyway, that was different, I know. I wasn't guilty of any crime. And neither were either of you. Whereas Babcock—'

'Isn't either, Lady Swift.'

All three of them turned in surprise towards the sitting room doorway.

'Luna!' Eleanor murmured.

She was still wearing the same long black gown and hood Eleanor had seen her in each time. But as she swept the hood off, Eleanor had to stop herself gasping again. Even though she'd seen her at the lake without her hood on, it was still a shock. She looked so much... younger. Eleanor had pictured her in her fifties, the same age as Pritchard when he'd died. But she appeared more like early forties.

Maybe even late thirties, Ellie.

And she was almost breathtakingly beautiful. Her long, jet-black hair swirled around her shoulders in loose waves. But it was her piercing eyes Eleanor was enchanted by. They were such a vivid sapphire.

Ansel, who was hovering behind, smiled apologetically. 'I'm

sorry for not announcing you had a visitor. Perhaps I should leave you to talk?'

Mrs Butters nodded imperceptibly at Polly and Lizzie. 'We'll rustle up some more tea for our new visitor, m'lady.' She bustled out with the two maids. Ansel gently closed the door behind him.

For a moment, there was an awkward silence. Eleanor waved at a chair. 'Do sit down, Miss, er, Lyndseer, isn't it?'

She smiled. '"Luna" will do fine.'

'And "Eleanor" will do fine.'

Clifford took her cloak as she sat down. Underneath she had on a simple cotton navy dress.

For a moment, there was silence again. Eleanor swore she saw a faint smile play around their visitor's lips. Luna turned to Seldon. 'You can call me "Loony Luna" if it's easier. All the villagers do.'

He coloured. 'Good gracious, no.'

Mrs Butters entered with another cup and saucer and a fresh pot, accompanied by Polly with a tray of yet more Christmas Day leftover sandwiches. As she began to pour, Luna waved her down.

'Really. Thank you, but I can do it myself.'

Mrs Butters carried on pouring, nodding to Polly to continue loading a plate with a selection of sandwiches. 'I'm sure you can, miss, but you're the reverend's guest. And as I'm standing in as a temporary housekeeper, like...'

Luna smiled. 'I was Constable Quilter's "guest" not long ago!'

Mrs Butters nodded sagely. 'True, miss. And I thought then at the lake, like I do now, the way you behaved showed you're a proper lady, whatever title others may give you. Now, our own mistress may have a title, but if it were taken away tomorrow, 'twould make no odds. She'd still be a lady, like yourself.'

As Mrs Butters closed the door behind her and Polly, Luna

shrugged nonchalantly. 'Well, that told me,' she said. But her nonchalance didn't reach her eyes.

Clifford cleared his throat. 'Please excuse Mrs Butters, Miss Luna. Lady Swift's staff have experienced an... unsettled period.'

Eleanor rolled her eyes. 'That's one way of putting it!'

'Actually.' Luna picked up a sandwich. 'Do you mind? I'm famished.'

'Thank goodness!' Eleanor took another. 'So am I. We can talk while we eat. After all, it is still Boxing Day and, close your ears, Clifford, rules can go hang!'

She grimaced again at her choice of words. Seldon quickly jumped in.

'Miss Luna, can I go back to your statement when you came in? You said that Mr Babcock wasn't guilty. Why?'

Luna swallowed her bite of sandwich and took a sip of tea. 'Because I don't want him to be.'

Eleanor blinked. It wasn't what she'd expected to hear. All she could think of doing was to repeat Seldon's question. 'Why?'

Luna took another bite of her sandwich and chewed slowly, sipping her tea again before replying. 'He was the *only* person... who has always believed in me.'

Seldon leaned forward. 'The evidence against Mr Babcock is damning. I agree it looked bad against you as well. But if it is found, as I assume it will be, that his fingerprints, and his alone, are on the murder weapon,' he shrugged, 'then I'm afraid what you, or I, or the wind, wishes will make little impact on a jury.'

Eleanor started. Luna was staring at her as she'd done the first time they'd met. And then again when she'd led her to Ned's body.

'Luna. If there is anything that you can tell us that might help Babcock, then tell now. And only the truth. We are too good at uncovering lies. Tell us everything and we'll find something useful. If it's there,' she murmured to herself. She raised her voice again. 'You know you can trust us. We didn't search your cabin that day. And we didn't lure you to the lake today for Constable Quilter to arrest you, I promise.'

Luna nodded. 'I know that or I wouldn't be here. And I didn't throw that knife! I don't know who did. It was foolish of me to follow you to the lake. But...' A strange look came into her eyes. 'It was your maid. The youngest. Polly, you call her. She was so full of joy. And wonder. I... I always dreamed of having children.'

Eleanor's heart clenched. If Luna and Pritchard had got together when she had been younger, she could have had a child around Polly's age by now.

Suddenly, Luna put her cup down and sat back in her chair, eyes closed. After a moment, she started to speak slowly...

'No one ever came to Lyndseer Castle. All our family, except my parents, had long ago deserted a sinking shire and moved on to richer counties. And my parents wouldn't tolerate mere villagers playing with me. Besides, by the time I was old enough to play, we barely had enough money to pay our bills, so most villagers kept away. But one day, when I was nineteen, I slipped out of the castle. My parents were away for the first time since I could remember. Some last surviving relative had died, and they were desperately hoping they might have been left a crumb or two. I crept out of the castle, over the bridge and then down to the river, not daring to take the road in case someone saw me. And then' – her hand strayed to her heart – 'I saw him. Augustus.'

Pritchard, Ellie.

Luna opened her eyes as if reliving the scene. 'He was fishing. He'd already seen me, so I couldn't run away.' A dreamy look came into her eye. 'I stayed with him until I realised the time. I had to get back to the castle before my parents returned.'

'What did you talk about?' Eleanor said.

Luna shook her head, her eyes misty. 'We didn't. We just stood next to each other in silence and he... fished, and then I told him I had to go.' She smiled weakly. 'We never mentioned meeting again, but we both knew we would.'

'But how did you manage it once your parents were back?'

Luna shrugged. 'As our situation worsened, Father drank more and more often in his study at the top of the main tower. While Mother went to bed earlier and earlier on sleeping tablets from the doctor. But I could still only slip out for an hour or so. And sometimes not for days on end.' She closed her eyes again and took a deep breath. 'One day Augustus told me he... he wanted to marry me. I told him Father would never give his permission, even though he had more money than we did. Father had vowed that I would never marry a man from Yorelow. He was too proud. None of them were good enough for our family.'

The bitterness in her voice made Eleanor wince. Then Luna's tone softened. 'One day, Augustus told me he couldn't go on like this. Only seeing me for a few snatched hours a week. If that. Always hiding. He threatened to march up to Lyndseer Castle and have it out with Father. I begged him not to, but he was adamant. I managed to dissuade him. Eventually. But a few weeks later, he did just that without me knowing. I was in Blackington accompanied by our old housekeeper, who doubled as my chaperone. I was seeing the doctor. He wouldn't do house calls to us any more, because we never paid our bills.' Luna swallowed painfully. 'On our return, even before we entered the house, I could hear Father shouting. When he saw me, he told me if Augustus ever tried to see me again or set foot in Lyndseer Castle, he'd have him arrested. Or shot! But he never got the chance.'

34

Eleanor pushed herself out of her chair and grasped Luna's arm as she swayed. She scanned her face in concern. 'Luna, you don't have to continue if—'

She placed her hand over Eleanor's. 'Yes, I do. The detective from Blackington will arrive tomorrow and take Babcock away. Constable Quilter told me the road should be open by the afternoon. And I doubt anyone in Blackington police station will take any notice of what "Loony Luna" has to tell them!'

Eleanor bit her lip and said nothing because there was nothing to say. It was often hard enough for a woman with standing to be taken seriously by the authorities. Let alone one who lived wild in the woods in a remote hamlet like Yorelow.

Luna took another deep breath and continued, her voice a little stronger. 'That night, Father got drunk. More than usual. I think he probably lit a cigarette and then passed out and...' She swallowed hard. 'The first I knew of the fire was when the old housekeeper came running into my room and dragged me out of the castle.' She shivered. 'By the morning, there was nothing left. And I knew my parents were among the ashes. And then... I noticed. The looks. The nudges. The servants had told everyone about Augustus's visit. They believed I'd set the fire. In the end, Quilter took me to the police station to question me.' She jerked upright so suddenly, Eleanor let go of her arm. 'And... he was there. Augustus. I thought he must have come to tell Quilter he was wrong. That I had nothing to do with it. But...'

Eleanor squeezed her arm again. 'You don't have to tell us, Luna. Constable Quilter told us what Augustus... said. Or didn't say.'

Luna shrugged. 'Then you know the rest. I didn't want to ever see him, or the villagers, again. But Yorelow was all I knew. So I stayed, but had as little to do with the village as possible. And nothing to do with... him.'

She reached for another sandwich while Clifford poured everyone a fresh cup of tea.

Eleanor sipped hers for a moment, then set it down.

'You visited Pritchard's... I mean Augustus's grave, though, didn't you? And Lyndseer Castle?'

Luna nodded. 'I've slept in the ruins of the castle once a month ever since that day. And... and sat by Augustus's grave once a week after midnight, ever since he passed away.'

Hence the ground-down clay pipe stems, Ellie.

'And the riddle on his gravestone?'

Luna nodded slowly. 'Augustus loved riddles. He'd tell me one when we met and then tell me the answer if I hadn't guessed it by the time we met again.'

A flash of understanding hit Eleanor.

'You married him, didn't you?'

Luna's eyes lit up as if recalling a joyful memory. But then just as quickly faded. She hesitated, then sighed. 'Yes. The day I was supposed to be seeing the doctor in Blackington. I slipped some of my mother's sleeping tablets I'd stolen to my old nanny in the park. She often fell asleep anyway. I left her by the bandstand and met Augustus. We were married in the local register office. It was the day of my twenty-second birthday, so finally I didn't need my father's consent. Afterwards, we had our honeymoon in a café and then parted. I went back to Nanny, woke her up, and we came home.' She hesitated again. 'Augustus beat us back to the castle and confronted Father. I think he thought he would have to accept him now we were married. Instead, Father swore he'd have the marriage declared illegal before the week was through and threw him out.'

For a moment, there was silence. Eleanor could see Seldon's policeman's brain sifting through what they'd been told. He cleared his throat.

'Miss, er, Luna, what did you argue so publicly with Mr Unwin about that you almost came to blows? And we know he came to your, er, cabin.'

'I didn't like him, even though he was Augustus's nephew. Babcock told me he only wanted to—'

'I'm sorry to interrupt, but you were meeting Mr Babcock *before* Mr Unwin's death?'

Luna looked confused. 'Yes. Babcock was the only one who believed I hadn't set that fire. I only knew this because I overheard two other villagers talking about it. Then, when... Augustus died, Babcock sought me out. Told me he hadn't felt it right, or his place, to do so before.'

'But now he did because you were the rightful heir to Waketon Court!' Eleanor breathed.

Seldon's frown deepened. 'In that case, Miss Luna, why didn't you claim your inheritance and move in?'

Luna shrugged. 'Why? It meant nothing to me. I was happy... enough where I was. The miserly stipend my parents still received from some long-dead relative wasn't sufficient to keep Lyndseer Castle in genteel poverty, let alone genteel grandeur. But it was sufficient for me to live my way. On my terms.'

'"Be yourself, for everyone else is taken",' Clifford murmured.

Eleanor remembered him writing that exact quote from Oscar Wilde and hiding it in her shoes when she'd only just inherited Henley Hall and was all at sea as to who she was.

She glanced at Seldon. His demeanour reminded her of when they'd first met and he'd warned her if she didn't stop interfering in the case he was investigating, he would have to arrest her. She shifted uncomfortably.

'Miss Luna,' Seldon's tone was measured, but firm, 'I asked what you argued twice with Mr Unwin about?'

She shook her head. 'Argued *once*. After Babcock told me what Unwin had come there for, I saw him.' Her eyes flashed. 'Sitting in *Augustus's* chair behind *Augustus's* desk in *Augustus's* study! I know it's silly, but I felt outraged. He didn't deserve to be there. And he was probably just working out how much he could sell everything in there for. So, I told him when I met him in the street if he touched anything, he'd be sorry!'

Seldon rubbed his chin. 'I see. You said that was the only time you argued with him?'

She nodded. 'Yes. But at first I thought the same as you do. When I found him some weeks later outside my cabin, I imagined he'd come to cause trouble. But he hadn't. While searching Waketon Court to find what he could sell, he'd came across Augustus's diary.'

The leather-bound diary with the bookmarks still in my dress pocket, Ellie.

'Being... the sort of man I mistakenly thought he was,' Luna continued, 'he read it.'

Eleanor's eyes widened. 'And found entries about... you?'

'And me being Augustus's wife, yes.'

Eleanor frowned. 'You said "being the man you mistakenly thought he was"?'

Luna nodded. 'I misjudged him. He was quite happy to sell

the contents of Waketon Court off piecemeal and the house itself. But only because he believed the clause in Augustus's will had been added by Babcock by bribing the local solicitor. He thought Babcock was just trying to hang on to his job and the house. After reading Augustus's diary, he realised it was genuine, and I was the rightful heir. So he offered to drop his challenge and leave.'

'Then why didn't he?'

'Because I asked him not to.'

Seldon, Clifford and Eleanor exchanged confused glances.

'Why?'

'Because I needed his help. I'd noticed Augustus's grave had been disturbed. I couldn't ask Quilter or anyone else in the village for help. Gossip had turned to folklore over the years, and half of them believed I was a witch. They still do.'

Eleanor winced, remembering Quilter's 'broomstick' remark.

'At first I thought the man they call "Digger" was bodysnatching. I caught him sneaking around the graveyard at night.'

Ah, Ellie! Hence Unwin accusing Digger of trying to steal Pritchard's body. He was probably just trying to avoid Ned after meeting Dora.

Luna frowned. 'But then, even after Unwin had warned him off, it continued. Augustus's grave just wasn't... the same. And there was more than one of them sneaking around in the yard after dark. I saw their lanterns. But before you ask, I never managed to get close enough to identify anyone. The night before Unwin was killed, they were there again. And this time I heard one of them. A man. And he said, "We'll do it tomorrow night for sure. The reverend will cover us!"'

The three members of The Byron Detective Agency shot each other a loaded glance. Eleanor felt an icy prickle slide down her spine. It couldn't be? Ansel had a cast-iron alibi! He was conducting... She gasped. Seldon had remarked how unusually long the Midnight Mass had been. Had Ansel arranged it as cover, so his associates could do whatever they had planned in the graveyard outside?

She glanced at Seldon again. It was clear he was thinking along the same lines. Even Clifford had raised an eyebrow.

'The ladies, Hugh!' she cried, jumping out of her chair.

Clifford's quiet but soothing cough stopped her.

'My lady, if I can offer an alternative interpretation of Miss Luna's statement?'

She slowly sat back down.

'I suggest that what the gentleman meant was, not that the reverend was complicit with their scheme. But rather that the length of the Mass itself would naturally provide cover.'

Eleanor breathed a sigh of relief. Seldon nodded. 'That's a more plausible explanation.'

'*Vetus Ordo.*'

They all turned. Ansel stood by the half-open door. 'Apologies. I heard someone call out.'

Eleanor blushed. 'Sorry, Reverend, that was me. What did you mean by, what was it again?'

'*Vetus Ordo.*' Ansel held his hands out. 'Everything in Yorelow is from the Middle Ages. As was my predecessor, as I mentioned. Which is why he still held the full Traditional Latin Mass.'

'The Traditional Latin Mass is the liturgy in the Roman Missal of the Catholic Church,' Clifford said. 'It was codified in 1570 and is celebrated almost exclusively in Ecclesiastical Latin. And is considerably longer than the standard Mass in the vernacular.'

Ansel nodded and left again, closing the door.

Clifford turned back to their guest. 'So what did you do, Miss Luna, when you suspected Mr Pritchard's grave was still being interfered with and was possibly going to be robbed?'

'I told the only two people I could; Unwin and Babcock.'

Eleanor clicked her fingers. 'Which is why Unwin sent that telegram. And why he insisted we arrive by midnight. To catch the culprits red-handed.'

'And why he gave no details in his telegram,' Seldon added. 'Had he put what he did know, we might have refused the assignment.'

'Which also explains the money paid into the agency's account, sir,' Clifford said. 'Whether we took the case or not. We could hardly not come after such a generous gesture.'

Luna bit her lip. 'I didn't know about the money.'

Eleanor let out a long breath. 'Thank you, Luna. What you have told us has filled in so many blanks. There's just one more matter that would be helpful if you could throw some light on it. Ned. Rumour has it he was Augustus's illegitimate son.'

Luna laughed mirthlessly. 'And that's all it was. A village rumour. Augustus assured me of that and I believed him one hundred per cent.'

Eleanor nodded. 'That's good to know. Now, we...' She tailed off, having caught Seldon's expression. 'What is it, Hugh?'

He hesitated, then turned to Luna.

'The evidence against you was relatively compelling before this conversation, Miss Luna. You were known to have argued violently with the deceased, Mr Unwin. There was evidence of your presence at the scene of his murder. You were also the one who led my wife to the body of Ned, the second victim. Again, traces of your presence were found in the vicinity.'

'But, Hugh. She explained about visiting both places regularly because—'

Seldon raised a polite, but firm, hand. 'And now, you have admitted to being friendly with the man whose fingerprints we will surely find on the murder weapon. A man who had a motive to do away with both men. And finally, by admitting you married Mr Pritchard, you have strengthened your motive for killing Mr Unwin. He was challenging you inheriting Waketon Court.' He stood up. 'Miss Luna, as a representative of The Byron Detective Agency I—'

Eleanor shot out of her seat. 'Hugh! You can't! Clifford, tell him!'

Clifford cleared his throat. 'I apologise, my lady, but on previous occasions, I have taken your side. But I'm afraid, in this instance, I feel Constable Quilter must be fetched and Miss Luna charged with being an accessory, at least.'

Eleanor looked from one to the other in disbelief. 'I'm telling you both now. You're arresting her over my—'

'Who said anything about arresting, my lady?' Clifford picked a piece of imaginary lint from his jacket sleeve. 'I do not recall the master uttering such a threat.'

Luna, who had been silently watching throughout, turned a puzzled brow to Seldon. 'Then what, as a representative of The Byron Detective Agency, do you intend to do, Mr Seldon?'

His face broke into a smile. 'Solve the case we voted to accept in Mr Unwin's absence; the apparent attempted graver-obbing of Mr Pritchard.'

'After all,' Clifford added, 'we have already received a generous initial payment.'

Eleanor's mouth dropped. 'You never intended... this was a set-up!'

Seldon's tone, and features, turned earnest. 'Apologies, Miss Luna, but I had to make sure you weren't going to run out on us. Again. If we're to solve this case, we will need your assistance. Especially if things get hairy. And I expect they will,' Eleanor's sharp hearing caught him mutter.

She held Luna's hands in hers. 'And I promise we will put Inigo Unwin and Ned's killer behind bars.'

She mentally crossed her fingers.

Let's just hope, Ellie, it's not Babcock. Or Luna!

Luna rose. 'Thank you. It's inadequate, but all I have at the moment. I must be going.'

They accompanied her to the door, Clifford opening it and standing to one side to let her through.

But she didn't move. She stood there in the hall, her eyes transfixed.

Eleanor followed her gaze. Sticking out of the middle of the holly wreath was a knife. The same kind of knife they'd encountered on Luna's veranda. And pinned by it to the door, fluttering in the stiff breeze, was a note written in what looked like blood: *Leave Yorelow in your fancy car tonight. Or in a pine box tomorrow.*

35

Over breakfast at dawn the following morning, the three members of the agency held an emergency meeting. The detective from Blackington was due sometime later that day, depending on when the road in and out was reopened, and they urgently needed more progress. Eleanor wished another snowstorm would blow in to delay him. Everyone had gone to bed so late the night before that once more, at Eleanor's insistence, only Mrs Butters was in attendance in the vicarage kitchen. Eleanor had asked for a simple breakfast of coffee and toast, given how early it was. Her rumbling stomach was now regretting the decision, however, but her conscience wasn't, as her housekeeper hadn't had to rise an hour earlier to prepare it.

Seldon rubbed his eyes as he yawned. 'I'm sorry, I'll come to in a minute. I just need... ah! Thank you, Mrs Butters.' He picked up the cup and took a large glug. 'Ah! Hot!'

Mrs Butters tutted. 'Would I be serving you cold coffee, sir?'

Eleanor hid a smile. 'Of course she wouldn't, Hugh.' She sipped her own carefully. 'Now, I know it's' – she peered at the clock on the mantelpiece and shuddered – 'hideously early, given how late we retired last night, but I still think it was the right decision, knife stuck in the door or no knife. All it proves is the killer is getting desperate.' She held up a hand. 'I know, Hugh. Which also means they could do something foolish. And possibly dangerous. We'll all take much greater care. But we were just wearing ourselves out with no result. It was far better to have had a little more Boxing Day fun all together and then sleep on it.'

Clifford nodded. 'Indeed, my lady. As William Blake said, "Think in the morning, act in the noon, eat in the evening, sleep in the night." Although perhaps it might be amended for my mistress. "Eat in the morning, eat at noon—"' He caught the napkin she threw at him with studied ease.

'I was the one who insisted on a light breakfast, if you remember?'

Seldon chuckled, then took a cautious sip of his coffee. 'I think we all agree, even though we're now really under pressure, it was the best we could do. And I've probably been far more guilty than most, staying up night after night trying to crack a case at the Yard, when one good night's sleep might have seen me solving it over the sausage and bacon.'

At the two words, Eleanor and Gladstone both stared around, then shared a look of resigned disappointment.

They both perked up, however, as Mrs Butters appeared a moment later with a mountain of hot, buttered toast. As Eleanor munched on her first slice, she slipped Gladstone one. Immediately, she felt an insistent pawing on her leg.

'Morning, Tomkins. I thought you were still asleep with the others.' She pulled him off a middle piece of the toast with no crust. The butter caught in his whiskers as he curled up next to the bulldog with his prize. Seldon took another swig of coffee and set his cup down. 'Actually, my brain is clearer already. I think I have an idea.'

She leaned forward eagerly. 'Wonderful, Hugh! Any idea is

better than none.' She winced. 'Sorry. That didn't come out right, but you know what I mean.'

'We are all ears, sir,' Clifford added.

Seldon rubbed his chin. 'Last night, we were all for blasting back around the village, cross-examining our suspects again. But now, in the cold light of day...'

She nodded. 'I know, Hugh. It does rather feel as if we're just repeating ourselves because we can't think of anything new. Or better.'

He see-sawed his head. 'Y-e-s. Don't get me wrong, we learned a lot of new information from our last round of questioning. But I'm beginning to fear it was mostly irrelevant, and it was only yesterday. I was going to say, "I think I have an idea what *not* to do. Which is to go around a third time!"'

She sighed. 'I agree. At least that's half a new idea.'

'Perhaps I could offer the other half, my lady?'

Eleanor spun around. 'I know that studiously casual manner of yours, Clifford. It means you've come up with not half an idea, but a complete whizz of a one!' Her tone became more serious. 'We could so use that now. Otherwise, by the end of today, I fear not only Babcock, but also Luna will be going back with that detective. Both in handcuffs!' She sighed. 'I genuinely believe Luna to be innocent of both murders. But I'm not absolutely convinced Babcock isn't our killer. But...' She shrugged.

'I concur, my lady. However, *I* am equally convinced of Babcock's innocence. He exhibits too many admirable traits of an old retainer. But I am also convinced he knows more than he is saying. Which is why I am putting forward a contrary suggestion. Which is this; rather than cross-examine our suspects again with their endless propensity for lying and half-truths as we have just agreed, why not cross-examine our *physical* evidence, which cannot lie? Well, not maliciously, unlike our suspects.'

Seldon finished his last dreg of coffee and slapped his mug onto the table. 'An excellent plan! I second the proposal.'

'And I third it, so long as we start immediately after breakfast,' she said firmly. She stifled the small voice of panic that told her if it didn't work, they would have no chance to try anything else before the detective arrived. Quilter had made it abundantly clear that whoever the detective took back with him to the Blackington cells would be the one who went down for the crime. Apparently, the brass at Blackington liked quick, clean results.

Clifford consulted his notebook. 'Fortunately, we do not need to wait until after breakfast, my lady.'

'In that case, I'll bring more coffee and toast,' Mrs Butters said.

As she turned back to the range, Clifford slipped an envelope out of his pocket.

'The telegram!'

'Indeed, my lady. The first physical item we have connected to this case. Although, whether it is in any way connected to the murders themselves, we cannot say for certain.'

'But the coincidence would be too great for it not to be. So I think we can continue with that working assumption,' Seldon said.

'Very good, sir.' Clifford produced his reading glasses.

'"Sir, madam. £300 deposited in agency bank account. Further £300 payable on accepting case. Further £300 payable on completion. Initial £300 to be retained regardless case taken or not." Signed "IOU Esq".' Clifford removed his glasses.

Eleanor fed her fresh piece of toast to the terrible two under the table. When she'd finished, still no one had spoken.

'Okay. So, on the positive side, the first physical item we have related to the case hasn't told us a string of lies and half-truths.'

'It has instead, my lady, called upon its statutory right to remain silent.'

Seldon chuckled. 'You have a wonderful knack of lightening the mood just when it's needed, Clifford.'

Mrs Butters, who was refreshing everyone's coffee, tutted. 'If you wants him to talk, sir, you need to get him a friend. Then he'll chatter sixteen to the dozen.'

Eleanor looked blank for a moment, then struck the table with the flat of her hand. 'You know, you're right!' She turned to the others. 'We need to compare our pieces of physical evidence with each other. Somewhere there'll be a discrepancy and then we can pounce!'

Seldon swallowed his toast with a glug of coffee. 'A fine theory, Eleanor. But who do you suggest as a "companion" to our mute telegram?'

'The recording, if I might be so bold, sir?'

Seldon's eyes lit up. 'Of course, Clifford. It's the second item we know came from Unwin. I've no idea if comparing the two will give us the breakthrough we desperately need, but let's find out!'

Quilter fumbled with the key. 'Gone and got himself stuck, he has,' he grumbled.

'Perhaps I can help, Constable?'

Clifford smoothly removed the stuck key from the lock, reinserted it, and pushed the door open.

'Thank you, Mr Clifford. Reckon that's done it. Thought for a moment it were the wrong 'un. I tooks several off Mr Babcock before I locked him up.'

Eleanor had to admit, as she entered Waketon Court with Seldon and Clifford, it was rather handy Babcock was out of the way. Dora didn't seem to be there, either. It meant they would have free rein.

The four of them hurried across the hall into the study. She shivered in the doorway. The whole place had an abandoned air. Still, they didn't intend to be there long.

Clifford slipped the record on the machine and a moment later Unwin's voice could be heard faintly above the crackling, hissing and popping...

'Good evening. I, as you have probably learned from Babcock by now, am Inigo Unwin. My apologies for asking you to come at short notice. Especially on Christmas Eve. But an urgent matter has arisen. You will have received the first amount of three hundred pounds I placed in your account earlier. The second instalment is in the top drawer of the desk. I shall wait while you confirm this for yourselves... So, you know now I am deadly serious in wishing to engage your services. But if you choose to accept the case, you must do so by midnight tonight. Now, the reason for my calling you down here...'

They waited through the hissing, the sound of the microphone falling over, and the other faint noises. Then Clifford stopped the recording.

Eleanor looked around hopefully. 'Well? Did it "speak" to anyone?'

Quilter shuffled his feet, while Seldon grimaced in apology. Clifford said nothing for a moment. Then she realised he was writing in his notebook.

'I am not sure, my lady. But one thing did strike me. I have transcribed the recording so we can study it alongside the telegram.' He placed both on the desk and she, Seldon and Quilter crowded around. 'Now, this gave me pause for thought.' He pointed to a line in his notebook from Unwin's recording: "You will have received the first amount of three hundred pounds I placed in your account earlier." Now, compare it to this line from the telegram: "Sir madam £300 deposited in agency bank account."'

Eleanor read, and reread, the two lines, Seldon and Quilter doing the same. All three of them exchanged blank looks.

Clifford pointed to the telegram. 'The word "deposited" is used here, but' – he pointed to the line from the recording – 'the word "placed" is used here. Similarly, in the line "Initial £300 to be retained regardless case taken or not," from the telegram, the word "initial" is used. But in this line in the recording, "You will have received the first amount of three hundred pounds I placed in your account earlier," the word "first "is used.'

Seldon's brow cleared. 'By Jove! Well spotted.'

Quilter still looked bemused.

'What Clifford is saying, Constable,' she explained, 'is that most people's vocabulary is very set. They always tend to use the same words, not variants of. "Deposited" for example is a... posher, or more precise word for "placed". Same with "initial" and "first".'

Quilter's eyes widened. 'So that there disc wasn't recorded by Mr Unwin?'

Clifford shook his head. 'Unfortunately, I do not think we can draw that conclusion yet. There is the added complication in this instance, that people write very differently when composing a telegram.'

Quilter nodded. 'That's very true, sir. They be charging you by the word, so you wants to make sure if one word will do, you don't use two. And also, the man at the telegraph office is going to read what you wrote in front of you. So you don't want to sound as if you ain't had no education.'

Seldon rubbed his chin. 'But if you're observations are accurate, Clifford, it means Unwin may not have written that telegram. In which case—'

'We've been set up from the start!' she breathed.

'Blimey!' Quilter shook his head. 'That would be a turn-up for the books and no mistake.'

Clifford nodded. 'I agree, Constable. But it is merely a possibility at the moment. And, perhaps, a remote one.'

'Remote or not,' Seldon said grimly, 'we need to find out urgently. But how?'

Eleanor was already out the door. 'As Mrs Butters would say, we find our telegram and recording some more "friends",' she called over her shoulder. 'And see if we can't get one of them to slip up and reveal whether we've been played from the start!'

36

Quilter and Clifford started on the ground floor of Waketon Court, while Seldon and Eleanor started in the attic. Even though it was most likely they'd find something in the obvious places such as the study and Unwin's bedroom, Eleanor pointed out that they hadn't last time they'd looked. And this time, they were equally unsure exactly what they were looking for. So it was best just to look everywhere.

The top floor took little time to search, consisting purely of the servants' rooms, Babcock's being the only one in use. Eleanor shook her head. It seemed it hadn't occurred to the valet that he could have had any room in the house. She doubted Clifford would have, either. Babcock's room was as spartan and ordered as she'd expected. The only nod to any real comfort was an old wingback chair with a copy of *Whose Body?* by Dorothy L. Sayers on the arm. Eleanor smiled. She hadn't pictured the stiff Babcock as a lover of crime fiction.

Seldon grunted as he stood up from searching under the bed. 'Nothing! Shall we try the next floor?'

The second floor consisted mostly of bedrooms, none of

which were now occupied. She shivered as Seldon reached for the first door.

'Are you alright, Eleanor?' he said.

She nodded. 'It all feels so forlorn. Everyone from this house is either dead or in prison!'

Seldon grimaced. 'I hadn't really thought of that. It is a little like a ghost house at the moment.' He pushed the door open and stepped to one side to let her enter first. From the size, it was obviously the master bedroom. And would have been Pritchard's for sure, Eleanor thought. But much to her surprise, it was as impersonal as the guest bedrooms on the floor above. And, a search revealed, devoid of any personal belongings. She had rather thought that Babcock would have kept it exactly as it was when his master had died. It seemed not.

The next three bedrooms were the same; empty of any personal effects. And the final room, Unwin's, was exactly as last time she'd been there. Only colder. The four-poster sat unslept in, still covered in packing paper, string and magazines. The wardrobe revealed the same modest selection of clothing, whilst the dresser was still piled with boxes, more magazines and newspapers. Eleanor was glad Seldon was searching the room with her this time. The time before, Clifford's horror at the general untidiness had been palpable.

She set to, with Seldon dealing with the more... gentlemanly areas of the room. It didn't take long. She was soon left looking through Unwin's obsession with the latest gadgets again; an electric shaver, a vibrating cocktail plate, a self-propelling pencil, press studs which looked like buttons on the outside and—

'Oops!'

One of the studs slipped through her fingers and dropped down the side of the dresser. She crouched down. The gap between the dresser and wall was slim, but she reckoned she could get her fingers in there if she twisted her arm sideways. The trouble was, there was no natural light down there, and she couldn't see the stud. Clifford probably had a pocket torch on him somewhere, along with a myriad other things a normal person would never need or want to carry around, but, she had to admit, often came in rather handy. She figured she could do without light on this one occasion. The gap was so narrow, the stud had to just be on the small sliver of carpet between the dresser and wall.

So long as an eight-legged surprise isn't lurking there as well, Ellie.

She steeled herself and slid her arm into the gap, fingers reaching. Instead of feeling carpet, or a stud, however, they touched something else. For a brief moment, she almost withdrew her hand. She scolded herself. It hadn't been a spider. It was far too—

'Round. Hugh!'

Seldon was over to her side in an instant. 'What is?'

'This!' She triumphantly held aloft a black disc.

Downstairs, back in the study, they were still debating her find.

'I really can't say either way, Constable. It might have been hidden. On the other hand, it could just have slipped down there and been forgotten. You couldn't see it as there was no light, you see.'

'I think if we play it, it might answer the question for us,' Seldon said.

She nodded. 'We did think it rather odd there were no more recordings as apparently Unwin was mad for them.'

'True, my lady,' Clifford said as he placed the record on the apparatus. 'But they are not inexpensive. So, a man of Mr Unwin's... cautious fiscal outlook—'

'Parsimonious, you mean, Clifford?'

'Perhaps, my lady. But not where Miss Luna and his uncle

featured, it seems. In that regard, he was the epitome of generous.'

She held her hands up. 'It was just a joke to lighten the mood.'

'Although, to be fair, both are correct,' Seldon said. 'Our Mr Unwin seemed to have quite a contradictory character.' He stroked his chin. 'Where have I come across that before...?'

The small cushion caught him squarely in the stomach.

'You'll have to learn to dodge better than that, Hugh,' she said. 'I'm sure Clifford will teach you. Now, let's see if this recording throws a searing spotlight onto any Machiavellian machinations that might have been going on before we arrived!'

Clifford started the disc spinning. They listened without interruption. It wasn't a long recording. As Clifford replaced the needle in the cradle, Seldon broke the silence.

'Well, it certainly answered the question of what Unwin liked to accompany his roast lamb.'

'And, I think, sir,' Clifford said, 'as to whether the record was hidden, or merely misplaced.'

'Well, if it was hidden,' Quilter said, 'I reckon it would have been Babcock or Miss Dora what done it.' He shook his head. 'If my old pa, may he rest in peace, had recorded what he wanted for his dinner, my mum would've boxed his ears!'

Eleanor noticed Clifford was writing in his notebook again.

'Transcribing it?'

'Yes, my lady. To compare the syntax to the original recording initially. Or should I say "first"? And then to the telegram. I confess nothing struck me on first listen except the same poor quality of the recording. But then again, although not inexpensive, it is a relatively new invention and only recently available for the home market. I'm sure the quality will improve.'

She laughed. 'I'm not sure that will happen in time to help our investigation! But hopefully, if we run through this transcription, it might answer those discrepancies you noticed between the telegram and first recording.'

It didn't.

In the study, Quilter scratched his head. 'Well I don't mind admitting I'm flummoxed proper. What does it tell us?'

Seldon stared at the three different texts. 'That Unwin made both recordings? And that he probably also wrote the telegram. What do you think, Clifford?'

He examined the texts again. 'I honestly couldn't say for sure, sir. One may be phoney, or they may both be genuine. I—'

Of course, Ellie!

'Constable Quilter!'

The policeman's head shot up in surprise. 'Er, yes, my lady?'

'We need to go fishing!'

Seldon stared at her in puzzlement for a moment, then groaned. 'That is your worst pun, yet, Eleanor! And more to the point, why?'

She tapped her nose knowingly. 'Tag along and find out, Hugh.'

He shook his head. 'Clifford? Oh! Of course, you weren't there when we first went to Constable Quilter's police house, so this will mean nothing to you.'

'Indeed, sir. For once, I am the one in the dark. But on a different note, I know earlier I suggested we shouldn't waste any more time interviewing our suspects. However, I feel now there is an exception. Mr Babcock.'

Seldon shrugged. 'If you think so. Although he made it very clear he had no more to say. We can visit him in his cell after we've been on Eleanor's bizarre fishing trip if that's alright with you, Constable?'

Quilter nodded. 'No problem on my side, sir.'

'Excellent, Constable,' Clifford said. 'However, with apologies, sir, may I suggest I alone interview Mr Babcock? If we all go, I believe he will indeed have nothing more to say. But, as a fellow valet and butler, I feel I could persuade him to see things from a different viewpoint.'

As they hurried out, Eleanor grimaced. She hoped Clifford succeeded. Otherwise Babcock might soon be seeing things from a very different viewpoint – that of a hangman's noose!

37

We'll never get it all done in time, Ellie.

Having gone fishing and caught a very big fish indeed, they hurried back to Quilter's home-cum-police station to meet Clifford. On the way back to the vicarage, they filled him in.

'So we got Professor Pike—'

Clifford groaned. 'Now, I understand the "fishing" pun, my lady.'

She laughed. 'I know. Excellent, wasn't it? When Hugh and I first went to Quilter's police station, he was in the one and only cell, behind the curtain. Quilter told us he used to be a professor of "phoney" English. But this evening, I realised he'd meant phonetics! Anyway, we dragged him back to Waketon Court and Pritchard's study and played him the original recording we listened to and the second one of him ordering his dinner.'

'Only,' Seldon added, 'the first recording *wasn't* Unwin!'

Having revealed who Professor Pike insisted had really recorded the first disc, Clifford filled them in on his interview with Babcock.

'Fortunately, I was correct in my assumption that he would be more willing to listen to a fellow valet and butler.'

'And how!' Eleanor said. 'I can't believe you got him to confess so much. Especially why his fingerprints, and his alone, are on the murder weapon.'

Seldon nodded. 'I have to admit, no one is going to believe that story. Especially the Blackington police, from what Quilter has told us about them. Although, to be fair, I have trouble believing it myself. And the evidence of an alcoholic ex-professor may not hold that much sway in court either. Even if it did, it doesn't prove the person who actually put his voice to the recording we first heard in Pritchard's study is actually Unwin's murderer. Although, it would help give teeth to the prosecution's case.'

'Either way,' she said firmly, 'we need to carry on with our plan no matter what.'

Half an hour later, while pacing the vicarage sitting room, she glanced anxiously at the mantelpiece clock for the third time. 'What is he doing?' she whispered, nodding towards the table in the far corner.

Seldon shrugged. 'Examining the fragments of clay we found at the scene of both murders.'

'I know that,' she said more tartly than she'd intended. 'I mean, what's he looking for?'

He shrugged again. 'I guess we'll discover that when he finds it. Or doesn't.'

They glanced at Clifford as he took another fragment of clay from one of the two labelled piles and meticulously scraped a few shavings off with his pocketknife.

'That's destroying evidence, that is,' Quilter grumbled. He was perched on the edge of the settee. 'Or at least, tampering with it.'

'You can't make an omelette without breaking eggs, Constable,' Seldon said firmly.

'Or catch a vicious killer, I'll warrant, either, sir. You go ahead and break whatever eggs you need. I'll pick up the shells when that fancy detective arrives.'

Once again, she found herself warming to this country constable. Hugh was right. He really was more interested in justice than glory. If Hugh had been born in a village like Yorelow, she could see him turning out a little like Quilter. And Clifford, Babcock.

And you, Luna, Ellie?

As if he could hear her thoughts, Clifford stood up. 'Constable, we need to pay a visit to Miss Luna. Immediately.'

Luna met them on the veranda of her cabin.

'Constable. It was very kind of you to let me have my liberty. But have you come to rearrest me already? I had a suspicion you believed I was, at least, an accessory in one or both murders.'

Quilter coughed into his hand. 'No, miss. Can't exactly arrest you even if I wanted to. I've only the one cell and I couldn't countenance you in there with a man. Even if he is Babcock.'

Eleanor caught Clifford's horrified nodding out of the corner of her eye.

'Actually, Luna, we're here because Clifford needs to ask you some questions. And we are running desperately short of time,' she added earnestly.

Luna nodded in understanding, shot Quilter a look, hesitated, then ushered them inside.

The tiny wooden building only had two rooms, it seemed. A diminutive sitting room-cum-kitchen-cum-whatever was needed. And a curtain off to what Eleanor imagined was Luna's bedroom and washing facilities. The similarity in layout to Quilter's roundhouse didn't escape her. Luna's place, however, was sparsely furnished with a simple stove, an obviously homemade wooden table, and a shabby, but exquisitely upholstered, button-back leather chair. Luna followed her gaze.

'From the castle. It was the one in my bedroom. For some reason, someone dragged it out. Maybe they had some idea they could rescue the furniture and stuff before the whole place caught fire. This was all they managed, though.' She laughed mirthlessly. 'Took me an age to walk it here.' She turned to Clifford. 'Now, what do you need?'

'But two things, Miss Luna. A sample of a recent pipe of yours, along with directions as to where you get the clay. And secondly, on your monthly visits to Lyndseer Castle, where you sleep.'

She looked at Eleanor in puzzlement. She shrugged. 'I've no idea, but if he needs to know, it's not on a whim.'

Luna turned around and took a small box covered in mother-of-pearl off the shelf.

'That's beautiful,' Eleanor breathed.

Luna nodded. 'It was my mother's. It's the only other possession I have apart from the chair that survived the fire. I keep it because it's just a handy size to put... things in.' Her nonchalant tone rang false. She opened it and passed Clifford a pipe. 'I get my clay from the hill just behind here. Go up the road about a hundred yards and you'll see a small clearing. You can see where I scrape the clay from. And I stay... in my old bedroom. It's one of the few parts of Lyndseer Castle that still has some of the roof remaining. So even in wet weather, I remain reasonably dry.'

'Thank you, Miss Luna.' Clifford was already heading for the door.

'I'd better stay,' Luna said in a subdued voice. 'In case, you know.'

Eleanor went to follow the men, then turned and threw her arms around a surprised Luna. 'Don't worry,' she whispered. 'Clifford and Seldon are a pair of Jack Russells when they get going. With them on the case, you and Babcock will be fine.'

She mentally crossed her fingers.

As they carried on through the trees, Luna called from the veranda, 'Thank you for believing in me, Lady... Eleanor. Whatever happens, I'll never forget it. Or you,' Eleanor's sharp hearing caught her add as they turned the corner.

Having collected a small scraping of clay, Clifford producing a 'sample bottle' and a disposable pair of gloves from goodness-knows-where, she, Seldon and Clifford set off to the castle. Quilter, meanwhile, set off back to the police station to make sure everything was in order when the detective arrived.

'I may have to return shortly for Miss Luna if he insists, my lady,' Quilter explained. 'Apologies if it's so.'

So that's why she stayed behind, Ellie. She promised she would not run any more.

Assuring Quilter he was only doing his job, they parted company.

Despite it being further, they stuck to the road, Eleanor not trusting herself to retrace her way through the densely packed woods without Luna leading her. As they went, she noticed the temperature was visibly rising, the snow dripping off the ends of the trees, the ground no longer slippery underfoot, but muddy. The three of them exchanged a worried look. They all had the same thought; the road in and out of Yorelow couldn't be closed for much longer!

The ruined castle appeared, brooding, high on their left. They picked up their pace and were soon crossing the ancient stone bridge to the steep, narrow path that led to the entrance. Hurrying under the gateless arch, they followed Luna's directions past blackened, snow-topped stone walls to the only part of the building that was still roofed, if badly. They soon identified Luna's old bedroom. It was just bare stone walls now, blackened by the fire like the rest. But on the floor they spotted fragments of clay, as they had around Unwin's body. And Ned's.

Clifford collected a selection, placed them in another sample pot he produced from the depths of his coat, and carefully wrote on the blank label. Returning it to his pocket, they set off back into Yorelow.

But before they'd gone far, a horn blasted them to the side of the road. An ancient truck lumbered past. She groaned. The road was open. They'd run out of time. Without speaking, they all exchanged a determined nod. They'd keep going.

But in her heart, she knew it was hopeless.

Dispiritedly, they straggled into town and straight to the police station. At least they could have their say— But before they were even within calling distance of the diminutive round hut, Quilter appeared, waving his arms. He hurried up to them.

Seldon nodded dourly. 'We know, Constable. The road's back open.'

'Indeed, 'tis so, sir,' Quilter said. 'But,' a note of jubilation crept into his voice, 'there ain't no detective!'

Seldon grabbed his arm. 'Are you sure, man?'

Quilter nodded gleefully. 'Blackington station just rang. Apparently, he should be here by now. But he hit a patch of black ice 'bout a mile outside the town and binned the car in a ditch. A farmer pulled him out, but axle were broken. And there were no more cars free.'

'And the upshot is, man?'

'That he won't be here until tomorrow morning!'

'Right!' Eleanor said determinedly. 'We've been given a brief reprieve. Let's make it count! Clifford, go do whatever wizardry you need to with those samples and stuff you collected. Hugh, you come with me. Oh, and if you're free, you too, Constable.'

Quilter nodded enthusiastically. 'I'm free, m'lady. But for what?'

She smiled grimly, a glint in her eye. 'So far, our clues have opened up under interrogation and talked to us. And I don't believe they've lied. Hopefully, when we return, Clifford will be able to tell us what his lumps of clay told him. For the moment, we need to interrogate another clue.'

And it might just be the most difficult, but vital one, to get to open up, Ellie.

38

In the churchyard, the three of them stared at Pritchard's last resting place.

Silent as the grave, she thought with a shudder.

Let's hope we don't have to open it up to unearth its secrets, Ellie.

Quilter cleared his throat. 'Er, I know you explained, m'lady, but what are we looking for?'

'As you know, we found Unwin's body slumped over this gravestone, Constable.' She pointed to it. 'It was obvious from the way it was placed that the killer wanted it found. But it was more than that. They could have placed it on any gravestone. But they chose Unwin's uncle's. Why? Something to do with the riddle, we hazarded a guess earlier. After all, Unwin was killed with a herald trumpet, which is possibly referenced in the first line.'

'Or maybe it was just a red herring. Designed to throw the police off the real reason for Unwin's death,' Seldon said. 'Either way, something here knows and can tell us as clearly as if we were asking one of our suspects.'

Twenty minutes later, the phrase 'silent as the grave' came back to haunt her with a vengeance. She sighed. 'Any luck?'

Seldon and Quilter shook their heads. They'd scoured every inch of the grave and gravestone to work out the connection between it and Unwin's death. They'd all tried to decipher the riddle as well, but got no further than they had before.

Seldon straightened up. 'The light's fading fast. I... Reverend?'

Eleanor turned around to see Ansel and the ladies descending on them.

'Good evening, as I suppose it now is,' Ansel said. 'Mr Clifford asked me to let you know he should be finished in quarter of an hour or so. In the meantime, he suggested you might need some help.'

'Absolutely!' she cried. 'All hands to the pumps before it's pitch-dark out here.'

Ten minutes later, she wasn't sure it was such a good idea as the ladies and Ansel bumped into each other as they crawled around the grave and gravestone like wasps around a picnic. All, however, without disturbing the grave itself.

Seldon stood by her, scratching his head. 'I can't see how... ah! Just the lady we need.'

'As if there aren't enough people already,' Eleanor muttered. Luna appeared and smiled at her.

'Something told me you might require a hand.' She stared at the crowd around the grave. 'But I see you have enough already.'

'Actually,' Seldon said, 'you're exactly the person we *do* need. In what way was Pritchard's grave disturbed, so much so that you thought Digger was trying to rob it? I, in fact, we *all* have examined the grave itself, and we can't spot any sign of it being disturbed.'

Luna shook her head. 'No. Not the grave itself. Only the gravestone. It had been moved. It was at an angle.'

Eleanor grimaced. 'We noticed that, too. Unfortunately, Clifford worked out that it was due to worms.'

Luna looked incredulous. 'I don't want to disagree, but do you know how much a gravestone weighs?'

'One of this size, approximately two hundred pounds, Miss Luna.'

'Clifford!' Eleanor cried. 'I thought you were still back at the vicarage.'

'I was, my lady. But I have finished my examination.'

'And?' She tried not to sound too hopeful. He was under enough pressure already.

'The results were very... satisfactory.'

'Good man!' Seldon said fervently.

Clifford held up his hands. 'However, I feel there is still a major part of the puzzle missing. And without it, our case will collapse like a house of cards.' He paused, his brow furrowing. 'Excuse me, my lady, but you were saying to Miss Luna something about "worms"?'

She rolled her eyes. 'I know, Clifford. You used some fancy word or other to describe them, but—'

She paused in amazement as he raised his hand, something she or Seldon normally did to him when he was starting on some long explanation.

'I apologise profusely, my lady, but time is painfully short. And you have just made me realise that I may have made a dreadful mistake. I stated that I believed the action of earthworms, or *"lumbricus"*, were responsible for the partial subsidence of Mr Pritchard's gravestone.'

'*Lumbricus*', *Ellie. It was on the tip of your tongue.*

'However,' he continued. 'I was missing a crucial piece of information. Constable Quilter provided it later, but I failed until now to realise its significance.'

Quilter scratched his head. 'I did, Mr Clifford? Blow me down if I can remember.'

'You told me, Constable, that Mr Pritchard died only five years previously. Therefore, earthworms would not have been able to move a sufficient quantity of soil in that time to account for its subsidence at one end.'

'So something, or someone, else moved that gravestone!' Seldon said thoughtfully. 'But why?'

'Gladstone! Get down, boy!'

They all turned to see the bulldog, front legs up on the back of Pritchard's gravestone.

Polly tried to pull him off without success. 'I'm sorry, your ladyship. It's most disrespectful to poor Mr Pritchard, I know.'

Lizzie lent a hand, but the stubborn bulldog refused to budge, sniffing the back of the gravestone as if looking for treats.

Clifford shook his head. 'Master Gladstone! Heel!' He strode over and grabbed the dog's collar, gently, but firmly, pulling him down.

By now the light was so bad, the ladies had all lit lanterns. Eleanor jumped as Lizzie's swung past the gravestone, illuminating it.

'Wait!' She hurried over. 'What was that?'

'What, my lady?'

'That... odd shadow?'

Lizzie shone her lantern on the gravestone again. Clifford peered at it as Eleanor pointed at a dark green-brown line that ran along a section of the back.

'Just lichen, my lady. There are several more on—'

'Let him go, Clifford,' she said quietly, but in a tone that brooked no argument.

Once free, Gladstone padded back to the gravestone and heaved his front legs up the back of it again, furiously sniffing the line of lichen.

Eleanor stared at it for a moment, then turned to Seldon. 'Remember what Clifford said about never underestimating a dog's sniffing ability? Even one with a short snout?' She turned back to the gravestone. 'Does anyone have a small, flat—'

At least three items were pressed in her hand. Choosing a nail file, she gently slid it under the beginning of the lichen and lifted. The line came away in a long strip.

Clifford's torch light clicked on.

'What the...!' she breathed.

In the sitting room of the vicarage with the curtains tightly closed, Eleanor watched Seldon pace up and down with a hint of amusement. It was normally her impatiently pacing. Clifford's raised eyebrow showed the irony wasn't lost on him either.

In front of the fireplace, Seldon turned to face them, his features etched with concern.

'This changes everything we thought we knew about this case.' He threw his hands up. 'Everything!' He paced up and down again, before stopping once more. He rubbed his chin. 'Eleanor. Did the reverend see what you discovered?'

She shook her head vigorously. 'No, Hugh. I'm certain of it. In fact, he had already gone into the church at that point and didn't come out until we'd secreted whatever those sheets of paper were.'

'Good. The fewer people who know about this, the better.'

She looked at him quizzically. 'Even the reverend?'

'Yes. Even him. If only for his own safety.'

'And Constable Quilter, sir?' Clifford said.

Seldon hesitated, then nodded firmly. 'Yes. Now, the ladies?'

'They know only that something unexpected was found in the gravestone itself, sir. And that it obviously wasn't the gravestone originally placed there when Mr Pritchard died. They also know not to mention either fact to anyone, under any circumstances.'

Seldon's face broke into a half-smile of relief. 'That's good enough for me.'

'Do you need to report this to the Yard?' she said. 'Or... someone even higher up?'

'Yes. To both.' He hesitated. 'I'm telling you in the strictest secrecy. Those "sheets of paper" we found in Pritchard's gravestone were Professor Hunt's top-secret plans. The professor was the man mentioned in one of those headlines Clifford showed you before we got that fateful telegram. The one that read, "Police confirm man killed in Butterton in Staffordshire was inventor working for government". Well, the plans are for a type of radio wave that detects objects long before they are visible to the eye, with or without a telescope.'

Clifford uncharacteristically raised both eyebrows. 'Indeed, sir! Such a capability on board, say, a naval vessel, would give them an unparalleled advantage over an enemy vessel without such. Also, it would mean the vessel could move at night and in thick fog when other vessels would be severely hampered.'

Seldon nodded. 'Apparently, the invention is only in its infancy, but if it were to fall into the wrong hands...'

Clifford nodded gravely. 'If I might suggest, anyone capable of stealing such plans and selling them to the highest foreign bidder would also have the wherewithal to tap Constable Quilter's police line.'

Eleanor slapped her forehead. 'Of course! Chaps! We were wondering if we'd been set up from the start. If Quilter's line was tapped before we even arrived...'

Seldon groaned. 'Like Yorelow at the bottom of this wretched Devil's punchbowl, we've unwittingly fallen down a rabbit hole just as deep. But way more deadly.'

And I'm beginning to think, Ellie, just as full of devils.

39

As she went over their final plan to trap the killer that evening with Seldon and Quilter, Eleanor was still reeling from the totally unexpected direction the case had taken. For the umpteenth time, she glanced at the desk drawer where the plans they'd discovered hidden in Pritchard's gravestone were under lock and key. The plans that had probably been taken from Professor Hunt's dead body!

She shook her head. Ansel was out on his mercy rounds and Clifford was next door, analysing the murder weapon to see if it too had any more secrets to give up. And they would need every one they could get if they were going to trap such a cunning and dangerous enemy.

Dragging her attention back to the matter in hand, she glanced at the meticulous list of items they needed to do just that. Clifford had insisted on writing it out again after casting a jaundiced eye over her initial efforts.

'"Sample of hay", my lady? I do not recall collecting and analysing such,' he'd said, raising an inquiring eyebrow.

'It says "clay", as well you know.'

'Conceivably from some angles, my lady. However, I also do not recall examining an "angel's strumpet?"'

'You're just being obtuse, now. You know it says "angel's trumpet",' she'd huffed.

In the end, she'd let him rewrite the list. It was quicker. And now, as she swiftly looked down it, she was glad he had. The less chance of error at this stage, the better.

She turned back to Seldon. 'Right, let's check each item off: Telegram from Unwin to Agency, original recording from Unwin to Agency, and "hidden" recording found in Unwin's bedroom?'

Seldon ran his eye over the table. 'Check!'

'Clay samples from the vicinity of Unwin's and Ned's bodies, the hill outside Luna's cabin, Lyndseer Castle and the stonemason's yard?'

The last one they'd obtained from Jarrett's closed workplace on Clifford's insistence only a short time ago.

'Has he had a chance to analyse that last sample yet?' she asked hopefully.

'Indeed, my lady,' Clifford said, entering the room. 'And, fortunately, the samples do not match. When I examined them closely, I noticed a definite difference between their make-up.'

'One that confirms our belief that we know who the killer is?'

He nodded.

She let out a deep breath. 'Thank goodness for that. You can drop that bombshell when needed.'

'Them's all present and correct, my lady,' Quilter said. 'Sorry, I mean "check!"'

'Could you pop out and see if the reverend is around, Constable?' Seldon said.

'Right you are,' Quilter replied willingly.

She winced as he left. She was still uneasy they were keeping him in the dark about the latest developments, but at the same time, completely understood Seldon's stance. Suddenly, this case was bigger than just The Byron Detective Agency. Or Yorelow.

She glanced back at the list. 'Top-secret plans recovered from Pritchard's gravestone?'

'Check!' Seldon threw her a congratulatory glance. She'd wanted to bring the false gravestone itself as evidence, but practical considerations stopped her. And she felt poor Pritchard's grave had been desecrated enough already. Seldon collected Professor Hunt's plans from the locked drawer and slid them carefully inside the bag holding the clay samples.

'And last, but not least,' Clifford said, entering the room. 'The murder weapon.' He laid the herald trumpet on the table. 'Plus one short strand of Mr Unwin's hair found lodged in it.'

'Check!' She ticked it off the list.

'That's everything, then,' she said.

Quilter came back in. 'Mrs Butters has said how the reverend is still out on his rounds, sir.'

'No matter.' Seldon started gathering the items up. 'We'll need to store these securely over in your place until tonight, Constable.'

Quilter nodded. 'So long as youse is okay with them being locked in the equipment trunk, sir, as I can hardly lock them in the cell with Babcock, can I? What if he interferes with the evidence?'

Seldon smothered a laugh. 'Actually, a good point, Constable. And no, I'm sure they will be secure there. I'll help you take them over now.'

With Seldon and Quilter gone, Clifford and Eleanor found the ladies in the kitchen preparing dinner.

'The reverend, my lady?' Mrs Trotman said without pausing in mixing several ingredients in a large bowl. 'Like Butters told Quilter, last I heard, he was still out.'

'He's joining us for dinner, I assume, though? After all, it is his vicarage!'

'Mind you,' Mrs Trotters said, 'you wouldn't believe it, m'lady. The way he's made us feel at home, and as if it was our home at that. Reckon we're all going to miss the reverend when we leaves here.'

'I am in agreement, Mrs Trotman!' Kofi passed them, balancing a stack of serving dishes. 'He is a most delightful host. And the skating was such a treat!'

'I also agree, my lady,' Clifford said, looking at her quizzically.

His tone made her pause. 'What do you mean, exactly?'

'I mean, my lady, that since arriving in this singular hamlet, we have had little but trouble and calamity. Yet, in some inextricable way, I believe you will miss it when we are gone.'

She shook her head disbelievingly. 'I've finally come to accept that you can read my thoughts, Clifford. But what I can't understand is how you can tell me them before I even know I have them myself? You're right. For no good reason I can explain, this... place has... bewitched me.' She shook herself. 'I blame it on festive feelings being allowed to run rampant. That's what you're here for, Clifford. To bring the cold, emotionless weight of logic to bear to stop such nonsense. Now, enough of this. It is still Christmas in spirit, and I'm sure I can help the ladies with preparing dinner.'

His eyes twinkled. 'If you are referring to a Lady Swift's definition of "helping", which some might find indistinguishable from "hindering", then yes.'

'My lady!' Mrs Trotman said sternly. ''Pologies for talking out of turn, but that be my best rolling pin. If you are going to assault Mr Clifford, please use this one. 'Tis only me second best.'

By the time Seldon had returned, via the Angel's Summons to collect a change of clothes for himself and Eleanor for dinner, peace had been restored in the kitchen. And food was near enough ready. Mrs Butters had suggested something light, given everyone would have to be on high alert later on. One wrong move on their part and the plan could fall apart in a moment. And one unexpected move on the killer's part, and things could get very hairy indeed.

They'd discussed just passing all the evidence they'd gathered over to the Blackington detective in the morning. But they'd come to trust Quilter's judgement. And his viewpoint was, once the Blackington brass had an easy conviction under lock and key, they were unlikely to be interested in looking for other suspects. Any contrary evidence handed over would probably disappear or be mislaid, until well after the trial.

'I mean, sir, why risk a bird in the hand for one in the bush, as it were? Especially when you needs to go through a lot of fiddlesome and time-consuming work to do so.'

Seldon had nodded firmly. 'And we have to face the facts. In the cold, harsh glare of the courtroom, this "evidence" we've collected so far could easily be torn apart by an experienced, and amoral, defence lawyer. We need to flush the killer out in the open to be sure of a conviction at the trial.'

So, they'd unanimously voted to stick to the original plan to do just that.

That sorted, and the terrible two fed, dinner proper started. Being a little less formal than usual, and in someone else's kitchen, Mrs Trotman introduced the fayre.

'Chestnut and apple soup to start, my lady, followed by curried mutton. Then pear and Stilton crumble with fake brandy cream to finish as I thought the reverend would be eating with us.'

'I'm sure he'll turn up soon, Mrs Trotman,' Eleanor said. 'He must have been delayed.'

Forty-five minutes later, and all that remained was for her to spoon up every last drop of the cream. 'I say, Mrs Trotman, you'd hardly know there wasn't real brandy in there.'

'Thank you, m'lady,' Mrs Trotman said.

'Weren't really no point, though,' Mrs Butters added. 'Seeing as the reverend never made it.'

Eleanor frowned. 'I know. I hope one of the poor parishioners he's gone to see hasn't taken a turn for the worse. Or...' She couldn't bring herself to say it. There had been enough death in the tiny hamlet of Yorelow for a hundred Christmases.

Seldon finished his dessert and put his spoon down. 'Well, dinner was absolutely wonderful, as always, Mrs Trotman. But how on earth did that constitute a "light" meal? Dinner, or otherwise?'

'Well, sir, we could have started with oysters or glazed ham, with roast duck and—'

'Yes, I get the idea,' he said quickly. 'But we'd better be getting over to Waketon Court and set up—' He was interrupted by a timid knock. 'There you go. That must be the reverend now.'

'Not meaning to disagree, your lordship,' Polly said. 'But why would the reverend be knocking on his own back door?'

Seldon frowned. 'Good point, Polly.' He strode to the door and opened it. 'Constable. Come in.'

Quilter shuffled in.

'Shame you were too busy to join us for dinner,' Seldon said. 'And excuse me getting straight to business, but time is short. What did the brass at Blackington have to say about the latest developments down here? Bet that knocked them for six, eh?'

Quilter coughed. 'Actually, sir, they didn't say nothing. On account of me not having spoken to them.' At Seldon's confused look, Quilter continued. 'Line's down.'

Eleanor's brow furrowed. 'But it can't be the snow. The road's open and it's melting fast.'

Quilter nodded. 'You're right there, m'lady. 'Tisn't the snow. Don't rightly know what it is.'

An icy prickle slithered down her spine. Her frown deepened. 'Constable. You seem... a little ill at ease? Is there something else you came to tell us?'

Quilter swallowed hard as all eyes turned on him. 'Er, yes. It's... it's gone.'

She, Seldon and Clifford exchanged a baffled look.

'Constable,' Clifford said, speaking evenly to ease the policeman's obvious nerves. 'What *exactly* has gone?'

Quilter spread his hands out. 'The lot, Mr Clifford. The whole, bleedin' lot!'

40

Eleanor took control. 'Constable, sit down,' she said firmly. Once he was seated at the table, she continued. 'Now, tell us from the beginning what happened.'

Quilter fumbled with his helmet in his hands. 'It was like this, your ladyship. Mr Seldon and me had just locked them items of evidence in the trunk.' He looked at Seldon for confirmation.

'Absolutely. I saw you lock it securely and pocket the key.'

'Exactly, sir,' Quilter said eagerly. 'Well, once you'd left, I tried ringing Blackington police station but couldn't get through. Odd thing was, normally there's still some crackling, or popping like on the line, but this time nothing. Only usually happens like that when it comes down 'cos of snow or a storm. Well, there weren't neither.'

The prickle of dread she'd felt earlier increased. 'So what did you do then, Constable?'

'Naturally, I puts the kettle on. Thought I'd try again in ten minutes. But, blow me down, I'd only just turned the gas on, when a blood— Sorry, m'lady, a bleedin' great rock comes smashing through me window and lands right at me feet!'

Seldon groaned. 'Did you, by any chance, leave the police station in pursuit of the culprit, Constable?'

Quilter nodded vigorously. 'Of course, sir! Went straight after the bug— er, assailant. These old feet can move a sight faster than you might think to look at them when I'm riled, like.'

'I'm sure they can, Constable. But did you catch the culprit?'

Quilter looked crestfallen. 'Almost, sir. I just about kept up with him. And I can tell you, he led me a merry dance.' He dropped his gaze. 'Truth is, though, I lost him in the end.'

Eleanor's breath caught, remembering Luna leading her to Ned's body.

Seldon glanced at her and Clifford. She braced herself. 'And when you returned to the police house. You found...' At Quilter's hesitation, she stepped in again. 'That the trunk was open and the' – she swallowed – 'evidence gone, perhaps?'

Quilter kept his eyes down. 'Yes, m'lady. I realise now that it were all a ruse. The rock thrown through me window was so I chased them. And they kept themselves just in view, so I'd keep chasing. But far enough away, so I couldn't recognise who it were in the dark.'

She kept her tone neutral. 'Constable. Could you say whether it was a him? Or a her?'

He shrugged. 'Couldn't rightly say, m'lady. They was too cunning. Avoided any lit areas, they did.'

She groaned to herself. It wasn't what she wanted to hear.

Seldon's brow was increasingly furrowed. 'Had the lock on the trunk been forced? Or sprung when you returned?'

'Sprung, sir. There weren't no sign of force being used.'

Seldon shared a meaningful look with Clifford. She understood. The lock had obviously been a strong one. Otherwise, Seldon would never have agreed to place the evidence in the trunk.

Quilter scratched the back of his head. 'I feel like I'm missing something here, sir.'

'For someone to have opened a lock of that type that quickly,' Clifford said. 'Given that you were away from the building a matter of minutes only I'm sure, Constable?'

'Five or six, Mr Clifford.' He fiddled with his helmet again. 'Well, maybe ten at most.'

'Which denotes,' Clifford continued, 'organisation and skill beyond that of the ordinary local criminal.'

'And,' Seldon continued, 'that even though we may not be dealing with more than one murderer, we are definitely dealing with more than one criminal. An accomplice must have taken the evidence while the first person kept you occupied.'

She groaned. That only reinforced the possibility that... Her eyes widened. 'Constable, did Babcock see anyone breaking into the trunk?'

He shook his head. 'Curtain were drawn. I drew 'em as I left. Don't rightly know why, but I always do when leaving if someone's in the cell. Babcock did say as how he heard someone, though. He called out, but there weren't no reply.'

She slapped the table. 'But at least it proves Babcock wasn't one of the criminals, as he was locked in a cell at the time. Surely even the Blackington detective would agree with that?'

Seldon see-sawed his head. 'Not necessarily. Babcock definitely saw Quilter and me put the evidence in the trunk. The curtain was open before we left. I remember.'

Clifford nodded. 'So Miss Luna, or another suspect,' he added quickly at her look, 'could have distracted Quilter long enough for Babcock to have picked his cell lock and then that of the trunk. Whoever was capable of one would have been capable of the other. Most rural cell locks are crude in the extreme. No slight on yourself, Constable.'

'None taken, Mr Clifford,' Quilter said.

'So,' Seldon continued. 'Babcock hides the evidence just

outside... possibly round the back, say, in the woods, and hurriedly returns and relocks his cell.'

'Remembering to pull the curtain closed, sir.'

'Exactly, Clifford. I'm sorry, Eleanor, but the only way to prove his innocence, or Luna's for that matter, is still with our plan tonight. And that's, well...'

'In tatters!' she finished for him.

They were interrupted by Ansel coming in. 'Hello. Sorry, am I interrupting?'

Eleanor tutted. 'Of course not, Reverend. It is your vicarage. We missed you at dinner.'

His face fell. 'Oh, yes! Mrs Jordan was rather worse than usual, so I offered to stay with her longer.'

Mrs Trotman appeared in the doorway. 'We made sure there was some dinner left, in case you was still hungry when you got back, Reverend.'

'That was very thoughtful, Mrs Trotman,' he said with a beaming smile. 'Do excuse me all, won't you? I am rather famished.'

As Ansel left, Eleanor caught Quilter mutter something.

'Sorry, Constable?'

'Oh, nothing, m'lady. I was just thinking out loud to meself that I thought only this morning old Mrs Jordan were on the mend. Goes to show, you never knows, do you?'

Her chest tightened.

Or do you, Ellie? The reverend was rather conveniently absent when someone threw a large rock through Quilter's front window.

She shook herself. They knew who the murderer was, didn't they? She was just becoming increasingly paranoid!

Quilter cleared his throat. 'I owe you an apology, sir. You offered to help me solve these here murders. And you've kept your end of the bargain. But all I've done, I feel, is undone all the good work you've put in.'

She, Seldon and Clifford looked at each other in discomfort. An unspoken agreement passed between the three members of The Byron Detective Agency.

'Constable,' Seldon said, shaking his head. 'I have a confession to make on behalf of the agency. And an apology to give you. I kept important information back from you when it was your case. And more damningly, when I should have realised having a man like you in the know would have been invaluable.'

Quilter stood straighter and looked Seldon in the eye. 'I'm sure you had your reasons, sir. But perhaps it might be better in future if I'm kept up to date with developments, as it were?'

'You have my word,' Seldon said without hesitation, bringing him up to date immediately. When he'd finished. Quilter scratched the top of his head.

'Crikey, sir! I can see why you wanted no one, including me, to know 'bout this. Fewer the better.'

'Thank you for your understanding, Constable. Unfortunately, the only update left is the unpleasant truth that with the evidence gone, no jury would ever convict anyone we, or the Blackington detective, put in front of them. It probably wouldn't even get as far as a trial!'

'Shouldn't imagine it would, sir.'

Seldon grimaced. 'But equally important, if not more so, is the loss of the items Eleanor discovered hidden in the gravestone. That is a serious blow on its own.'

'Mrs Butters!'

Eleanor's housekeeper jumped. 'Sorry, Mr Clifford. Missed the cup there.'

His eyebrow rose. 'I have never observed you "miss" a cup while pouring tea, Mrs Butters. Is something ailing you?'

'Er, no, Mr Clifford.' She shot Eleanor a worried look.

Seldon glanced between them. 'Why do I get the impression everyone is in on something, and I'm not?'

'Don't feel so good, does it?' Eleanor's sharp hearing caught Quilter mutter to himself.

'Actually, Constable, my husband, and Clifford, are as in the dark as you are. The thing is... I had a... sort of premonition. Well, maybe nothing quite that strong. I think I was just loath to part with our new find or take even the smallest risk it might disappear.'

Seldon turned to Mrs Butters with a quizzical look. At Eleanor's nod, she coughed.

'Well, her ladyship might just have asked me to sew... certain items into her petticoat.'

'That is enough information, thank you, Mrs Butters,' Clifford said hurriedly.

Seldon's look of stupefaction slowly turned into a grin that spread across his face. 'I imagine you are referring to our recent find?' At the housekeeper's nod, Seldon switched his gaze to Eleanor. 'You are quite amazing! So, what exactly was that hidden with the clay samples?'

'Oh, that, Hugh?' she said nonchalantly. 'Just some of Mrs Butters' old sewing patterns.'

He laughed uproariously. 'So, there you go, Constable. I got dished some of my own medicine! And grateful I am for it!' His expression sobered. 'We've won half the war, for the moment, thanks to you, Eleanor. And to your sewing prowess, Mrs Butters. Now, what can we do about the other half? Without the rest of the evidence, what we've got left is still not enough to convict anyone. Unless their fingerprints are found on it, and I can't believe anyone running this kind of operation would be that sloppy.'

'Nor me, sir,' Clifford said.

Seldon let out a deep breath. 'So how do we trap the murderer and his accomplice, with most of our evidence gone?'

A steely smile slowly spread across Eleanor's face. 'Exactly as we originally intended, Hugh.'

At his, Clifford and Quilter's confused look, she nodded slowly. 'Think about it! The killer will still have to show up tonight, otherwise they are going to appear mighty suspicious. And they must be itching for a chance to get their ill-gotten gains back. They know we must still have them. And as we believe they have cut the police line, they know we haven't had an opportunity to tell anyone about our find yet.'

'Well done, my lady,' Clifford said. 'You are right! The killer, and his, or her, accomplice, are the only ones who actually know we have basically no evidence now. But they dare not show it, or they will blow their cover.'

'Exactly!' Her eyes glinted again. 'And there's one other ace we have. Or will have. Which, again, the killer and accomplice won't be able to do anything about without revealing themselves.' She clapped her hands. 'Tonight we go on the counterattack and hoist them with their own petard!'

'I'm game!' Quilter grunted. 'Or would be, if I knew what that meant.'

She laughed. 'It means we'll string them up by their own under—'

'My lady!'

41

Despite Eleanor's fighting words of only a few hours ago, she felt a rush of nerves stepping into the room. They'd gone over as many scenarios as they could think of, but in her heart she knew they could never have all angles covered. When you cornered a poisonous snake, it would lash out. That much was certain. But when you cornered a cunning killer, you could never second-guess exactly how they would respond.

And the killer had already proved how cunning they were. Stealing evidence from under their noses as well as falsifying that recording. But tonight they were going to turn the killer's audaciousness and arrogance against them.

If they turn up, Ellie!

She went to the window and stared out again, searching in the gloom. But no one was hurrying up the drive. She rolled her shoulders back. She couldn't put the moment off any longer.

Her entrance into Pritchard's study caused a ripple of anticipation. And, she noted in some quarters, unease. On either side of the desk stood Seldon and Quilter. Facing them on various chairs were Mathilde, Blythe, Dora, Digger, Jarrett, Dunstan and Luna. Sitting to one side, nearest to Quilter, was Babcock, handcuffed. On the other side, nearest to Seldon, sat Ansel.

With more confidence than she felt, she walked over and stood in front of the desk, trying hard not to think about the empty desktop behind her. The one that should have been laid out with evidence from the trunk in Quilter's police station.

Okay, Ellie. So, it was round one to the killer. Now, it's your turn.

'Good evening, ladies and gentlemen, I'm sorry for dragging you over here at this late hour. But as the detective from Blackington can't take Mr Babcock away until tomorrow, we thought we'd make productive use of the time and clear up a few loose ends concerning Mr Unwin and Mr Yearth's deaths. So when the dust settles after the terrible events of the last few days, there are no recriminations. After all, we'll soon be ringing in the New Year, so it will be good to start with a clean slate, won't it?'

'That might be,' Mathilde grumbled bitterly. 'But it's nigh on midnight and I've to be up early as ever tomorrow. Angel's Summons don't run itself, you know.'

Eleanor nodded understandingly. 'Of course. You do have your sister to help you.'

'Fat lot of use she is,' Mathilde muttered.

'Why you—' Blythe exploded.

Eleanor frowned as if suddenly recalling something. 'By the way, Mathilde, wasn't it around the time Unwin was killed you told us that Blythe had slipped out of the Angel's Summons?'

Blythe rounded on her sister. 'Why, you little sneak! And... and liar!'

'Shut up!' Mathilde hissed.

'Ladies!' Seldon's strenuous voice called. 'The sooner you let Lady Swift say her piece, the sooner you can all go home to your beds.'

It's working, Ellie.

Quilter and Seldon had roused everyone out of their beds and bundled them straight down to Waketon Court with the minimum of explanation. Hence tempers and nerves were already frayed. Which was just what they needed if they were going to have any chance of unmasking the killer.

'Thank you, Mr Seldon,' Eleanor said. 'Now, where was I? Oh, yes, the late hour is necessary. This is around when Mr Unwin was murdered, which is a fitting time to have this little chat, I'm sure you'll agree? And we are in his uncle's study, because, well, you'll find out why soon enough.'

She half-turned towards the desk and then spun back.

Drat it, Ellie. Remember, there's no actual evidence to show them. Yet.

'Mr Seldon?'

He shot her a quizzical glance. She shrugged apologetically.

Where the devil is Clifford, Ellie? The whole show is about to collapse before it's begun.

Seldon took her place in front of the desk. He cleared his throat. 'Right. Er, let's start with Mr Unwin's death. He was killed between midnight and twenty-five past on Christmas Eve—'

''Ere, 'ang on!' Digger looked suspiciously at Seldon. 'How can you be so definite, like?'

'Babcock obviously confessed and told Quilter when he done it,' Mathilde snapped.

'If he had,' Blythe said, turning on her sister, 'he'd have known the exact time, wouldn't he, clever clogs!'

'We'll explain exactly how we know this later,' Seldon continued quickly. 'Now, he was killed in the churchyard, not outside his study by a prowler, which is what we believe the killer initially intended the police to believe. However, the killer was forced to change his plan because of a telegram Mr Unwin had already sent to The Byron Detective Agency. It was our imminent arrival that led the killer to drape Mr Unwin's body over his uncle's gravestone.'

Digger shook his head. 'That never did make no sense to me. Why didn't Babcock hide 'im?'

'Constable?' Seldon said with a hint of desperation Eleanor hoped only she noticed.

'Because, Digger,' Quilter said, nodding understandingly and smartly switching places with Seldon, 'he didn't have time to hide the body. And he'd already been forced to bash 'im on the head, so he couldn't pass it off as an accident, could he?' Quilter hesitated, glancing at Eleanor. She quickly stepped in.

'Exactly, Constable. You see, Digger, we are sure now it was nothing but a red herring to try and throw us off the scent of what was really happening in that graveyard that night.'

She paused, looking pensive. 'Although, if I'm being completely accurate, in one way, Mr Pritchard's grave had nothing to do with Mr Unwin's death. But, in another, everything.'

The room erupted into chaos. She held up her hands.

'I'm not being purposefully obtuse. All will become clear shortly. Dora?'

The young woman jumped. 'What?'

'Sorry. I was trying to attract Jarrett's attention and as he's sitting next to you... Do you mind?'

'You've got my attention, Lady Swift,' Jarrett said stiffly.

'Good. I was wondering when you agreed to make Mr Pritchard's gravestone, if you ever imagined it would be responsible for two deaths?'

The whole room fell silent. All eyes swivelled to Jarrett. He licked his lips, but kept her gaze. 'I have no idea what you are talking about. How could I poss—'

She raised a finger imperiously. 'Actually, you are right. It was a silly question. Mr Seldon?'

As they swapped places again, Seldon caught her eye and

nodded imperceptibly at the clock on the mantelpiece. She nodded back grimly.

How much longer can we keep this delaying tactic going, Ellie? Where the devil is Clifford?

The door to the hallway opened a fraction and the man in question poked his head in. She didn't catch what Seldon said, but it was enough to turn all eyes, and ears, his way. Taking advantage, she slipped out of the room.

'Where have you been?' she hissed. 'We're winging it in there by the seats of our—'

Clifford shuddered. 'I can well imagine by the seats of what, my lady. And my apologies. Professor Pike, or our "secret weapon" as you refer to him that we went "fishing" for earlier, was waiting in his house as arranged.'

'Then what took you so long?'

'I had to sober the gentleman up sufficiently first to remember who I was,' he said drily. 'And then who he was. And most importantly, to remember what he had promised to assist us with this evening.'

Her mouth fell open. She let out a long breath of relief. 'Anyway, thank goodness you got him sobered up and here. Now, the real fireworks can begi—' Her heart sank at his expression. 'Clifford. He isn't here, is he?'

'No, my lady. He is at the vicarage. Mrs Butters is at this moment forcing a litre of strong black coffee down his throat accompanied by another litre of my quickest acting hangover cure. She will bring him straight here afterwards. I estimate that to be between five and ten minutes' time.'

She groaned. When the hero in the penny dreadful novels she devoured regularly arranged a showdown with the villain, it was never this farcical! If their secret weapon wasn't there soon, sober or not, it could mean the difference between catching a killer. Or not.

'Right.' She cocked her ear. 'By the sound of that lot in

there, they're ready to mutiny and leave. I've no choice. I have to start the real show now. Wish me luck.'

Go knock 'em dead, Ellie.

She winced at her choice of words and walked back into Pritchard's study where it had all begun three nights ago when she, Seldon and Clifford had first listened to that recording. And tonight, it would end the same way.

42

Eleanor walked back into what seemed like a full-on riot. On seeing her, Quilter raised his voice.

'Right, you lot! Anyone who isn't in their seat in the next ten seconds is going straight to my cell until the morning! And I don't care how many of you are in there at once. I'll fit the lot of you in if needs be!'

With bad grace, their audience reluctantly retook their places, grumbling loudly.

'And I want quiet so Lady Swift can hear herself speak!'

Eleanor recalled the first time they'd met Quilter, and the way he'd commanded the villagers to go home after Midnight Mass. Behind his easy-going exterior, there was a streak of steel.

Once everyone had quietened down, she held her hands up. 'Listen, please. I'll only say this once. At the start of this little soirée, I said I wanted to clear up a few loose ends concerning Mr Unwin and Mr Yearth's deaths. Well, the main "loose end", as it were, concerns the culprit. You see, Mr Babcock did not kill Mr Unwin. Or Ned. We will now show you all incontrovertible evidence that will reveal the true killer.'

Dunstan was the first to break the stunned silence. 'That's a bold claim, Lady Swift. How exactly do you intend to prove it?'

She held up a finger. 'Ah! I'm glad you asked that.' She stepped to one side and indicated the desk. 'The astute among you may have noticed the empty desktop behind me. It was supposed to be laid out with the evidence I just mentioned. However, it was stolen earlier this evening.'

Jarrett smirked. 'A little careless, I must say.'

She smiled sweetly. 'You see, the killer bungled this evening's burglary as comprehensively as they did their amateur efforts at disguising their disgusting deeds. Not only did they fail to regain the very thing they desperately wanted and had originally hidden in Mr Pritchard's gravestone, but they also failed to steal one vital piece of evidence. The one piece of evidence that is going to see them hanged!'

On cue, Clifford entered the study. 'The first evidence we will present tonight is this.' He produced several handfuls of clay fragments and placed each carefully on the desk. Their audience craned their necks forward and then exchanged puzzled glances.

Eleanor crossed her fingers. They'd had no time to go back and collect new samples and analyse them again, so each pile was exactly the same clay, hurriedly collected from around Luna's cabin. But, she thought grimly, only the killer would guess that. However, as they'd worked out, they couldn't say anything without blowing their cover.

'I must remind everyone,' Clifford said, 'that Miss Lyndseer was actually accused of these crimes before Constable Quilter arrested Mr Babcock. And she is still currently under suspicion for aiding and abetting him. Kindly keep that in mind.' He indicated each pile as he spoke. 'The first sample was found in the vicinity of Mr Unwin's body. The next in the vicinity of Mr Yearth's. One would, therefore, expect them to be the same if Miss Lyndseer had committed both crimes. However, they are not. The first sample does indeed match the clay Miss Lyndseer collects from a quarry near her to make her pipes. However, the second found at Lyndseer Castle near Mr Yearth's body does not. It does, however, match clay found... elsewhere.'

It seemed as if Eleanor's attention was fully focused on Clifford. But, in reality, she was watching a certain person who had just developed a full-blown facial tic.

'From which we conclude,' Clifford continued, 'that the real killer placed the second sample by Mr Yearth's body in an attempt to incriminate Miss Lyndseer. But in doing so, has instead incriminated themselves.'

There was a general shuffling among their audience.

Seldon stepped in. 'The second piece of evidence we will present wasn't stolen, but, ironically, can't be produced as it is rather bulky. I am referring, of course, to Mr Pritchard's gravestone.'

'You see,' Eleanor said, 'when I told you that Mr Pritchard's gravestone had nothing to do with Mr Unwin's death, and yet, at the same time, everything, I wasn't being obtuse.'

Seldon nodded. 'The reason being, Mr Pritchard's gravestone had indeed nothing to do with it. But the *replica* gravestone that it was replaced with, did!'

Digger shook his head in disbelief. 'You telling us that there gravestone on Pritchard's grave ain't real?'

'Oh, it is real, alright, Mr Dilkes,' she said. 'It just isn't the one Jarrett originally made. Is it?' She flashed Jarrett a quizzical look, and then looked away before he could respond. But, in that brief glance, she swore she saw murder in his eyes.

Clifford cleared his throat loudly over the general hubbub. 'The lack of extensive lichen growth and the sinking of one end of the gravestone both provided the evidence. Evidence that shows the current gravestone was placed there not five years ago, but considerably less than five *months* ago. Initially, I misinterpreted the subsidence as the action of worms, but now realise that it was the action of humans, not bedding in the replica sufficiently. Although, to be fair, as the reverend will confirm, they were acting by torchlight and were disturbed.'

Ansel nodded. 'I can indeed confirm that, having been the one to unwittingly disturb them.'

Jarrett jumped to his feet. 'You can't really have us believe this nonsense?'

She shook her head pityingly. 'Oh, dear! I hadn't realised just how much you've been kept in the dark. You really have no idea what we found in the hidden compartment you made within the replica gravestone, do you, Jarrett?'

'A most ingenious design, I have to say,' Clifford said. 'Concealing the opening with real lichen taken from other gravestones was genius.'

Jarrett spun around.

'Stay where you are!' Quilter blocked his path, brandishing his truncheon menacingly. 'If you don't want a nasty crack on your head like the one you gave Mr Unwin and Ned, I suggest you sit down. And listen to the rest of what we got to say.'

Reluctantly, Jarrett sank back into his chair.

Eleanor let out a deep breath. That was the first half of the plan executed successfully. The easy part. The second part would be the tough one. So far, the evidence they'd presented wasn't enough to convict anyone. And she was sure Jarrett knew it. He'd just panicked for a moment. But it wouldn't last. They needed to keep turning the screw.

43

'Now,' Seldon said. 'We need to go back to Miss Lyndseer. Just like Reverend Ansel, she also "met" the killer, and their accomplice. The night before Mr Unwin's murder. Although, unlike the reverend, they were unaware of her presence.' He turned to her. 'Would you kindly repeat what you overheard in St Cuthbert's cemetery that night?'

Luna nodded. 'The man said, "We'll do it tomorrow night for sure. The reverend will cover us!"'

All eyes spun to Ansel. Seldon raised his hand.

'I need to make it unequivocally clear that Reverend Ansel had no part in this. The Midnight Mass he conducted was used unbeknown to him to cover up—'

'Poor Unwin's murder!' Blythe sobbed.

'Actually,' Eleanor said, 'no. But we're getting ahead of ourselves. If you remember, Mr Seldon told you that Mr Unwin was killed between midnight and twelve twenty-five. Let me explain now how we know this.'

She bit her lip. Jarrett had shown no reaction at the last few revelations. He looked as if he was set in stone. And the next one was their last throw of the dice.

She half-turned and then stopped. 'Actually, we won't show you. "Seeing is believing" is normally a good adage, but in this case, hearing will be much more convincing!'

As Clifford uncovered Unwin's home recording unit, Eleanor held up a finger. 'Earlier, I said I'd explain why we needed to have this meeting in Mr Pritchard's study. This is why.' She waited as Clifford produced a black disc and placed it on the turntable. She stiffened, sure she saw Jarrett move. Obviously Quilter thought so too, as he raised his truncheon threateningly.

Clifford lowered the needle and a perfect replica of the recording they'd listened to in that very study on Christmas Eve floated across the room. She held her breath. But Clifford had done an amazing job imitating the original voice and recording it onto the one remaining blank disc they'd found stored with the machine. Mixed in with the crackling, popping and hissing, his voice was indistinguishable from the original Babcock had passed to them when they'd first arrived at Waketon Court. And the wording was exactly the same, as he'd read it off the transcription he'd written out.

With grim satisfaction, she could see utter disbelief showing on Jarrett's face.

'You thought you'd stolen it, didn't you?' she muttered. 'And yet, here it is!' *Make what you will of that!* she thought grimly, knowing again he daren't say anything without fear of blowing his cover.

As the voice ended and the odd noises started up, she put her finger to her lips. 'Listen carefully, everyone! What can you hear, excluding a microphone falling over, a chair scraping back and French windows being opened? Anything?'

A series of head shakes and shrugs answered her.

Clifford stopped the recording.

She let the silence grow. Finally, Mathilde spoke up. 'So we didn't hear anything. What does that prove?'

'We know the recording was done during Midnight Mass. And yet, there was no sound of organ music. Or singing. Both would have registered otherwise. Even faintly. We checked. Especially as the French windows were opened towards the end. Now, we were shown into this very study on the night in question at just gone twelve thirty, so the recording had to have been made before then. Reverend Ansel, you started Mass around eleven thirty, isn't that right?'

Ansel nodded. 'Yes. Although it was probably more like eleven forty, allowing for stragglers.'

'And what did you do initially?'

'I played a few appropriate organ pieces while Dunstan made sure everyone was settled and had the order of service and hymn books. Then I played, and the congregation sang, some festive carols to get us in the mood for the Mass proper.'

'So when did you stop carolling and organ-ing, as it were?'

'Just before midnight. After a few essentials, I basically went straight into my sermon. A little unorthodox, perhaps, but what isn't in Yorelow? And I'd found from previous Masses that the congregation's attention span can, er, wane rather early.'

'Which means,' Eleanor said, 'the recording must have been made between midnight and twelve-twenty-five during the reverend's sermon as earlier there would have been the background sound of an organ, or singing. And any later, and we couldn't have listened to it when we arrived.' She hesitated. 'There is one minor detail I must mention, however. That recording you just heard is fake.'

This time Jarrett didn't try to hide his fury. 'What the devil are you trying to pull here?'

'Nothing,' she said innocently. 'I'm sorry for any confusion. To be crystal clear, what I meant was, it was never recorded by Mr Unwin.'

Well, the original we copied never was, Ellie.

For a moment there was complete silence, then Blythe spoke. 'Then who was it recorded by?'

'The killer, of course,' Eleanor said nonchalantly. 'Jarrett.'

Jarrett flew out of his chair. 'How dare you make such an accusation! There's no way you can back that up.'

'Oh, but there is. Clifford?'

'Yes, my lady.' As he walked out of the study, everyone held their breath.

'Oh, by the way, while we're waiting,' she said casually, 'I promised to explain the difference in the clay fragments found near Mr Unwin's body as opposed to those found near Ned's. The ones planted by the killer. The former were pure clay. Whereas the latter were contaminated with sand. We took a sample of sand from your mortar supplies, Jarrett. And we also found a few fragments of clay you carelessly hadn't cleared up properly when you made that clay pipe you subsequently ground into fragments and then scattered near Ned's body. They both contained the same type of sand. The sand we took from your yard.'

For a moment, she was sure Jarrett was going to leap over the chairs in front of him and attack her. He was visibly shaking. Clifford's return seemed to make him change his mind. She waited on tenterhooks until... Pike entered. Eleanor felt her knees almost give way with relief.

Clifford led him to the front of the desk.

'Good evening, Professor Pike,' Seldon said. 'I know most people know you in Yorelow, obviously. But could you just state your area of expertise?'

She scrutinised him. You could only really tell he'd been drinking if you looked closely at his still slightly bloodshot eyes. Or noticed one hand holding the desk gingerly behind him.

'Er, I'm a professor of phonetics.'

'Has anyone here seen George Bernard Shaw's fascinating

play, *Pygmalion*?' Clifford said conversationally. 'I believe it toured the provinces a few years ago.'

Apparently, nobody had.

'Perhaps you'd better explain what a professor of phonetics is an expert in then?' Seldon said.

Pike's eyes lit up. 'Well, er, in the application of phonetics obviously. And phonology, of course. And in language acquisition. Also sociolinguistics, speech science, language patterning and so forth. In broad terms...'

Eleanor groaned. Never again would she tease Clifford about how long-winded and obscure his explanations were!

Seldon came to the rescue. 'In layman's terms, would it be fair to say you are an expert in the study of human speech, Professor Pike? Specifically, how it sounds?'

Pike nodded enthusiastically.

'And therefore,' Seldon continued, 'you can readily match a recording of someone's voice with that person? Even if it is of poor quality and the person has deliberately tried to disguise their voice?'

'Oh, yes,' Pike said, almost disinterestedly. 'I thought Mr Clifford had a real challenge for me.'

'Which means,' Seldon said gravely, 'you should be able to readily identify which of your neighbours' voice it is on this recording?'

Pike shrugged. 'Nothing easier!'

Eleanor allowed herself a grim smile of satisfaction as Clifford picked up the disc to place it on the player again.

Only he got no further. Jarrett leapt up and turned on Dunstan. 'You lied to me from the start, you cur! You set me up from the beginning!' He lunged and pulled... a pistol from what she could only imagine was a poacher's pocket in Dunstan's coat. 'I didn't help you steal that damn recording for you to hand it back to them so they could put a noose around my neck!' In a flash, he vaulted over the row of chairs in front, just as she'd imagined him doing. She closed her eyes instinctively as he aimed and fired.

As the roar of the gun echoed off the walls, she opened her eyes to see Jarrett crumpling to the floor as Quilter brought his truncheon down on the back of his head. Quilter's eyes glinted. 'You can make a fool of me once, Jarrett. But not twice!' she heard him mutter.

She spun around to see Clifford brushing shards of black disc off his jacket.

'Are you alright?' she demanded breathlessly.

'Perfectly, my lady. Jarrett's shot was most impressive. Dead centre. Alas, the recording is no more. But perhaps?'

He nodded towards Seldon who was aiming a revolver at Dunstan, everyone else having crowded to one side of the room. She walked over with Clifford who searched Dunstan's poacher jacket, producing a rather familiar knife.

'So, Dunstan, what do you have to say for yourself?'

He glared at her. 'I have no idea what you mean. I have nothing to hide.'

'Except, it seems, a gun, and a knife that was part of a set of three, I think. We still have the other two.' She shrugged. 'It doesn't matter whether you say anything or not. Once he regains consciousness' – she nodded at Jarrett still lying on the floor – 'he'll sing like four and twenty Christmas blackbirds to save his own skin. You see, you were far too cool a customer to crack under any pressure we could bring to bear, I'll give you that. But your accomplice, Jarrett? That was a different story. And all we needed was for him to incriminate you. Which, with the few pieces of evidence we do have remaining, will be enough to convict you of the murder of Inigo Unwin and Ned. And complicity in the murder of Professor Charles Hunt and the stealing of plans of national importance to this country. Goodnight. I'll see you at the trial.'

As Seldon and Quilter made sure the two men were

securely handcuffed and then led them away, she suddenly had an overwhelming urge to be sitting at a kitchen table with her ladies—

'And the terrible two nestled either side, along with a glass of Mrs Trotman's home-brewed sloe gin, perhaps, my lady?'

She shook her head. 'You know, Clifford, if you become any better at mind reading, they will definitely hang you as a witch!'

44

'But how did you know it was Dunstan, m'lady?'

Eleanor looked around the bustling kitchen. It was the following morning, and the ladies were preparing a celebration lunch, while she and Seldon drank coffee and filled them in on the drama of the night before. Everyone having been far too tired and wrung out to do so when they'd finally returned to the vicarage in the early hours.

'To be completely transparent, Mrs Butters,' she said, sipping her piping-hot coffee with care, 'we didn't suspect Dunstan any more than most of our other suspects. And a good deal less than some! Until, that is, we discovered the plans hidden in the gravestone. That changed everything. It was immediately obvious that Unwin's murder, and almost certainly Ned's too, was tied up with the theft of Professor Hunt's plans. And not the result of any feud going on in Yorelow itself.'

Seldon nodded. 'The theft of the plans and the professor's murder were obviously the work of an organised gang. One who knew exactly what they were doing and how they were going to sell the plans afterwards. To the highest bidder, irrespective of whether they were enemies of this country or not, I can guarantee! And they were smart enough to realise the police would probably suspect them immediately and pull them. Several of them already had form.'

'Which basically means they were known to the police, as you know,' she added.

Seldon nodded. 'Therefore, they had to divest themselves of the stolen plans as soon as possible. Then, they could collect them again later when things had calmed down.'

'And what better place to hide them than Yorelow, the most out-of-the-way hamlet in England?' she added. 'Especially as they had a contact here. Dunstan.'

'The first clue that singled him out was that he hadn't lived in Yorelow long,' Seldon said. 'Which meant there was more chance he had links to the gang than our other suspects. Excluding the reverend, that is, who also hadn't been here that long. But he had a watertight alibi. And even at the time, I didn't buy Dunstan's cock and bull sob-story about splitting up from his wife. We reckon now he had to hide away in Yorelow, either because he did a job that went wrong, or he upset someone he shouldn't have.'

'The second clue,' Eleanor continued, 'was that Dunstan also had the perfect cover. As a delivery driver, he could meet with the gang in some remote spot and be passed the plans without anyone knowing. And all without any of the gang having to come to Yorelow. Which was essential. They had no direct link with the place in case the police did pull them in.'

'The third clue,' Seldon said, 'was Dunstan mentioning that Staffordshire was one of the counties he covered as a delivery driver. And Professor Hunt's house is in Butterton in Staffordshire.'

'I remember the newspaper Clifford originally showed me back at Henley Hall mentioning it,' Eleanor added.

'And,' Seldon raised a finger, 'clue four. Why would a chap from Birmingham volunteer to be the churchwarden the minute he moved to Yorelow? That was odd in itself. But the clincher was when Clifford mentioned the duties of a churchwarden as laid down by the Canons of the Church of England, Dunstan looked completely blank. And once we found the plans hidden in the churchyard, his behaviour became more than suspicious!'

'All this was enough on its own to make Dunstan our leading suspect,' Eleanor said. 'But there was one last clue on top of that. One that meant only Dunstan could be the killer.'

By now all work had temporarily ceased as Polly and Lizzie stood at the other side of the table, wide-eyed, Mrs Trotman and Mrs Butters beside them.

'And what clue was that, your ladyship?'

'The timing of Unwin's death, Polly. Between midnight and twenty-five past, as we told our captive audience at that little showdown last night. Although, we'd actually narrowed it down further to between midnight and at the latest ten past, but we thought it would sound too unbelievable.' She laughed. 'And from the look on your face, I can see I was right. Ah! Clifford. Perhaps you'd like to explain?'

Clifford entered the kitchen, Kofi skipping in ahead of him. 'I too want to hear the rest of this remarkable tale!' the boy said. 'Mr Clifford has only told me some.'

'Well, young man.' Clifford put his arm around the boy's shoulders. 'Knowing what we knew at that stage, it was reasonable enough to assume Mr Unwin was killed because he disturbed Dunstan hiding the plans in Mr Pritchard's gravestone. Now, ask yourself; why did Dunstan need Reverend Ansel to cover him hiding the plans in the first place? Everyone would have been in the church until well gone one a.m. Why did the killer choose then to hide the plans specifically during the reverend's sermon? My lady?'

She took up the thread. 'Then we realised. The reverend said before the sermon he played the organ while Dunstan dealt with stragglers, and then the congregation sang hymns and

Dunstan handed out hymn books and so forth. And during other parts of the Mass, Dunstan, as churchwarden, had other functions. Only during the sermon did he have a reasonable period of time when he wasn't required. When he could slip out of the church without anyone noticing. Only Dunstan among all our suspects would have benefited from this. And when he did, the congregation would think nothing more than he'd gone for a...' Out of the corner of her eye she saw Clifford's horrified expression. 'For a comfort break and a cigarette was all I was going to say,' she fibbed.

Seldon hid a smile. 'Which basically wraps up why we knew it was Dunstan. But how did we know how he actually committed the murder? And why we know it must have been between the times we said? Well, he slipped out when the sermon started, but Unwin was already poking about the grave. So Dunstan grabbed the first thing he could lay his hands on, which happened to be the herald trumpet, and bashed Unwin on the back of the head with it. So that must have been between the start of the sermon at midnight, and at the most five to ten minutes later.'

'And from Babcock's confession to Clifford before our little showdown,' Eleanor continued, 'we know Dunstan used the bench seat to wheel Unwin over to Waketon Court. He hoped to make it look as if an intruder killed him in a bungled robbery. Babcock interrupted him and, to cut to the chase, at gunpoint Dunstan forced Babcock to place his fingerprints on the murder weapon, having wiped his own off first.'

'And everyone in Yorelow knew Babcock wanted to get rid of Unwin,' Seldon continued. 'So when Dunstan told him he'd tell the police he'd heard a disturbance while having a cigarette break during the sermon, come over, and' – he spread his hands – 'caught Babcock with Unwin's body and the murder weapon, Babcock had no choice but to cooperate. Having checked with Babcock that we'd never heard Unwin's voice, he returned to the graveyard and placed Unwin's body on Pritchard's grave as a red herring. Then he returned to the church before the end of the reverend's sermon, dashed off what he wanted Jarrett to say and sent him over to make the recording Babcock was to give to us. Which is why we knew it would panic Jarrett into action when we played the fake recording we made. He was convinced Professor Pike would recognise his voice.'

'Although,' Clifford said, 'there was always the small possibility that the professor might have realised it was someone else trying to sound like Jarrett. Luckily, however, Jarrett reacted immediately.'

'All of which is why,' she said, 'we knew there was no point in trying to panic Dunstan into revealing he was the killer. He was obviously far too quick-thinking and cool under pressure for that. The way he dealt with Ned reinforced that.'

'Speaking of that, m'lady, why was that other poor man done in?' Mrs Butters said.

'Ned? Well, we knew he had been shadowing Babcock because he was helping Dora and Digger meet. So, we reckon he was keeping an eye on Waketon Court that night. And he either got discovered and dealt with. Or saw what was going on and foolishly tried to blackmail Dunstan. Dunstan killed him with the same murder weapon he'd used on Unwin. But I imagine he put on gloves so he didn't smudge Babcock's fingerprints. Then he got his accomplice, Jarrett, to make a clay pipe, a simple job for him. Dunstan then ground it up and scattered some of the fragments near Ned's body to incriminate Luna at the same time as Babcock. I assume, Dunstan had come to the conclusion by then that Luna was too much of a threat to leave be.'

Lizzie shook her head. 'Ah cannae believe it! Whit a terrible man, m'lady. His heart must be made o' stone!'

'Granite, I think, Lizzie. Which is why we went for the

softer target, Jarrett. Who only works with stone as opposed to being made of it!'

Mrs Trotman rubbed her eyes. 'Thing that's still puzzling me, m'lady, is why that man Dunstan went to all the trouble to fake Mr Unwin's voice and make that there recording?'

'Well, Mrs Trotman, Babcock told us he was forced to tell Dunstan about the telegram Unwin had sent the agency. And when Dunstan demanded to know who Unwin had asked to investigate, he hit the roof! He told Babcock he knew of Detective Chief Inspector Seldon alright. He'd put away several of his criminal colleagues over time. And he'd also heard of me and Clifford. Reputations do seem to proceed us. The upshot was, he told Babcock he needed a much more sophisticated plan if he was going to pull the wool over the agency's eyes.'

'Which is quite the compliment, is it not?' Kofi said.

'I suppose it was. Anyway, as our arrival was imminent and he couldn't disguise Unwin's death as anything but murder, the recording was supposed to make us think Unwin was disturbed in his study and then killed. Dunstan added the theatrical touch of draping Unwin over his uncle's grave as he figured we'd soon work out where he'd actually been murdered. He hoped we'd be wrong-footed by the whole set-up, including the riddle on the gravestone and Unwin's connection with the grave's owner, his uncle Pritchard. Which we were! We chased that red herring for a long time before we realised it smelt just a little too fishy to be true.'

Seldon and Clifford both groaned at her terrible pun.

'But why stow the plans in a stane o' the dead, m'lady?'

Eleanor blinked. 'I'm sorry, Lizzie? Could you repeat that?'

The young girl laughed. 'Awa' times ah forget ah'm no' back at Ranburgh Castle. Ah was meanin', why did he stow the plans in a gravestone? It seems awful complicated?'

'Ah! I see. Hugh?'

'Well, a few years before, Lizzie, the police had actually

been tipped off that a similar gang had hidden the proceeds of a robbery in a coffin. So they got a court order, dug it up and opened it. And it was jammed full of jewels from various robberies. Obviously, the gang were all arrested. It was in the newspapers and also criminals hear things through the grapevine. So we reckon this lot thought they'd be cleverer. And if Reverend Ansel hadn't seen Dunstan and Jarrett, and Miss Lyndseer heard them, I'm not sure anyone would ever have known. It really was most ingenious.'

'May I ask another question, please?' Kofi said.

Clifford nodded. 'Yes, but this is the last one. Her ladyship needs to change for lunch.'

She rolled her eyes. 'Yes, Clifford, I'm sure I do. But I can answer you first, Kofi.'

'I am most grateful,' Kofi said, beaming. 'My question is, how much did Jarrett know about Dunstan's evil actions?'

'That, Kofi, is an excellent question. And the answer is... we don't know.'

Seldon nodded. 'Obviously, when Dunstan asked Jarrett to make a replica gravestone and add a secret compartment to it, Jarrett must have known it was for something illegal. But I'm pretty sure he had no idea it involved killing Professor Hunt and stealing government plans to then sell to the highest foreign bidder. And I don't believe Jarrett had anything to do with Unwin's murder, or Ned's either. Yes, Jarrett wasn't very good with money and has a rash streak, but I genuinely think it was the old story. He made one bad decision and then was led down the slippery slope. By Dunstan on this occasion. Which doesn't excuse Jarrett's actions, especially not turning Dunstan in when he must have realised he'd killed Unwin. But,' he shrugged, 'that is not mine, or the agency's business. It would be wrong of us to question Jarrett. And could possibly cause problems for the Blackington police. No. We've handed him and Dunstan over to

Quilter now. And tomorrow, they will be the Blackington police's problem.'

Eleanor sighed in relief. 'That's right, Kofi. As far as we can know, we have completed the case Unwin asked us down here for. So, after lunch, we can all pack up and go home.'

'Oh, I don't think so, Lady Swift!' a voice called. 'I don't think that would do at all!'

45

Eleanor spun around.

Then did a double-take. It was Luna's voice she'd heard. But the transformation was amazing. Gone was the long, black, hooded cloak. In its place was an elegant navy-blue wool coat and a pair of stylish leather boots.

Luna shrugged self-consciously. 'The coat was my mother's. One more thing salvaged from the fire.'

'It's beautiful,' Eleanor said genuinely. 'And it fits you so well.'

'Thank you. I had to do a little altering here and there. But even witches are occasionally allowed to dress in something other than black, aren't they? Besides' – she brushed her arms – 'I've been in mourning so long people will mistake me for our poor departed Queen Victoria.' She laughed. 'Well, maybe not, but I think it's time I looked to the future, rather than the past. And, Lady Swift,' her voice caught, 'you have given me a second chance to do just that. To have a future. The first time I saw you in your car in the woods near the lake, I knew there was something... of an angel about you. A guardian angel.'

Eleanor laughed. 'I don't think so, although it is very kind of you to say so. And, really, you need to thank Hugh and Clifford. And Constable Quilter. And what happened to "Eleanor?"

'Tell me then, Eleanor,' Luna said earnestly. 'Do you believe in fate? Because I believe all those years ago the Frishams' tavern was named "the Angel's Summons" because one day it was fate. Fate that you would be summoned like an angel to this remote spot to bring justice, and hope.'

Eleanor blushed. 'Again, it's very kind of you to say so.' She froze. 'You said "hope"?'

Luna nodded. 'Yes. Why?'

But Eleanor didn't hear her. Eyes closed, she was remembering what Clifford had said and the line from that fable. The fable in one of the treasured books she'd had as a child. And still had on her bookshelf in her bedroom at Henley Hall: *And when she slammed the lid closed, only hope remained.*

'Eleanor?' a voice called in concern.

She opened her eyes. 'I'm fine, Hugh.' She turned back to Luna. 'You mentioned "hope". But I brought something else with me besides hope.' Her voice wobbled. 'Something that I'd like to bury here once and for all. Alongside poor Unwin and Ned. And Augustus. And your parents. And mine,' she added quietly.

Clifford was staring at her quizzically. Then understanding dawned in his eyes. 'What am I?' he murmured.

She nodded.

'Regret!' Luna breathed. 'First out of the box, first in if pine. Created by the hand of man, destroyed by the divine. Springs into existence in an instant, then burns bright for all time. Free to own, yet costs the sun, the moon and the stars.'

'Of course!' Seldon muttered. 'Regret. One of the ills that escaped Pandora's box and afflicted mankind. And the first thing a man is buried with. His regrets!'

Clifford nodded. '"Created by the hand of man", because "to err is human", and one can only regret one's errors. And "to forgive is divine", because you can only forgive yourself your regrets.'

"'Springs into existence in an instant, then burns bright for all time",' Eleanor murmured. 'Because it takes but an instant to regret a decision or action. But from then on it is burned onto your retina like a lightning strike.' She turned to Luna. '"Free to own". Because regret costs nothing.'

'Yet,' Luna choked, '"it costs the sun, the moon and the stars."'

'Of course!' Seldon said again. '"Luna!"'

Clifford nodded. 'Latin for "the moon". Luna was also considered by the Romans to be a goddess.'

Eleanor nodded sadly. 'But you were more than just his moon and goddess, Luna. You were Augustus's sun and stars. His dreams and hopes for the future.'

'"Wish upon a star",' Seldon muttered.

Eleanor stepped forward. 'It's still the festive season, Luna. The season of goodwill. And good cheer. And good decisions. And new starts. I'll bury my regrets not with me, but without me, if you will. My regret at growing up without parents from nine. Of not knowing what happened to them. And of not being able to stop it happening. And of not appreciating when I was growing up how much those around me' – she glanced at Clifford – 'loved me and were trying their best for me. And a thousand other smaller regrets I don't have the time, or desire, to waste my breath listing.'

Luna nodded, tears running down both cheeks. 'It's a deal, Eleanor. I'll give up wishing... everything had been different.'

The two women hugged each other. But then Luna pulled away. 'But only on two conditions.'

Eleanor drew back in surprise. 'Which are?'

'Firstly, you stay for New Year. I have so many plans for Waketon Court, and for Yorelow, I want to run past you. I've already talked to the Frisham sisters about taking advantage of the national spotlight that is bound to be shone on the village when the trial begins.'

Eleanor looked around the room. 'It's not my decision alone to make. After almost every other adventure, I've been desperate to get back home. But I've finally learned the truth of the saying that "home is where your heart is". And much as I love Henley Hall and will always live there, my heart is with my family.' She pointed at Seldon, Clifford, Kofi and the ladies. 'So I'm already home. Which means that's a yes from me.'

'And a yes from us!' the ladies chorused, Seldon, Clifford and Kofi nodding in agreement.

Eleanor took Luna's hands. 'Then that's settled.'

'Actually, my lady,' Clifford said, 'I believe Miss Lyndseer had one more stipulation?'

Luna nodded. 'Yes. It's that everyone stops calling me "Miss Lyndseer!" I might be happy to lose the moniker "loony" but not "Luna".

Clifford half bowed. 'It would be an honour, Miss Luna.'

She laughed. Then her expression clouded over.

'What's the matter?' Eleanor asked in alarm.

Luna bit her lip. 'It's just that... I imagine the Blackington police will want to speak to Babcock the minute they check the fingerprints on that trumpet. I know Jarrett all but confessed his part in things, but—'

Quilter, who had been standing mutely while the women talked, cleared his throat. 'Don't rightly see why they should, Miss Lynd— sorry, Miss Luna. Weren't no sign of prints last time I looked. I reckon Dunstan must have wiped it clean after killing poor Ned after all.'

Seldon stared at him. 'What the—'

Quilter shrugged. 'I don't mean to speak out of turn, sir, but I'd rather retire in disgrace, but with a clear conscience. Rather than with a commendation and with regret, as what you've been talking about so eloquently, in me heart. Only reason Mr

Babcock didn't do his duty and go to the police and tell them about Dunstan was because of them same police who had made it clear by their actions over the years that the only upshot would have been him banged up in jail for a murder or two he never committed. And a nice open and shut case it would have been too. Whatever the evidence told or not.'

All eyes swivelled back to Seldon.

He rubbed his chin. 'Well, Constable, I don't recall any prints either. We certainly didn't dust for any, did we, Clifford?'

He shook his head. 'No, sir. We just took Mr Babcock on his word.'

'So,' Seldon continued. 'Let's call the matter closed, shall we?'

'Agreed, sir.'

The two men shook hands.

Seldon glanced over Quilter's shoulder. 'Joking aside, though, aren't you worried about leaving Dunstan and Jarrett alone together in your cell? There may be another double murder in Yorelow if you're not careful, And I think we'd all agree, there's been enough!'

'Right you be on that, sir,' Quilter said. 'Although it would save a lot of trouble bringing 'em to trial! Only, don't fret, 'cos they're not in my cell.'

Seldon's brow furrowed. 'Good heavens, man! They haven't—'

Quilter shook his head vigorously. 'Course not, sir.'

Seldon held up his hands in apology. 'I'm sorry, Constable. After last night, I shouldn't have doubted you can more than handle them.'

'Thank you, sir. But actually, the detective from Blackington just turned up. Well, him and another. I rang and suggested they send two along. Upshot is, anyways, they've been and gone and taken Dunstan and Jarrett with 'em.'

'And good riddance!' Luna said forcefully.

'I agree!' Eleanor held up a finger. 'And another matter that I think we can agree is closed, is the case Unwin asked us down here to investigate. However, as we are all being so desperately honest at the moment, I have to point out that we cannot accept the money he left in his desk drawer.'

'I concur, my lady,' Clifford said. 'Mr Unwin stipulated most clearly that the second payment was only to be taken when the agency had accepted the case. And further, only if it were accepted before midnight.'

'Exactly, Clifford. And we were late.'

Luna shook her head. 'But surely—'

'I'm sorry, Luna, but the agency must stick rigidly to its rules. I mean, rules were made to be adhered to. Isn't that so, Clifford?'

He raised an eyebrow. 'Absolutely, my lady, even though I never believed I would hear such a statement from yourself. Regardless, rule number, er, seventeen states that the three hundred pounds must therefore be given to a worthwhile cause.'

She turned to Mrs Butters. 'Could you fetch the reverend?'

A moment later, Ansel appeared.

'Ah, Reverend,' Eleanor said brightly. 'Excuse us disturbing you, but I believe you have a leaky roof that could do with mending? Would a three hundred pound injection of funds for a rainy day help?'

Seldon groaned at her pun.

Ansel, however, didn't seem to notice. 'Absolutely! Especially as we shall need the church for a wedding.'

Eleanor and Luna both stared at each other, then Ansel.

He nodded. 'Yes! Dora and Digger have just asked if I will marry them as soon as possible.'

'This calls for a celebration all of its own!' Eleanor cheered. 'Ladies, how long until lunch is ready?'

Mrs Trotman did a quick reckoning. 'About half an hour, m'lady.'

'And can you fit in Miss Luna and Mr Babcock, as well as Dora and Digger? If, of course, you don't mind, Reverend?'

Ansel shook his head. 'As everyone will be at the vicarage having lunch, I was going to suggest inviting the Frisham sisters as well, as they will have no customers!'

Eleanor turned to her ladies. 'That's an awful lot more people than originally intended.'

Mrs Butters tutted. 'Not at all, m'lady. Trotters and me had anticipated some such.'

'In which case,' Luna said, 'I'll pop past the Angel's Summons to tell Mathilde and Blythe, and then Waketon Court to pick up Babcock.' She turned and hurried out.

Fifteen minutes later, Waketon Court's strident doorbell rang out. Babcock strode across the hall. On opening the door, he stepped to one side.

'Welcome to your new home, Miss Luna.'

In the dining room, ear pressed to the door, Eleanor nodded at Clifford. Then opened the door just as the ladies in the bedroom above hurried out and heaved the cloth over the rail of the galleried landing.

Dumbfounded, Luna spun around, looking up as a banner unfurled above her head:

WELCOME TO YOUR NEW HOME, MISS LUNA!

Before she could respond, the hall was full of ladies, The Byron Detective Agency, and the villagers of Yorelow.

Eleanor gave the stunned woman a hug. 'A house isn't a home without a house-warming party, Luna. So we all thought we'd better shift lunch from the vicarage to here. It's already set up in the dining room.'

Babcock cleared his throat. 'I hope I didn't overstep the mark, Miss Luna?'

She laughed through happy tears. 'Of course not, Babcock!'

Eleanor tutted. 'Although I should warn you, Luna. My experience with Clifford shows if you give them an inch, they'll take a mile!'

'Is that husbands or staff?' Seldon chuckled, putting his hand around her waist.

'Both,' she said emphatically, slipping her arm around his. 'And I wouldn't want it any other way!'

HISTORICAL NOTES

TELEGRAMS

Telegrams in Britain used to be the province of private companies until the post office started a national service in 1870. This lasted until 1982, when it was finally stopped due to declining usage. Who needs telegrams when everyone has a mobile phone? The same is somewhat true of home recording nowadays as well. You can make a professional quality recording on your mobile. One person who harked back to the days of Inigo Unwin, however, was the British comedian Spike Milligan of the Goons fame. Rather like Unwin, while upstairs in his house, he used to send his wife, who would be downstairs, telegrams telling her what he fancied for dinner!

INFLATION

The declining spending power of the British pound in one's pocket is a common lament. And one equally heard across the world, whether it be US dollars, euros or Turkish lira! Which is why the original down payment Unwin made to The Byron

Detective Agency was £100. As were the subsequent two payments. However, even though it is roughly equivalent to £6,000 today, it doesn't sound much to modern ears. Hence, upping it to £300, which still doesn't sound that much. Certainly not for the inconvenience, discomfort and danger Eleanor, Seldon and Clifford had to go through to earn their money.

HOME RECORDING

In 1877, Thomas Edison invented the phonograph and recorded the immortal words 'Mary had a little lamb'. Quite why he chose those words to commemorate what is generally regarded as the first ever recording of human speech I'm not quite sure. What I am sure of is that, like Eleanor in her showdown with the murderer, Laura and I exercised a little 'artistic licence' here. Home-recording machines like the one Unwin used were not really available until a few years after the book is set. But they were originally developed largely in America. The initial discs were aluminium until RCA Victor made shellac discs the norm in the 1930s. They originally recorded at 78 rpm with a paltry three to five minutes duration. Which was fine for Unwin's dinner demands, but meant a standard opera, for instance, had to be recorded over twenty discs or more!

THE ANGEL'S SUMMONS

The murder weapon, taken from the Frisham sisters' tavern sign, is a nod to a similar sign outside what used to be our local police station in Béziers, France. Above the entrance were two angels, one holding an actual herald trumpet. As we had breakfast each morning in the café opposite, we discussed using it one day as a murder weapon in a book. That book became this one.

MIDNIGHT MASS

We might owe the population of Yorelow a slight apology for this one. Reverend Ansel suggests they might be stuck in mediaeval times because they still celebrate the *Vetus Ordo*, or Tridentine Mass, or the Traditional Latin Mass, to give it some of its numerous names. To be fair, this Mass was not officially replaced until 1969 by the Mass of Paul VI. However, we felt most modern readers would be more used to this version. Perhaps a double apology is owed, as scholars tend to agree that the mediaeval period, or 'Middle Ages', ended in 1453 with the fall of Constantinople (now known as Istanbul). The older Mass, sung mostly, if not exclusively, in Ecclesiastical Latin, had been around since 1570, so was not really 'mediaeval' anyway.

DARWIN AND EARTHWORMS

I used to live in Down, Kent, and knew the churchyard where Charles Darwin studied the very earthworms Clifford mentions. I also had a copy of his book, with the riveting title: *The Formation of Vegetable Mould, through the Action of Worms, with Observations on their Habits*. It was actually very interesting. (I also had a collection of fossils collected by Charles Darwin.) It also illustrates how diverse the inspiration for a single Lady Swift novel can be. The death in a graveyard idea came from a graveyard in Sussex, England, we used to walk through, while the sinking gravestone came from Charles Darwin's book and the murder weapon from a police station in the south of France as mentioned before.

PANDORA'S BOX

In the tale of Pandora's box, there is no mention in the versions I have read of 'regret' itself. But as all of man's ills apparently escaped, it must have been one of the first out of the box, if not the first. The thing most people don't appreciate about this ancient fable is the role 'hope' plays in it all. With our modern tendency towards looking for the positive, the later tellings of the tale emphasise that Pandora slammed the lid closed, leaving hope outside the box, so despite all the ills released, there was still... well, hope. However, in a lot of the ancient tellings of this tale, Pandora slams the lid of the box closed (originally actually a jar) trapping hope inside... so mankind is devoid of hope as well!

PYGMALION

I've always loved accents. One of the wonderful things about being brought up in London was the multitude of accents. And not just non-London ones either. London has at least four distinct accents of its own, and Britain over forty. Identifying all of them might just give Professor Pike the challenge he felt he was denied. (He never even got to identify the voice on the recording. Which was just as well for The Byron Detective Agency, as it was Clifford's!)

RECIPE

Mrs Trotman's (Beeton's) Plum Pudding Recipe

Mrs Trotman is a great Mrs Beeton fan, although she does violently disagree with her on a few points. Well, Mrs Butters and Clifford might suggest on most points. The truth is Mrs Trotman is fiercely proud of her unique cooking skills and recipes. However, even she acknowledges that Mrs Beeton's Plum Pudding recipe in her iconic *Beeton's Book of Household Management* (1861) is perfect as it is.

INGREDIENTS

1 1/2 lb. of raisins
1/2 lb. of currants
1/2 lb. of mixed peel
3/4 lb. of bread crumbs
3/4 lb. of suet
8 eggs
1 wineglassful of brandy

METHOD:

Stone [**unless seedless**] and cut the raisins in halves, but do not chop them; wash, pick, and dry the currants, and mince the suet finely; cut the candied peel into thin slices, and grate down the bread into fine crumbs.

When all these dry ingredients are prepared, mix them well together, then moisten the mixture with the eggs, which should be well beaten, and the brandy; stir well, that everything may be very thoroughly blended, and *press* the pudding into a buttered mould.

Tie it down tightly with a floured cloth, and boil for 5 or 6 hours. It may be boiled in a cloth without a mould, and will require the same time allowed for cooking.

As Christmas puddings are usually made a few days before they are required for table, when the pudding is taken out of the pot, hang it up immediately, and put a plate or saucer underneath to catch the water that may drain from it. The day it is to be eaten, plunge it into boiling water, and keep it boiling for at least 2 hours; then turn it out of the mould, and serve with brandy-sauce. [**Faux-brandy sauce if a man of the cloth like Reverend Ansel is present at the table.**]

On Christmas-day a sprig of holly is usually placed in the middle of the pudding, and about a wineglassful of brandy poured round it, which, at the moment of serving, is lighted, and the pudding thus brought to table encircled in flame.

The pudding, like a speckled cannon ball, so hard and firm, blazing in half of half-a-quartern of ignited brandy, and bedight with Christmas holly stuck into the top!

~ *A Christmas Carol* by Charles Dickens, 1843

Time: 5 or 6 hours the first time of boiling; 2 hours the day it is to be served.

Average cost, 4s. [**Not allowing for inflation – see entry Inflation**]

Sufficient for a quart mould for 7 or 8 persons.

Seasonable on the 25th of December, and on various festive occasions till March.

Note: Five or six of these puddings should be made at one time [**especially if a hungry Lady of the Manor or bulldog is invited**] as they will keep good for many weeks, and in cases where unexpected guests arrive, will be found an acceptable, and, as it only requires warming through, a quickly-prepared dish.

A LETTER FROM VERITY

Dear reader,

I want to say a huge thank you for choosing to read *Murder on a Frosty Night*. If you did enjoy it, and want to keep up to date with all my latest releases, just sign up at the following link. Your email address will never be shared and you can unsubscribe at any time.

www.bookouture.com/verity-bright

I hope you loved *Murder on a Frosty Night* and if you did I would be very grateful if you could write a review. I'd love to hear what you think, and it makes such a difference helping new readers to discover one of my books for the first time.

I love hearing from my readers – you can get in touch through social media or my website.

Thanks,

Verity

www.veritybright.com

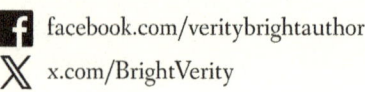

facebook.com/veritybrightauthor
x.com/BrightVerity

ACKNOWLEDGEMENTS

Thanks to all my fellow authors who encouraged and helped me to write and release *Murder on a Frosty Night*. And to the ever professional and hard-working team at Bookouture who made sure it was in tip-top form for release.

PUBLISHING TEAM

Turning a manuscript into a book requires the efforts of many people. The publishing team at Bookouture would like to acknowledge everyone who contributed to this publication.

Audio
Alba Proko
Melissa Tran

Commercial
Lauren Morrissette
Hannah Richmond
Imogen Allport

Cover design
Tash Webber

Data and analysis
Mark Alder
Mohamed Bussuri

Editorial
Kelsie Marsden
Nadia Michael

Copyeditor
Jane Eastgate

Proofreader
Liz Hatherell

Marketing
Alex Crow
Melanie Price
Occy Carr
Cíara Rosney
Martyna Młynarska

Operations and distribution
Marina Valles
Joe Morris

Production
Hannah Snetsinger
Mandy Kullar
Nadia Michael
Charlotte Hegley

Publicity
Kim Nash
Noelle Holten
Jess Readett
Sarah Hardy

Rights and contracts
Peta Nightingale
Richard King
Saidah Graham

RAISING READERS
Books Build Bright Futures

Dear Reader,

We'd love your attention for one more page to tell you about the crisis in children's reading, and what we can all do.

Studies have shown that reading for fun is the **single biggest predictor of a child's future life chances** – more than family circumstance, parents' educational background or income. It improves academic results, mental health, wealth, communication skills, ambition and happiness.

The number of children reading for fun is in rapid decline. Young people have a lot of competition for their time, and a worryingly high number do not have a single book at home.

Hachette works extensively with schools, libraries and literacy charities, but here are some ways we can all raise more readers:

- Reading to children for just 10 minutes a day makes a difference
- Don't give up if children aren't regular readers – there will be books for them!

- Visit bookshops and libraries to get recommendations
- Encourage them to listen to audiobooks
- Support school libraries
- Give books as gifts

There's a lot more information about how to encourage children to read on our websites: **www.RaisingReaders.co.uk** and **www.JoinRaisingReaders.com**.

Thank you for reading.

Made in the USA
Middletown, DE
13 December 2025

24743165R00191